MOTIVES FOR MURDER ...

When fascinating Sandra Gould is found dead, it is easy to rule out suicide. Sandra gave all too many people cause to kill her.

The list includes almost everyone who knew Sandra, as the redoubtable Colonel Primrose discovers when he sets out to solve the baffling crime.

Then, unexpectedly, the murderer strikes again . . .

"A baffler with a skillful plot, delightful characters, eerie atmosphere . . . top-notch reading"
—BOSTON TRANSCRIPT

THREE BRIGHT PEBBLES
WASHINGTON WHISPERS MURDER
THE BAHAMAS MURDER CASE
THE PHILADELPHIA MURDER STORY
MURDER IS THE PAY-OFF
BY THE WATCHMAN'S CLOCK
MURDER IN MARYLAND
RENO RENDEZVOUS
INVITATION TO MURDER
MURDER COMES TO EDEN
ROAD TO FOLLY
THE GIRL FROM THE MIMOSA CLUB
THE DEVIL'S STRONGHOLD
ALL FOR THE LOVE OF A LADY
BURN FOREVER
HONOLULU MURDERS
THE MURDER OF A FIFTH COLUMNIST
MURDER IN THE O.P.M.
MURDER WITH SOUTHERN HOSPITALITY
OLD LOVER'S GHOST
THE TOWN CRIED MURDER
DATE WITH DEATH
TRIAL BY AMBUSH
FALSE TO ANY MAN
SIREN IN THE NIGHT
THE WOMAN IN BLACK

LESLIE FORD
ILL MET BY MOONLIGHT

WILDSIDE PRESS

Ill Met by Moonlight

Published by Wildside Press LLC
www.wildsidepress.com

OBERON: Ill met by moonlight, proud Titania.
—A Midsummer Night's Dream, II.1. 60

CHAPTER ONE

I've been trying to remember if there was anything different about April Harbor the Saturday Rosemary Bishop and her father came back for the first time in seven years. It was stiflingly hot, but it often is in August, especially when a thunderstorm is brewing over Chesapeake Bay. But whether there was any hint of the ghastly business that was to turn April Harbor inside out and scatter our private lives in a shower of printer's ink over the front page of every newspaper in America—that's what I've been trying to remember.

I told Colonel Primrose not, the next morning, when he started asking me questions. In fact I was quite positive about it. But I think he sensed the reservations I was keeping carefully guarded in the back of my mind. He'd have been a fool if he hadn't, and I never heard anyone call him a fool, except himself, and perhaps Elsie Carter. Elsie calls practically everybody a fool, so nobody bothers much about her.

"Does *everybody* spend Saturday morning in the A & P, my dear Mrs. Latham?" he asked me.

And of course they do. April Harbor is like any other village that's been practically taken over by a group of city people who descend on it late in May when the schools are about to close and stay until school opens again in September. Some have been staying on till November, since 1929, and Bill and Louise Chetwynd even stayed a couple of winters, when their town place was being sold to pay up their margins. Everybody was hit, of course, because everybody virtually lives off stocks and bonds—the older people own them and the young crowd sell them. They sell other things too, mostly the sort of things everybody stopped buying immediately: architecture, divorces, ten-thousand-dollar portraits and unnecessary operations. Except Elsie Carter's husband, who's a glorified grocer of some sort and at April Harbor only because Elsie married him. Elsie's father was my father's law partner, and the two of them drew up the charter for the April Harbor Association thirty years ago when a group of young married people decided to

5

buy three hundred acres of the Poplar Hill Estate and make a summer camp. They were mostly Baltimore and Washington and Philadelphia then. That was before the days of airplanes. Now most of the younger crowd live in New York and the men charter a plane to come down for week ends.

Elsie Carter's family lived at one end of the Estate and mine at the other, and Elsie and I got on just as well—which means no better—when she was thirteen and I was five as we do now that she's forty-six and I'm thirty-eight. The fact that I'm a widow with two sons, and that Elsie might as well be one, with nothing to do but manage other people's lives, doesn't seem to have drawn us any closer. Possibly the fact that Ferney Carter never flies down for a week end except when he has to explain her constantly pointing out to me that if Dick hadn't been in such a hurry one time, and had taken a train instead of a plane, I shouldn't be a widow. Or perhaps I know it's true and just can't bear to be reminded of it so often. However, why I should object so much to Elsie's minding other people's business when the whole story of Jim Gould and his wife and Rosemary Bishop is a veritable epic of me as a busybody, I'm sure I don't know. Except, I suppose, that in a way I wanted to keep April Harbor the romantic spot for my youngsters that it had been once for me, and Rosemary and Jim became sort of a test case.

April Harbor is a tiny fishing village on the Eastern Shore of the Chesapeake Bay. In the winter it's as dead as the people who sleep under the lichen-stained slabs and crooked headstones that cluster around the old ivy-colored red brick church at the top of its one street. Then from the end of May the street is alive with the summer colony. The quay at the bottom is a bright tangle of white boats and bronzed laughing people in all degrees of undress. April Harbor is a teeter-totter, balanced between Church Circle and Dock Street, winter and summer; dirty sails and oysters in winter and white sails and colonists in summer. All the shops along the sloping street, except Mr. Toplady's, are boarded up in the winter. In the spring they're painted and opened again, and alive with people, mostly laying in food for the influx of week-end husbands and guests from Washington and Baltimore.

The morning of the Saturday when the Bishops were to come back wasn't any different. Except for the fact that the Bishops were coming. They hadn't been back to the Harbor since Chapin Bishop, Rosemary's older brother, was drowned and Rosemary and her father had gone abroad.

That, of course, was the thing about April Harbor that morning that I wanted to keep as quiet as I could, for a lot of reasons—even before the Bishops came; in fact, before anything was supposed to be known about their coming.

I hadn't, of course, counted on Elsie Carter's extraordinary nose for news. Elsie is a large and efficient woman. She was standing in front of a bushel basket of cantaloupes, pressing them with her two thumbs and smelling them in the professional manner that when I try it always nets me perfectly green and tasteless melons. She caught sight of me in the long mildewed mirror over the bakery shelves and abandoned the cantaloupes immediately.

"My dear!" she cried. "Isn't it marvelous about Rosemary Bishop? I'll bet you're thrilled to death!"

I'm afraid I looked blanker even than I'd intended to.

"Oh, don't try to pretend.—About her engagement to Paul Dikranov. He's coming with them today. I expect she wants to show Jim Gould that she can marry a foreigner too if she wants to. I must say I've always thought that business about not coming back here on account of Chapin was a little farfetched."

She picked up a box of shiny blackberries and turned them out in her hand to see the bottom. I always spill them when I try it. "Still, as you say . . ."

I'd said nothing, except from time to time for seven years that there was no use trying to make out that Chapin Bishop, aged twenty-five, had been murdered just because he'd been found one moonlight night face down in three feet of water at the cove. Everybody knew Chapin Bishop drank more than was good for any ten young men and had spent many a night lying face down somewhere or other where there'd just not happened to be any water.

"It'll be interesting to see how she and Sandra make out. Have they ever met?"

I said I didn't know. But I did. They'd never met. In a sense they never could meet, not on any common ground. Sandra Gould was Jim Gould's wife, and Rosemary Bishop and Jim Gould had played together at April Harbor when they were babies, quarreled there when they were children, fallen in love there when they were adolescents, become engaged there when Rosemary was eighteen and Jim a midshipman home for a month's leave, aged twenty-two. They hadn't had their big quarrel there. That had been in China. It seemed horribly

7

sardonic now that Rosemary Bishop should meet Jim Gould's "foreign" wife at April Harbor.

"I don't really see what she wants to come here for," Elsie Carter said.

"It's her home," I said curtly, and was annoyed because I let Elsie Carter get under my skin the way I do.

"They've been mighty anxious to sell for a long time."

She turned her attention to the problem of lettuce. I looked out into the street, filled with a gaily chattering crowd—on foot, in station wagons, in big cars and little ones, some properly dressed, a lot of girls and men in shorts, with dogs and children—all people I'd known all my life or all theirs. Except the girl now coming into the store.

I'd known Sandra Gould only four years, if indeed I could say I knew her at all. She was smiling, her fine white teeth gleaming between brilliant red lips slashed across a warm, incredibly petal-like face, with dark eyes, flashing now but always smoldering someway, and gorgeous smoky black hair, crowned now by an enormous dusty pink cartwheel of dull soft straw with a brown ribbon round the shallow crown. She had on a pink linen dress without much back. Her own was more than adequate. I could see Elsie Carter staring at it.

I moved away quickly. I didn't want to be a party to what I could see was bound to happen. It was cowardice, of course, but I simply didn't want to know how Sandra Gould was going to take Rosemary's return. Because I like Rosemary and I like Jim, and I've never particularly cared about Sandra. But there was never any getting away from the fact that she was bright.

She came forward instantly now, like a lithe young panther about to confront a mouse. Elsie Carter did quake a bit.

"Hello, Grace! Hello, Meeses Cahtair!"

She shook a crimson-nailed forefinger at us. We both backed a little against a crate of spinach.

"You were talking about me! Oh, I know, I read the face. You are all thinking 'Poor Sandra, she'll lose Jeem now that Rosemary Bishop is coming back!' "

She tossed her head, clinging lightly to the edge of her hat with her fingers, and laughed happily.

"No, no! You are all wrong. Look at my Jeem. Does he look so sad?"

Dr. Potter, who was engaged in the business of buying a tin of prezels just behind Sandra, turned and gave me a sardonic half-smile as he caught my eye. We both followed Sandra's finger pointing towards the street. Jim Gould, in an old gray sweat shirt and a pair of paint-spotted corduroy slacks, was out in the middle of the street with his brother-in-law Andy Thorp and a young chap from Wilmington refereeing a crap game for four minute colored boys. They all looked anything but sad.

"I suppose Jim knows they're coming?" Dr. Potter said. He looked at Sandra. There was no smile on his face. I remembered—but, thank Heaven, I never admitted it to Colonel Primrose, not even innocently, as I might so easily have done, and certainly not wittingly when I discovered it was decidedly significant—that he didn't smile, and that Sandra clapped her hands with such a delighted little gesture that the contrast was quite marked.

"Of course Jeem knows!" she cried. "I told heem myself—as soon as six, or"—she shrugged charmingly—"maybe thirteen, kind friends call me up thees morning to see eef I know!"

One thing about Sandra Gould is that the more charming she wants to be the rottener her English gets. She can lambast the butcher like a native.

"You are all ver' ver' weecked to poor Sandra," she laughed mischievously, and added, suddenly very serious, her dark eyes flashing, "but I weel not let her 'ave my Jeemy. You weel see, Meeses Cahtair! In my country we do not let othair women take our husbands!"

Since no one that I ever met knew just what Sandra's country was, there was no use arguing the point. I extricated myself from the spinach and moved away. Adam Potter followed me.

"Rather had us, what?" he remarked with a wry smile, as we came out together in the hot sun-baked street. "I only hope she's right."

"She probably is," I said. "After all, people don't go on being in love seven years. Not these days. Anyway, it's none of our business. Jim's as decent as they come and so's Rosemary."

Adam Potter looked at me a shade too steadily, I thought.

"Meaning Sandra isn't?"

"Not at all. But I think that if anybody made a scene it wouldn't be the other two."

"It's too bad the child died," he said slowly.

"Not if—"

"Nobody ever knew how true any of that was, Mrs. Latham," he interrupted sharply, knowing the village gossip even better than I. "Anyway, she's a damned attractive woman."

He turned on me with a sort of desiccated irascibility.

"My dear man, have I said anything to the contrary?"

He laughed and wiped his forehead with his handkerchief, pushing back his new wide-brimmed panama.

"No, of course not, Grace. Anyway, I wish they weren't coming back. It's bound to make trouble."

"Not unless we all insist on it. They've never actually admitted their not coming back had anything to do with Rosemary and Jim."

"I know," he said. "It's always been because Chapin was drowned here."

We were standing on the steps of Mr. Toplady's general store in the shade of what the telephone company had left of the big sycamore near the old slave block. Both of us were quite unconsciously watching Jim Gould, bareheaded, sun-bronzed and healthy, there in the middle of the street blocking the road.

"It's been five years since they busted him out of the Navy," Dr. Potter said after a moment. "Pretty hard medicine.—She's not the same girl now, of course."

"They didn't bust him out," I said, "He resigned."

He shrugged his thin shoulders.

"Worse. He doesn't get any retired pay."

I followed his tired eyes up and across the sidewalk in front of the tea store. I remembered later how they'd lighted up a little, involuntarily. Sandra was coming out, barelegged in white sandals, moving lithe and sinuous, different, somehow, from the other women, so that you noticed the difference instantly.

"Why, Jeem! Andy!" she cried in mock consternation. "Lucy Lee, make them stop! Please, Lucy Lee!"

Lucy Lee is Andy Thorp's wife and Jim Gould's sister; hence, consequently, Sandra's sister-in-law. More important at the moment, she is young Andy's mother, and young Andy had just at that moment fallen off his tricycle at the curb and was yelling as if he had been killed. Lucy Lee was trying frantically to pick him up with one hand and hang onto the baby and her bundles with the other.

One of the nice things about both Sandra and Andy is that it wouldn't ever occur to either of them to help her. Lilies of the field both of them, each in his own fashion; Sandra the tiger, and Andy a lily only in that he toiled very little and did nothing so practical as spinning. The trouble with Andy is that he was brought up with too much money and never counted on his father's marrying again.

10

"Oh, do make them stop, Lucy Lee!" Sandra cried prettily. Lucy Lee threw her a look over her shoulder that was understandable, certainly, but that surprised me nevertheless.

Most of us thought of Lucy Lee's face as pretty without much in it except tired lines, these days. Nothing like the sudden pent-up anger—almost hate—that I saw there now, before Lucy Lee remembered herself and smiled.

"Sorry, darling; you manage them," she called, and went back into the little group of her own friends who'd come to her rescue.

I glanced at Dr. Potter, expecting him to say what everybody at April Harbor had been saying all summer—"I wonder how long Lucy Lee and Andy will last." But he wasn't paying any attention to Lucy Lee. He was still watching Sandra and Jim and Andy. Lucy Lee's problem, I suppose, was the kind of thing he sees every day, without the glamour of the girl with the dusty pink cartwheel hat and dusky eyes. I was annoyed. I suppose it was sort of an instinctive defending of my own kind against something from the outside, although it was absurd of me to identify it with Rosemary Bishop rather than Lucy Lee and little Andy. At that, our instincts are wiser than we are.

"You know, Dr. Potter," I said, "I think we're all being pretty objectionable."

He looked a little surprised, and flushed almost as if I'd caught him being personally indiscreet. Which is quite unthinkable.

"I mean, Jim doesn't seem to be taking this very hard, and Rosemary's been having a pretty exciting life in Washington and Europe all these years. I haven't seen her, but I've seen pictures of her. She seems to be bearing up pretty well. After all, twenty-seven isn't an appallingly great age. I mean, it isn't as if she'd not married and was fifty, is it? It's quite conceivable that she just never met anyone she wanted to marry—until now."

"Now?"

"She's bringing her fiancé down. Didn't you know?"

Dr. Potter shook his head, definitely relieved, I thought.

"So it seems to me that if we just act as if Sandra and Jim are well and truly married, and Jim's forgot Rosemary, and Rosemary's forgot Jim—except as sort of childhood sweethearts—and *everybody's* forgot Chapin, and if we'd quit standing around like a lot of ghouls just out of the churchyard—well, it'd be a lot better."

11

. He nodded. "You're right," he said soberly. "At least, I hope you are.—Well, I'll be getting along. Drop in and see Maggie. She'll want all the news."

I watched him cross the street, a lean stooped figure in a wrinkled seersucker suit, his bag of groceries in his hand, walking rather slower than he used to, as if he were tired too, like Lucy Lee. I wondered with a little shock just how long it had been since I'd dropped even the formality of inquiring about Maggie Potter's health. It's curious how callous one gets about people who are always sick with nothing much the matter with them. Maggie Potter hadn't been out of the old red brick house on Church Circle for years—just moving from her chair by the front window to her bed and back again. Chapin Bishop's funeral was her last public appearance. Not that anybody missed her. And Elsie Carter was the only person I ever heard suggest that the poor man kept her an invalid for purposes of his own. Just what they might be, besides the privilege of doing the marketing, not even Elsie could guess.

I suppose I stood there grinning, because somebody behind my left shoulder said, "What's so funny? I'd *like* a good laugh."

I started and turned to find Jim Gould beside me on Mr. Toplady's steps, a bright new monkey wrench in one hand and a can of turpentine in the other. I had a horrible guilty feeling that he'd been there for some time, so that he must have heard what I'd said about him and Rosemary.

I smiled, but he didn't. In fact, he looked pretty sober—and when he does his face gets extremely hard, and it's difficult to remember that he's just thirty-two, not a lot older, and that he's a grand person, not somebody you'd rather not cross. That's the way he looked just then. I found myself a bit surprised to feel glad, all of a sudden, that he wasn't taking Rosemary's return simply in his grinning stride, as it were.

He was looking past me at Dr. Potter's old car. Then he did grin, and shrugged as if something amusing and sardonic had occurred to him. He put down his can of turpentine and pulled a blue bandanna out of his pocket to mop his brow.

"Lord, it's hot."

He squinted his light blue eyes up at the sky through the sycamore leaves.

"Hope it holds off till after the race. Then it can rain a week and suit me down to the ground."

"I'd like it to rain now," I said. But Jim wasn't paying any attention to me. He had the bandanna still in his poised hand, staring across the street, two puzzled lines between his brows.

"Who's that guy over there in front of the post office—in the linen suit?"

"Some city slicker probably," I said. "Though it's not one of the ground rules here that all the men have to look like unemployed painters *all* the time."

I looked anyway, and had a sudden hollow feeling in my stomach.

"It looks like George Barrol, Grace," Jim said incredulously.

"Maybe it *is* George Barrol," I said. I knew from Rosemary's letter that he was coming down early, to open up the house before the rest of them came. George Barrol is Rosemary's cousin and Mr. Bishop's bailiff, steward, estate manager and general handy man.

Jim was still staring oddly at him. "What's he doing here?" he said. Then he turned to me abruptly. "Grace, have they sold the house?"

I looked at him blankly, and caught myself just in time. Or was it? I'm not so sure now. I was sure then, because I saw the pallor that whitened the corners of Jim Gould's mouth as suddenly as if he'd been struck. His hands trembled as he pulled a flattened pack of cigarettes out of his pocket.

I knew instantly, of course, that Sandra had lied to us—that Jim didn't know Rosemary Bishop was coming to April Harbor that very day. I held my lighter to his cigarette. It wasn't very steady, but neither was the cigarette.

"That must be it," he said.

I should have said then that that wasn't it, that the Bishops were coming back to spend August at the old stand. But I didn't. I've wondered a lot what difference it would have made. I should have told him. Not doing it was nothing but the ghastliest sort of passing the buck. I thought then—or so I like to think—that I was really just passing it to George Barrol, who spends his life doing other people's dirty work. He had spotted me and was coming across the street. But even then, there's something about Jim Gould, even when you've known him since he was three and you were nine, as I have, that makes it hard to go barging into his private life. And anything connected with Rosemary, in spite of what I'd said to Dr. Potter, was intensely that.

George Barrol could do it better, I thought, watching him wait there in the middle of the street for a car to pass.

"I guess I'll get some cigarettes," Jim said abruptly. "I'll be seeing you."

The bell over Mr. Toplady's door jingled before I could say "Wait, Jim." He was gone. I wondered who'd tell him now.

"Hello, Grace! How's everybody?"

George Barrol and I shook hands. George hadn't changed in the seven years since I'd seen him, except that his light hair was a little thinner, with a touch of gray here and there. Perhaps he was a little more rotund, in a dapper way, and a little more perennially bachelorish. He was as precise and immaculate as ever, with the same slightly worried air as if things mightn't get done in time.

"It's nice to see you back," I said.

"It's nice to be back. Rosemary's dying to see you. They're getting here about four."

He looked about.

"There's a lot of new people."

He laughed, shaking his head. "Just think—seven years! A lot of water's flowed out of the Harbor."

"An awful lot," I said.

He laughed again and patted his moist forehead with his neatly folded white handkerchief.

"Wasn't that Jim Gould you were talking to?"

I nodded.

"Guess he didn't recognize me," he said cheerfully. "I say, Grace—who's that child in the pink hat?"

"Do you mean Nancy Thorp?" I inquired, seeing Lucy Lee's daughter, aged three and in a pink sunbonnet and practically nothing else. But of course I knew whom he meant. "Or possibly you mean Sandra Gould. Jim's wife."

He looked at me and raised his eyebrows. "Really. Not bad, eh? Foreign, isn't she? Brazilian, or something?"

"Something, anyway," I said.

George Barrol looked at Sandra again. She was standing on the opposite curb, looking about for Jim.

"She's got Rosemary beat," he remarked. I was annoyed. I don't know whether it was with him for saying that or with Sandra for her definitely breath-taking effect on men of all ages.

"What's Rosemary's young man like?" I asked.

"Paul's a good sort. Loads of money—oil concessions sort of thing—and darned attractive. Georgian, but he was educated in England. He's completely cosmopolitan, you know, the way those chaps get. Even Uncle Rod's sold on him. You'll like him. Well, I've got to be getting to work.—Ah . . . I say, Grace."

14

He hesitated, reddening just a shade, and patted his brow again.

"I mean . . . you'll lend us a hand, and all that, won't you? I mean, I don't think Rosemary's counted on . . . on Mrs. Gould's being such a . . ." He stopped and shook his head a little. "I mean, she's heard all about her being a swell boatman and swimmer, and all that, but I . . ."

"You mean she's not prepared to find her beautiful as well."

George got still redder and hotter.

"Well, you know—she saw her, once. In Shanghai."

"She did?"

"Well, not officially. It was before Jim married her. And she's . . . she's got the wrong idea."

"I wonder," I said.

George laughed. "You women are all cats. You'll stand by, anyway, won't you?"

I nodded. He crossed the street again.

Somebody spoke behind me: "Hello, Grace." I turned. Jim's mother was coming out of Toplady's with young Andy by the hand.

"Wasn't that George Barrol?" she asked.

I nodded.

Mrs. Gould's face is a strange combination of her two children. She looks like Lucy Lee except that her curly hair is white instead of chestnut, and her face is gentler, with more repose, as finely cut and delicate but rather determined in a way that Lucy Lee's isn't.

"You know the Bishops are coming today?" I asked. "For a month."

"Elsie Carter told me. Rosemary's engaged?"

I nodded.

"Jim doesn't know yet, does he?"

"Oh yes," she smiled. "Sandra told him this morning. I don't think anybody else would dare. Of course he *had* to know."

You can't very well tell a woman her daughter-in-law isn't telling the truth . . . at least you couldn't tell Mrs. Gould that. She's the only person who's always been unfailingly loyal to Sandra, and if most of us have thought it was just a deeper loyalty to Jim we've had no reason for it.

"Somehow I'd got the notion he didn't know," I said casually.

"It's rather difficult to know what Jim knows," she replied, laughing. "I think I'll go rescue Sandra. Look—I never knew George Barrol was so resourceful."

I followed her glance across the street. George was there with Sandra, his hat in his hand. They were laughing merrily, but it was Sandra's bundles they were picking up, so I doubted how much of the resourcefulness was his. Still, it made it simpler, George knowing her before the others came.

The clock on the church tower at the top of the road struck eleven. Across the street Mrs. Gould was shaking hands with George and presenting him properly to her son's wife. In a moment a little crowd had gathered, and by the time Julius had brought my car around from Dock Street George had greeted half the town.

Only Jim Gould was still in Mr. Toplady's general store buying a pack of cigarettes. Poor old Jim, who except for the girl in the dusty pink cartwheel hat across the road would be somewhere on the seas in a white uniform—or so they say—and Rosemary Bishop wouldn't be coming back to April Harbor engaged to somebody else.

CHAPTER TWO

I ought to explain April Harbor a little, in view of what happened there later, although the papers carried maps of it for days. Most of the things they said about it weren't true, however. Nobody there is fabulously wealthy, for instance, or ever was, and we don't have armed guards to protect us from the natives who burn down our garages.

Actually April Harbor Colony is a group of people most of whom have grown up together in the summers there, merely by the accident of their fathers' and mothers' having bought part of the old Lloyd estate on the bay, which was called Poplar Hill. My father had been chiefly interested because he wanted me to be some place near Alice Gould during vacations, after Mother died. Rodman Bishop came in later for much the same kind of reason, although it was Elsie Carter's notion that it wasn't for Rosemary and Chapin so much as for himself. But that was Elsie, even then.

I don't think any of us ever spent a summer away from the Harbor until Jim went to Annapolis. I married here when I was twenty-two, and I was here when Dick was killed, Rosemary had gone by then, and the days when I'd chaperoned her to hops in Annapolis were gone too. I remember the two of them so well one afternoon in a walled garden there, young and serious and sure of their own future, asking me if I'd come to China and stay with them. And of course it was in China that Sandra happened. I've always been sorry I didn't go. One of my youngsters was sent home from St. Paul's with whooping cough, and whooping cough lasts a long time. When he was over it Jim was married to Sandra, and Rosemary and her father and George Barrol were flying across Tibet or something on their way to Paris.

It's odd how all the houses in our row seem almost doomed. Judge Gould was drowned when his catboat capsized in a sudden squall. Chapin Bishop was drowned too, though not in the same way, and Dick was hurrying home from trying a case in Chicago when he crashed in the Ohio. Only the Carters

17

seemed to flourish till they have an odor of sanctity like the green bay leaf—and they aren't in our row anyway.

The Colony has a water frontage of something like a mile and a half, including an inlet where the yacht basin and swimming beach are. Overlooking it is the clubhouse, which was the old Poplar Hill mansion, with wide pillared porch and green lawn where the children play. It's all very rural and lovely— old trees and old gardens, and a couple of peacocks that sit on the marble urns that were brought from Italy before the Civil War. There are a lot of giant magnolias about, with their great white waxen blooms laden with yellow bees, and lilac trees, and tangles of roses and trumpet vine and wisteria.

To get down to the sandy beach and the big float there are stone steps, not elaborate but adequate, and there's a road too, down behind the clump of dogwood and wild cherry. The children play on one beach, under the watchful eyes of a couple of official nurses and a lifeguard; and out in front is the basin, dotted with gleaming sails and housing a few yachts— not so many as there used to be, but a few, and a new one or two this year.

The white cottages are dotted over the estate, most of them with an acre or so of private ground. Some of them are elaborate, like the Bishops', with oil furnaces and servants' quarters. Others are simple. Ours is, so we manage with a colored man and his wife. The Gould place is like ours. Sandra and Jim live in the main house with Mrs. Gould. Lucy Lee and Andy have a separate cottage that used to be a guest house when they were growing up. It happens that my cottage is between the Bishops', on my left, and the Goulds', on my right. To get to the Beach Club I drive out my back gate into the road, turn left past the Goulds' and another cottage that belongs to the Chetwynds, then left again at the Corner and on about a quarter of a mile to the club. When I walk, which most of us still do, I cut through the Goulds' yard past their garage, through their front yard and past Lucy Lee and Andy's cottage into a lane that runs along the bank the length of the waterfront.

I can, of course, go directly to that lane from my front garden. So can the Bishops, but normally they'd cut through my yard and through the Goulds', and into the lane that way. It's considerably shorter, and then we always went everywhere together, so it worked out most conveniently that way when we were younger.

I can see the Bishops' chimneys from my upstairs window,

18

out across our tennis court over the hedge of crape myrtle through the tops of the trees. I'd intended running over around five, but I didn't have a chance to. In the first place, Colonel Primrose, with his alarming bodyguard Sergeant Buck, arrived at the Chetwynds' where they'd been invited for the week end, and unfortunately all the Chetwynds' aunts and uncles arrived, uninvited, simultaneously. As I was one of the few people with a room available for the week end, Bill and Louise naturally overflowed into my house. They offered me an octogenarian aunt and uncle, but I have them of my own, so we compromised on Colonel Primrose and his sergeant.

I didn't, at the moment we were arguing about it and I was quietly but firmly declining the aged relatives, recognize that the voice was the voice of Grace Latham but the hand was the hand of Fate. At least, I thought, their colonel wouldn't be as completely embalmed in snuff, orris root, lavender, old lace and starched horsehair as all the elderly Chetwynds I'd met . . . and if anyone says horsehair isn't starched, then he's never met one of the Chetwynds of Richmond, Virginia. I was getting a pig in a poke, of course, but I did at least know that Colonel Primrose and Bill's father, whom I'd adored, were classmates at West Point. Bill and Louise had met him, years after, in Washington, where he still lived in the yellow brick house in Georgetown that Colonel John T. Primroses had lived in since the first one built it in 1730. It was confusing too, since they'd all been bachelors, but according to Bill it was part of their glory and quite easily explained by brothers or something.

However, if such a choice is ever offered me again I shall invariably and unhesitatingly take the aged aunts and uncles— snuff, stuffed shirts and lorgnettes included. If you take them, the probabilities are against somebody's taking pot shots at you in the middle of the night, just to mention one point. They also go to bed and stay there and are still there in the morning.

So I waited for them on my porch, watching the white wings of the sailboats dip and turn and dip again along the two-mile course in the bay. There must have been thirty sails out there. Even though I don't like to sail, and am terrified when the water rushes past with me balanced perilously on the gunwale, I like to watch at a distance. This afternoon, against the sultry horizon, lowering, steel-gray with the threatening storm, they gleamed white and lovely, almost unbearably graceful and swift across the dark water.

My guests came just as I'd about decided to give them up and run over to see Rosemary, and after that a lot of other

19

people came in, until it ended by all of us, Colonel Primrose included, going down to the club. It's rather a custom, everybody gathering there before dinner, and it was even before the days of cocktails. As I've said, the clubhouse is the old Lloyd Poplar Hill mansion. The big eighteenth-century drawing room is the cocktail lounge now, with no one under seventeen allowed. There were a lot of people there, otherwise I suppose we should have found a sofa and a table by ourselves. As it was, we joined Sandra and Jim and Andy Thorp. They were glowing with triumph. Andy's boat with Sandra at the tiller had come in first in the afternoon race. Lucy Lee, who'd been working like a beaver in the ladies' sailing class, wasn't there. She wasn't good enough yet for that race, of course, but anyway she'd never be as good as her sister-in-law. Wherever Sandra Gould had been born, it was certainly on the water. She was better than any of the men, any except Andy.

"Gosh, she was marvelous!" Andy was saying. "You should have seen her when old Bill's dory caught us astern! Have a drink, Grace—it's my night to howl!"

"We'll all have one," I said. Louise Chetwynd introduced Colonel Primrose. They shook hands.

"He's in the Army, or something," Louise said. "Jim here used to be an admiral, but they didn't like him so they put him out."

"I was much too good for them," Jim said, grinning. But he flushed a little as he shook hands with the rotund little man, who looks less like an officer than almost anyone I know.

"They put me out too," Colonel Primrose said with a smile. Someone pushed up a deep chintz-covered chair, but he shook his head. "That's why they put me out. I can't get up and down in club chairs like I used to, I'm afraid."

He sat down in a straight-backed chair and took the tall frosted julep growing with fragrant mint which the boy offered, his black eyes snapping with pleasure. Sandra, having looked the men over, moved to the arm of Bill's chair by him, and said, "Are you really a soldier?"

"Watch it, Colonel," somebody said. "She'll have your iron cross before you know it."

Everybody laughed . . . everybody but Jim.

Jim wasn't laughing at anything. He was sitting suddenly bolt upright in his chair, his face white as a sheet under its surface bronze, staring at the door.

I looked that way too. Rosemary Bishop was there. I said, "Steady, old man," under my breath, but it was too

20

late. The julep in his hand hit the floor with a shivering crash.

"Why, *Jeem!*" Sandra cried.

Everybody in the room looked around, including Rosemary.

"Oh . . . how grand!" she cried, and came towards us, her arms outstretched.

"Oh, Grace! It's marvelous to see you . . . I went by, through the old hedge, and they said you were here. Hello, Jim! Hello, everybody! It's so nice to see you all!"

Sandra, leaning languorously back in the chintz fireside chair, introduced herself before any of us had a chance.

"And I am Sandra Gould . . . because, you see, he ees *my* Jeem now."

I suppose it would have been all right in a New York speakeasy in prohibition days, with everybody making a point of not having any manners. Here and now it wasn't only ill-bred, it was stupid. It brought into a suddenly sharpened focus just the difference between herself and Rosemary. It was so obviously throwing the glove in the rival's face before it was decent.

Rosemary smiled.

"You're a lucky girl—your Jim's a very swell person!" she said, a barely perceptible emphasis on the "your."

She looked at Jim and smiled again. Poor Jim! He tried to smile too, but he couldn't.

"I . . . I didn't know you were coming back," he finally blurted out.

"Why, Jeem, darling! I told you this morning, at breakfast, and you said . . . what is eet so naughty you said? You said, 'What the hell I care?' Don't you remembair, Jeem?"

There was a little appalled silence as she looked at him, so wide-eyed.

Then Rosemary laughed. "Sounds just like him," she said. "Doesn't it, Grace?"

"Precisely," I said.

"But wait, here's Dad."

Rodman Bishop hadn't changed, even if his daughter had. He was a little thicker, perhaps, but he had the same tanned rugged square face under the same thatch of thick white hair. But Rosemary had changed in seven years from an extremely pretty girl to one of the loveliest women I've ever seen. Not particularly tall, but marvelously slim, with cool gray eyes, warm eggshell skin and pale gold hair. It wasn't only that she was lovely. There was something else; something cool and immaculate and well-bred about her that made Sandra's rather lush exotic beauty seem suddenly almost imperceptibly common. I looked at Sandra involuntarily. I think she realized it too. Her dark eyes smoldered. Two spots burned in her cheeks. But they might have been from the wind, or from the julep she had in her hand.

Rosemary looked around. "Where's Paul, dad?"

"Just coming, with George. Here they are."

If I hadn't been looking at Sandra at just that moment, I'd never have seen the sharp surprise in her face as she looked up at the door, or the unbelievably malicious smile that flicked one corner of her red mouth and died, and was then suddenly marked in the depths of her dark eyes. She opened her bag, took out a gold enamel cigarette case and opened it.

"This is Mr. Dikranov—Grace Latham, Paul, I'm always talking about. Mrs. Gould . . ."

Sandra looked up, her face blankly innocent.

She held out her hand. "I'm so stupeed about names," she murmured.

"Dikranov," somebody said. I watched him looking at her. He didn't seem to know her, or if he did he was a better actor than she was. There was nothing in his face that I could see. And a very handsome face it was, with fine chiseled features and olive skin, and black hair and brows. Paul Dikranov was tall and quite slender, and mature looking—I should have guessed he was nearer forty than Rosemary's age. On the other hand, he didn't look as old as George Barrol. Still, I should have been more sure that he hadn't recognized Sandra if he hadn't been so completely suave about Jim. Or maybe, of course, he'd never heard of either of them.

Just how Rosemary and I disentangled ourselves from that group I don't know—to powder our noses, I suppose. We wandered down the path towards the old mansion orangery.

"You haven't changed, Grace. Not much, anyway. You must miss Dick a lot. Why haven't you ever married again?"

"I haven't time, darling. And the boys are trouble enough just now."

"Where are they?"

"One of them's on a student tour in Europe, and the other's taken the boat and three friends for a week up the bay. I'm having a rest—or that's what I'd planned. And what about you?"

We'd stopped and were looking at each other. Rosemary smiled the cool smile that barely stirred the surface of her wide-set gray eyes.

"Nothing, darling, nothing."

22

She looked away. I saw the corners of her mouth quiver.

"She's quite beautiful, isn't she. Are they . . . happy?"

A long savage streak of lightning split the sulphur-gray sky across the dark water. A hideous clap of thunder shivered the air.

"They seem to get along well enough."

"George said she was beautiful and that all the men are mad about her."

"Your Paul's very handsome."

She nodded. "He's rather a dear. He wanted to meet Jim . . . that's one reason we came. I suppose I wanted to . . . see her."

She took my hand suddenly and held it very tight.

"I wish I hadn't. I knew the minute he dropped that glass it was all a horrible mistake. I shouldn't have come."

"Why don't you go back, tomorrow?" I asked.

She shook her head. "I can't."

"He'd understand. Your Paul, I mean."

"Dad wouldn't. Paul wouldn't either, not really. I . . . I couldn't let Jim down, anyway. Not in front of her. She'd love it, if she knew."

"She's not a fool."

"No, I suppose not. She'd never have got him if she was. You know about it, don't you?"

"Some of it."

"It doesn't matter now, I guess. It's absurd. I . . . I didn't care, yesterday—or today, till he dropped the glass."

If I'd told him in front of Mr. Toplady's store that morning, I thought, he'd never have dropped it. But something else would have happened, so I didn't worry about it just then.

Another flash of lightning slit the sky and grounded in the bay. It was quite dark all at once. In the club the lights went on first in one window and then another. We could hear the faint sound of laughing voices and the children shouting on the porch. Large drops of rain began coming down.

"We'd better go back—buck up, darling," I said. "Look out for Sandra. She'll make trouble if she can."

We went racing across the lawn between drops of rain as big as marbles. It was still poisonously hot and sticky, and the rain was cool on my arms and face.

"We'll all feel better when this is over," I said practically.

Rosemary's laugh was a strangled half-sob in her throat. "I hope so," she said.

23

CHAPTER THREE

I didn't go back to the lounge with Rosemary. The rain was starting in good earnest, we'd just had the second floor papered, and it would never occur to Julius and Lilac to see that the windows were closed, not if they happened to have company in the kitchen.

As it happened, I needn't have bothered. Julius and Lilac did have company, but that inestimable man Sergeant Buck had seen that the hatches were battened down. He had also seen that Aunt Carrie's ferns were put out on the lawn to catch the rain, the lawn chairs and the hammock brought in to the porch, the net from the tennis court neatly folded and stowed away in the garage, and my hat, gardening gloves and trowel brought in from the rock garden where I'd left them. All that should have given me some idea of what to expect from my week-end guest. Julius and Lilac were goose-stepping about the place in the most alarming fashion, completely regimented in half an hour's military dictatorship, beaming with pride and importance, and saying, "Yas, Sergeant, suh," "Yas, *indeed*, Sergeant, suh," every ten seconds.

Sergeant Buck, lantern-jawed, fish-eyed, granite-visaged, six feet and two hundred twenty pounds of beef and brawn, eyed me with what really could only be called a dead pan as I ducked out of the car onto the kitchen porch. It was our first meeting, and I could see he was definitely disappointed in me. He looked at me so forbiddingly, in fact, that I almost hesitated to go into my own house.

"Where's the Colonel, ma'am?"

He said it very suspiciously, almost as if I had him hid somewhere.

"I just slipped away to see if everything was all right here," I said meekly. "He stayed on. The Chetwynds will bring him along shortly."

Sergeant Buck nodded with some relief.

"You'll find everything in order, ma'am."

I started in.

24

"Excuse me, ma'am," he said coldly. "I understood we're staying here. I've unpacked the Colonel's bag."

"That's right," I said, turning round at the door.

"Excuse me, ma'am."

He hesitated a brief instant, and went stanchly on.

"It was my understanding we were staying with a widow woman."

"That's me," I said.

Sergeant Buck's face reddened a little.

"Excuse me, ma'am," he said again, frigidly. "But who's going to chaperon the Colonel?"

I stared for a moment, and Lilac, listening from the kitchen, threw up her hands with a scream of high-pitched colored laughter.

"Oh, *law*, Sergeant, suh, the Colonel he'll be all right! Miss Grace she won' 'noy the Colonel! *'Deed* she won'!"

Julius grinned and so did I. Sergeant Buck did not.

"I think it will be all right, Sergeant," I said soberly. "You see, Julius and Lilac live in the garage and your room is next to the Colonel's. I'm sure he'll be perfectly safe."

There was no expression of any kind on Sergeant Buck's face to indicate his acceptance of that. His face got a shade redder. "We understood you were a widow woman," he said stiffly. "I mean an old lady."

Colonel Primrose hadn't seemed particularly shocked that I was not of advanced age, although of course he may not have noticed it. Somehow I'd been feeling nearer sixty than thirty-eight all that day. The effect that a lot of people in love have on one, I suppose.

It was almost seven when Colonel Primrose came back from the club. The rain was over, for a moment or two, and I was out on the porch watching the bay, still turbulent and steel-gray under the lowering sky.

"Why did you leave so soon?"

"I had to get back to see about my family. Did I miss much?"

"A first-rate scene from modern melodrama," he said with a wry smile.

"Sandra Gould?"

He nodded. We stood silent a moment.

"I take it she knows Dikranov."

I said "Really?" I didn't want to talk about that.

"Her face, you know."

"How stupid of me not to notice."

Colonel Primrose smiled. He's very attractive, with thick gray hair and black eyes that seem to snap when he cocks his head down to look up sideways at you. It was a bullet in the neck at the Argonne that makes him have to cock his head before he can turn it. It's rather effective. And he's short and rather plump, with nothing in the least machine-gunnish about him—except possibly the sparkle in those keen black eyes.

"Stupid of *me*," he said, looking at me with a sort of amused calculation. "You know, I should have thought you did notice . . . Mrs. Gould and Dikranov, I mean. Anyway, she wasn't making much time with him while you and Miss Bishop were out. She's concentrating on George Barrol."

"George must be delighted."

"And a little nonplused, I should say. He seems to be a pleasant middle-of-the-road sort of chap."

Sergeant Buck appeared in the doorway.

"Well, I see I must go dress," the Colonel said. "You're going to the Chetwynds', and to the dance, of course?"

"Yes, indeed. It's Sail Cup Night. Rex Brophy's Band Wagon is coming down from Philadelphia."

Sergeant Buck's iron face looked at me over the Colonel's head. I'm afraid I flushed quite guiltily in spite of myself.

But Rex Brophy's Band Wagon broke down fifteen miles this side of Wilmington on the Du Pont Highway and didn't show up at April Harbor till eleven o'clock. Normally that wouldn't have been of any particular importance, and it wasn't now, actually, except that it left Sandra Gould at loose ends a bit too long.

I think we all knew we were in for trouble—all of us in our little crowd, that is. But just what horrible trouble, I don't suppose any of us—not even Colonel Primrose, who turned out· to be pretty well used to that sort of thing—even vaguely or remotely dreamed. We did, as I say, know that something would happen. If we'd been set in a circle and given a pencil and paper, and told it was a new parlor game and to guess what any three people in the room were going to do that night, I'd have written down

1. Jim Gould was either going to stay home and get stinko drunk, or come here and do it.

2. Sandra was going to raise as much hell as she could. And

3. Rosemary was going to come and be beautifully cool and sickeningly well-bred and ignore the whole wretched business.

Which showed how much *I* knew about it.

In the first place, Jim came, and so far as I know didn't touch a drop of liquor there the whole evening. A lot of us would have been happier the next day if he had. He wasn't cheerful, and he did act like a man with a terrible load on his mind, but nobody could blame him for that. He had one, in the shape of a wife who had never looked lovelier, or more like the female of the species, in all her life.

Outwardly Sandra was gentle and outrageously demure in a filmy sea-green chiffon frock with its little cape tied with long narrow grosgrain ribbons at the throat. It wasn't till you got close to her that you saw the suppressed excitement in the glowing depths of her dark eyes.

Rosemary, on the other hand, was definitely herself. She still looked like something pretty unattainable, however, with her dull gold hair parted in the middle and a thick coronet braid making a lovely sophisticated halo round her exquisitely shaped head. She had on a deceptively simple pink linen evening frock with a bunch of blue velvet flowers—one of those things that had Paris and New York written all over it and probably cost more than any six other gowns in the room. Beside her Paul Dikranov stood, courteously but definitely possessive, with the air of a man who would allow his property so much rope and not an inch more. There wasn't anything objectionable about it, however. In fact it was rather comforting in a way to have him there to be reckoned with.

But chiefly it was the lovely way he ignored Sandra that was noticeable. He talked to Mrs. Gould, he was positively charming to Lucy Lee, and I suppose he would have been to me too if Colonel Primrose hadn't sort of adopted me—Sergeant Buck not being there—to look after him.

People were standing about mopping their brows, waiting for something to do. The shower had been too short-lived to clear the air at all, and flashes of heat lightning, and the rumbling thunder still over the bay, made the hot sticky night seem closing ominously in on us.

Colonel Primrose, Mr. Bishop and I were standing in the window; Sandra, Jim, Andy and George Barrol were across the big room by the silver catboat, the presentation of which would be the high point of the evening. Sandra and Andy were receiving congratulations from people coming up, and George was sort of hanging about the offing saying, "Isn't she marvelous!" "*Lovely* child!" and what not.

They were having some kind of argument about sailsmanship, as Andy calls it, then. Lucy Lee, Paul Dikranov, Rosemary and some other people were playing monopoly. Mrs. Gould and the Chetwynds were talking to Dr. Potter, who'd put on a fresh linen suit and dropped in for his evening high-ball. It was just the ordinary sort of Saturday evening that you'd find in any country yacht club in America. Nothing on the surface suggested—or would have suggested to an outsider —that the room was packed with dynamite. Certainly not that the coolest, most detached person in the room was the detonating element.

Suddenly the argument in front of the model catboat broke into the loud "You can't possibly!"—"I can so!" stage. Everybody looked around, rather more amused and interested than surprised, for a moment. But only for a moment. There was something definitely alarming in the abrupt tenseness that was instantly apparent.

Sandra was facing her husband and Andy and the others. George Barrol was behind her looking a bit fidgety.

"I can *so!* Eef she could do eet!" she cried. "I show you! Andy will come with me!"

Lucy Lee's dark curly head went up with a jerk.

"Don't let him go, Jim!" she cried. Then she tried to laugh, her face quite white.

"Go where?" Rosemary asked.

"It's that old business. . . . Sandra wants to sail out to the lightship—in a storm—just because you did. It's crazy!"

Rosemary's eyes moved across the room and met Jim's, I imagine in the longest glance they'd yet exchanged. They were both remembering the night they'd gone out on a dare and almost never come back.

"But I will go!"

Sandra came across the room, head up, eyes flashing.

"Or maybe . . . your Paul will go weeth me!"

She stopped by Dikranov's chair, her hands resting lightly on her hips . . . rather more like the dancing Carmen than an intrepid young sportswoman.

"Just for old times' sake—hein?"

Her dark head tossed wickedly.

"But maybe you try to forget! Ah, naughty Paul!"

She shook her scarlet-tipped finger at him.

Paul Dikranov's face was as expressionless—in its own different way—as Sergeant Buck's. Rosemary stared at them both, her own face a pale mask, ivory-hard suddenly. Sandra made a quick pirouette away from them, like a dancer on a cabaret floor, and came to a stop in front of her husband.

28

"Ah, my Jeem! You theenk I don't know how much you don't like me tonight . . . but I weel show you!"

Jim's jaw tightened. He reached out to take her by the arm, but she eluded him with the grace of an apache. He couldn't very well chase her across the room with fifty people watching. So he took a deep breath and just stood there.

Sandra had whirled across to poor George Barrol and had him by the arm.

"*You* weel come with me, George! They are cowards—we weel show them!"

Poor George! He hates to get his feet wet, and even Rodman Bishop's yacht is torture to him in rough weather. But Sandra was the better man. She dragged him out of the open French windows and down the steps, the rest of us looking on dumfounded and horribly, horribly embarrassed . . . for Jim.

"Can't somebody stop them?" Mrs. Gould said quietly.

Rodman Bishop's deep voice brought all of us back to our senses. "We don't have to worry. George won't leave the dock —wild asses couldn't drag him into a boat tonight."

A terrible forked streak of lightning split the dark night. Jim and Andy went out through the windows. The rest of us looked at each other, breathed again and turned back to where we'd been. All except Rosemary. She sat erect in the white leather chair, as frozen as an icicle.

"Let's not play any more," Lucy Lee said abruptly. "I'm going outside."

Dikranov stood up and bowed formally. "Shall we go out on the porch, Rosemary?"

"No . . . thanks," Rosemary said quickly. Her voice was strained, almost harsh. Then she caught herself and said quite naturally, "You stay and talk to Dad. I'll go out with Lucy Lee. Come on, Grace."

We went, Bill Chetwynd coming with us. From the porch we could hear the sudden burst of applause that went up, and in another minute a saxophone blared. We knew that Rex Brophy's Band Wagon had arrived. I looked at my watch. It was just eleven.

Rosemary and I ran across the lawn. Lucy Lee had disappeared. Even when the lightning flashed so that we had a momentary picture of the entire scene we couldn't see her white little figure in it. We could, however, see a small boat with two figures in it bouncing on the dark waves, and on the dock two other figures in white flannels and dark jackets, running down, shouting.

"Is her boat out?" Rosemary whispered.

"Unless they brought it in tonight. They all thought the storm had died down for good."

We picked our way down the rock steps aided by the flashes of white light. Not that we needed it. Either of us could have gone from one end of April Harbor to the other in the dark with our eyes closed.

Suddenly, in front of us, was Lucy Lee, sitting on a step. Just sitting there.

"What's the matter, Lucy—hurt your ankle?" Rosemary asked quickly.

Lucy Lee shook her head.

"Go on down. I'm all right."

Rosemary went on. I stayed.

"What's the matter, Lucy Lee?"

She laughed . . . a ghastly tear-stained laugh.

"I'm just being a silly fool. Don't mind me. Go on down." I sat down beside her.

"Look, precious," I said. "You *are* being a silly fool. It's all right if you can't help it, but for Heaven's sake don't let everybody on the place know it."

She didn't say anything, just sat, a white-faced stricken child, with a thunderstorm playing havoc with her life.

"I'll go back up," she said suddenly. "Mother wants to go home early anyway. Tell Andy, will you? Not that he'll care, but it . . . sort of keeps up the joke."

CHAPTER FOUR

I watched her long white dress disappear up the hill, and went down to the float. A drop of rain hit my shoulder, and another. It was dark, but I could make out Andy with his flashlight, trying to untie a motorboat down by the No. 4 landing. I didn't see Rosemary or Jim. Not until another flash of lightning came, and then I wished I hadn't. It would have been easier the next day, and a lot easier when the State's Attorney began asking me questions. I don't imagine either of them had realized that meeting in the dark there where they'd spent so many intimate growing-up years would simply annihilate in one mindless instant all the bitterness and tragedy of those intervening years.

I ran on to the end of the pier where Andy Thorp was. He had given up trying to release the motorboat and was standing there dully, staring out at the tiny light bobbing up and down where Sandra and George Barrol were.

"No use," he mumbled. "She can handle it if anybody can. I should have gone with her."

"She won't try it, she can't! Not in this sea."

"She'll go, all right," he said.

"She's a fool!"

"I guess she thinks Rosemary's trying to get him back," he said doggedly. "He doesn't deserve a woman like her."

I stared at him.

"And I'm not saying I *do*," he went on.

"Well," I said, "of course, there *is* Lucy Lee."

"I'm not saying anything about Lucy Lee. I guess it's not her fault she's sort of all washed up."

It wasn't a particularly appropriate time, of course, to go into Andy's domestic and emotional difficulties. Not with Jim pounding along the dock towards us and Sandra and George out there in the squall, lightning flashing and the rain beginning to come down in torrents. The trouble with Andy is one of the great troubles with American colleges. He'd been one of those All-American everythings, from marbles to football, to whom

31

just the mere fact of being out of college for a couple of years is deflation enough for one ordinary twenty-five-year-old ego. Andy got the depression slapped on for good measure. Whenever I look at him, I hope my sons will be bandy-legged and cross-eyed so they can't be All-American anythings, and will escape the dreadful letdown and go into the world and not onto it.

"You'd better put this on." He pulled an oilskin coat out of the motorboat and put it over my head.

Jim was coming. He was alone.

Even then I don't think any of us thought Sandra was in any real danger.

"You going out, Jim?" Andy shouted through the rain.

"No." His voice was curt to the point of rudeness. "I'll stand by if she needs help. Rosemary's gone to have 'em put the lights on. Sandra can manage a boat better than we can."

He came back towards us.

"That sounds pretty damn offhand to me," Andy said. He was trying hard to control a sudden anger. "If she was *my* wife—"

"You wouldn't even be down here," Jim said angrily. Which was the first time I knew he had even noticed Andy and Lucy Lee lately.

"Yeah? What about yourself? I guess everybody here knows how you'd feel about it if she never got back in!"

"Andy . . . Jim!" I cried. "Shut up, both of you!"

I put my hand on Andy's arm. He shook it off angrily. "You keep out of this, Grace!" he snarled. They stood there face to face, staring at each other for an instant in the crashing storm and the rain and the lightning.

Then from above the twin beams of the great searchlights flashed out across the rain-lashed inlet. I didn't look for Sandra just then. I was looking at Jim. His tortured face was turned towards the water.

"So you'd be free . . ." Andy said deliberately.

Jim turned back.

"Steady," I said. "Andy doesn't know what he's—"

"The hell I don't. You think I'm too dumb to know what's going on? What do you suppose she brought her dago fancy man down here for!"

I don't think I'd have stopped it if I could. Jim took one swift step. His fist shot out. Andy's knees buckled like an accordion and down he went. He stayed there motionless a second, more surprised than hurt, and then leaped to his feet. Jim Gould stood square to meet him, back to the bay.

Then suddenly across the rain-driven water came a high-pitched scream of terror, and with it a man's voice shouting, "Help! Help!"

We looked. A white sail, half unfurled, dipped and pitched crazily in the wind and rain. The jib tore loose. I saw Sandra's slim figure, arms up, caught suddenly by the falling mast, careen and disappear.

We stood staring for one instant. Then Jim tore off his coat and dived. It's probably wrong to say that a dive could be impersonal, but I had that feeling very definitely, that he was going into it as he would have done if anything had been drowning—a suicide off Brooklyn Bridge, a coolie off a sampan in the Yangtze, or a dog overboard . . . just because that's the kind of person he is. I saw him strike out in a swift powerful crawl, his shirt sleeves molded to his arms making quick white arcs above the dark water. Then behind him was Andy. I was only reading into it again, probably, what I knew; but it seemed to me that there was a tensely emotional quality to the way he'd gone in and was fighting to reach Sandra first. I wouldn't have been surprised in the least if he'd caught Jim and pushed him back out of the way.

But he didn't. He didn't even catch him. I could still see him a few yards behind, picked out in the orange path of the searchlights playing frantically across the water. Behind me I could hear them shouting on the topside, and men pounding down the stone steps. Then I heard Sandra scream again, and all the laboring excitement in me went stone-dead.

Someone shouted from above: "They're hanging onto the boat!"

I turned away, feeling curiously unmoved. Joe Bates, our life guard, pounded up. "Jeez," he shouted breathlessly, "if she can hang on and bellow, why the hell doesn't she swim?"

I didn't say anything. I guess I'm pretty hard-boiled about people like Sandra.

"Why doesn't he let her drown, anyway?"

That was the voice of young Sally Parks, Lucy Lee's oldest and best friend, and actually about as cruel and cynical as a newborn babe.

"It's not right to talk like that," Joe Bates shouted.

"I would if I was him. But I hope somebody saves George Barrol. I'd *miss* him."

33

As it happened, they saved them both. Jim brought Sandra in and Andy brought George. Sandra was much the same as she was after any hard swim, except that she clung to Jim saying, "My brave Jeem!" until he shoved her off and said, "Skip it, for —— sake!"

But poor George! He was more dead than alive.

Joe Bates grabbed him and started pumping him up and down on his stomach, saying, "One, two, *three;* one, two, *three!*" But not much water seemed to be coming out of his mouth.

Everybody else was standing about in the deluge.

"Andy and Jim look the worst to me," Sally Parks remarked coolly, in her hard practical young voice. "I move we go up and give 'em a hot toddy."

"I'll stay here with Joe," Jim said stiffly. "Take Sandra up, will you."

"But, *Jeem,* you are wet, darling!"

"Stow it, will you. Go on up."

They went. I stayed down, looking at Jim. His face was a grim tragic mask, and on it was the sort of bitter sardonic travesty of a smile that I don't want ever to see on anybody's face again for a long, long time.

Joe Bates lifted George up and down. "Jeez," he said. "This guy ain't drowned, he's *fainted!*"

"Throw some water in his face," Jim said curtly.

Joe looked at me, completely bewildered.

"Pinch him," I said.

We eventually brought him around quite decently. He opened his eyes slowly, not sure apparently whether he was waking up in this world or the next. Then he struggled up, wiping the rain off his face, staring at me, the most utter and complete terror gradually dawning in his face.

"Sandra! Where's Sandra! Did they save her?" he gasped.

"Sure they saved her," Joe said cheerfully. "She's the original water baby. Couldn't drown her in the middle of the Atlantic."

"Where . . . where is she?"

"Up top. Where we're takin' you. It's your one chance for a free drink. You don't want to miss it."

I don't think the idea of free liquor was very tempting to George just then. He shuddered, felt tentatively for his heart, and breathed in a sort of experimental fashion to see if he was all right.

"I guess that was a pretty close shave," he said. His voice

shook and his face was still white with shock. "Why, I might have been drowned!"

"Sure," Joe said. "That's what some of 'em were countin' on, all the time."

"Really!"

"Don't be silly, Joe," I said. "Get him up."

Jim and I didn't even go to the club.

"They'll take care of him," Jim said. I imagine he didn't want another scene with Sandra doing the clinging lily. We passed by the club porch, however. We could see a big crowd in the lounge and in the ballroom Rex Brophy's Band Wagon was playing "The Music Goes Round and Round." We got into my car.

"What did she do it for, Jim?" I said.

"You've got me."

"She might have drowned poor George."

"She had him by the collar, holding him up," Jim said.

We rounded the Corner and turned down our road. The rain had stopped as suddenly as it began. A star or two appeared in the cloud rift.

"Why don't you come over to my place and have a good stiff drink before you turn in?" I said.

"O.K."

I turned in my back drive and we got out. Sergeant Buck opened the kitchen door and gave what in anyone less completely granite would have been a shuddering gasp. He must have thought I'd drowned his colonel.

"This is Mr. Gould, Sergeant," I said. "We've been swimming and we're going to have a drink and a fire."

I almost added "if you don't mind," but I caught myself.

"The Colonel's dancing at the club. I suggest you take my car and go wait for him."

Sergeant Buck looked a little uneasy. Then he gave the impression of clicking his heels and saluting without actually doing either. "Yes, ma'am."

Jim and I lighted a fire in the living room and I got him a drink with hot water and lemon in it and a bathrobe. It was a quarter to twelve by the clock on the mantel. We sat there, Jim hunched down on the middle of his spine, his chin forward on his chest, thinking God knows what. We sat there from quarter to twelve until ten minutes of one, neither of us having spoken a word. We moved then only because we heard Sergeant Buck bringing the Colonel up the back drive.

Jim got up. "I'll be shoving," he said, and grinned a sort of

35

twisted grin at me that brought quick hot tears to my eyes. I let him out the front door and locked it again. Then I gathered up the glasses and ash tray and took them out to the kitchen.

Colonel Primrose came in.

"I'm sorry we don't seem to have any other entrance to this house," I said. "Did you have a nice time?"

"Excellent."

"How about a nightcap?"

I noticed he glanced a little cautiously at Sergeant Buck's dead pan.

"Perhaps you'd rather have it upstairs. There's a tray on the sideboard. I'll see you in the morning. Good night. Good night, Sergeant."

I don't know about the Colonel, but I know Sergeant Buck was definitely and plainly relieved when I let the dog in and went upstairs, leaving them alone.

CHAPTER FIVE

I'm not quite sure now what woke me up. I thought as I waked that it was Sheila scratching at the door wanting to get out. But I knew it wasn't when I sat up in bed and heard her tail wag on the floor under the foot of the bed where she sleeps. I spoke to her, then I sat quite still, listening. The illuminated clock on the table said ten minutes past three. Sheila growled, gave a deep throaty bark and shambled over to the window. She stood there with her feet up on the sill, growling uneasily.

I put on my dressing gown and slipped out of bed. Sheila's head was thrust forward, her tail straight and stiff. I went over to the window and pulled her down. A pale quarter-moon was high in the clear sky. All signs of thunder and rain were gone. Sheila growled uneasily and retired to the rug in front of the fireplace when I told her to. I peered out, but I couldn't see anything.

I could, however, hear the motor of a car running quietly, rather close to me . . . then suddenly I realized that it was only Sheila breathing behind me in my own room. Why I didn't abandon the whole business then and there, and put it down to an Irish setter's nerves, I can't quite say. All I know is that suddenly, almost as if I'd seen handwriting on the wall, I had an intense and unanswerable conviction of something terribly, horribly wrong. I could no more have denied it than Joe Bates could a drowning child.

I slipped on a coat and a pair of sneakers, told Sheila to lie down where she was, opened my door and looked out down towards the guest wing. I half expected to see Sergeant Buck posted sentry in front of the Colonel's door, but the hall was empty. I closed the door and went quietly downstairs, taking the big electric torch off the landing table as I went.

Outside the night was quiet as the grave. I stood and listened. Still, somewhere near me, I thought I heard a car running quietly. I looked around for Sheila, but I knew she wasn't there. Then I heard someone, somewhere between the back of my house and the Bishops', moving quickly, and rather heavily, I thought. I crept to the end of the porch and looked out across the lawn.

A man was there. For an instant I didn't recognize him—not, in fact, until he heard me, if it was me he heard, and stopped. The next instant he was gone, slipping into the shadow of the big cherry tree by the end of the house. I stood there a little bewildered, wondering not very happily why Rosemary Bishop's fiancé should be dodging about my garden at that time in the morning. Then I heard the Bishops' garage door close, and again that low throbbing of a running motor, and I remembered then that Rex Brophy's Band Wagon had been expected to carry on till two-thirty, so that of course ten minutes past three wasn't actually late to be getting home.

I stood there, nevertheless, unable to get the sense of impending disaster out of my head. If Dikranov *was* coming back from the dance with the Goulds, why should he be so extraordinarily furtive about trespassing on my grounds? Or had he, I wondered, had a clandestine meeting with Sandra there? I waited, hesitating to go back inside, hesitating still more to go any farther forward, when quite suddenly a woman came through the hedge and stood in my garden, looking about. She started to turn back, then changed her mind and came on, towards the porch. She stopped under my bedroom window and called softly.

"Here I am," I said. "Down here."

Mrs. Gould started violently at the sound of my voice from the porch.

"What are you doing down here?" she said in a low voice, coming over.

"I couldn't sleep. It's so hot in my room, and Sheila's so restless. I just came down."

She looked at me a moment as if trying to make up her mind whether to believe me or not.

"Is anything wrong?" I asked.

"That's what I'd like to know. I can't find half my family."

"Sandra?"

"And Andy. Jim's in bed, Lucy Lee's pacing the floor.—I don't like to wake Hawkins at night, he barricades himself in."

Hawkins is her old colored butler and handy man.

She looked at me again. I noticed then that she still had on the print dress she'd worn that evening but she'd taken off her pearl necklace.

"Sandra's such an impulsive child," she said. "Sometimes I'd like to shake Andy. I know he hasn't a notion of how he upsets Lucy Lee. Who's a little ninny, of course."

She smiled wearily.

"I'm worried about Sandra, Grace. Do you realize that she tried to drown herself tonight?"

"She *what?*" I gasped.

Mrs. Gould nodded.

"She's been threatening to kill herself all day. She's got some horrible notion that she's ruined Jim's career and now she's ruining his life. She's so terribly impulsive!"

"You ought to go to bed, darling," I said—which was an easy way of putting it. "I'll walk back with you. Andy's probably home by now and so's Sandra."

I took her arm, and was startled at how curiously rigid her body was, and immovable.

"You're tired, Alice; do come back," I said. She relaxed suddenly. I could hear her long relieved breath.

"Thanks, my dear. I suppose I am." She pressed my hand quickly.

"And you're cold."

"No, no. I'm just . . . disturbed." She laughed softly. "My children are such—wretches."

The night wind shivered in the stiff magnolia leaves. The boys' pigeons in the side yard cooed and rustled as if something strange had passed them. Somewhere from the bay there was the faint sound of a guitar and voices singing. But that was far away. Around us in the dark was nothing but an eerie silence, throbbing and uneasy.

"Come along, darling."

We moved across the grass. It was cold through my slippers, and the tall blades on the edge, where Julius's sickle had missed, brushed against my bare ankles, sharply intense. At the hedge I pulled back a branch of white althea for Alice to pass. Released, it brushed, softly cool, against my shoulder. I started so that Alice stopped.

"What is it, Grace?" she whispered.

"Nothing, darling."

I pressed on my flashlight. A white moth dashed out of the dark, an enormous potato bug trundled across the dirt path.

"I'll just get my bag out of the car," Alice said. "If you'll lend me your light and give me a hand with the doors."

The garage loomed white and ghostly above the dark line of shrubs. We turned to the right along the narrow path that leads to the double doors at the end of the drive from the road.

Suddenly I knew what I'd been hearing . . . what it was that had given the throbbing undertone to the clear still night.

"Somebody's left his motor running," I said.

39

"That's one of Sandra's tricks," Alice Gould said. "She's back, then. It's funny the things that annoy husbands," she went on. "That's a much worse offense in Jim's eyes than burned rice pudding."

I tugged at the white door. The padlock wasn't on, but the doors seemed jammed tighter than usual. Finally I got them open, after skinning my knuckles and breaking at least two fingernails. I swung them wide, started in, and then remembered that I had no idea of how long the motor had been running and that the garage had been tightly shut.

"We'd better let it air out a minute," I said. Mrs. Gould nodded. We stood there a minute or two, looking in. Jim's car was parked in front of me, Andy's was in the other half.

"It's Andy's motor that's on," I said. "I'll turn it off while you get your bag."

I wriggled around behind Andy's sedan, squeezed along the running board to the door and reached inside to switch off the engine and take out the keys. My hand struck something woolly and hard. The smell of Scotch whisky hit my nose and almost took my breath away. I caught myself sharply. Mrs. Gould's voice was running along pleasantly as she fished around in Jim's car for her bag.

I caught my breath, and said, as casually as I could—knowing how she hates for people to drink too much, "Well, here's our precious Andy."

I could hear her suddenly stop her fishing about.

"Where?" she said.

"Right here. Fast asleep."

I turned off the engine and switched the lights on. Then I stood there motionless, my hand out in front of me.

It wasn't Andy Thorp under that wheel. It was Sandra Gould—and it didn't take the ghastly open-eyed stare on her strangely colored face to tell me she was dead.

Hardly knowing what I was doing, I took the flash from Alice Gould's paralyzed fingers and turned its beam on the lifeless girl. Her arms were sunk down at her sides. Clutched in one hand was the torn petal of a blue velvet flower.

I held the flash on it for a long time. Only in a strange remote part of my consciousness was I aware of Alice Gould's hands moving over the window ledge and quietly, calmly disengaging from that dead hand the evidence that might easily have hanged her son . . . or her son's lost lady.

CHAPTER SIX

Alice Gould's simple act of disengaging the torn and crushed velvet petals from her daughter-in-law's dead fingers was small and unobtrusive enough in itself. Its implications were appalling. Even at that moment, still balanced on one foot on the running board of Andy Thorp's car, with Sandra Gould sprawled inert and so terribly silent on the seat, I recognized a few of them. First, and above all, it meant that we tacitly and definitely accepted the fact that Rosemary Bishop was in some way involved in whatever had happened. Second, it meant that both of us pledged ourselves to keep the fact from getting out —lined up on Rosemary's side, as it were, against Sandra—and became quite simply accessories after whatever the fact might turn out to be.

"I'll stay here, Grace," Mrs. Gould said at last, quietly. "You go and get Jim and phone Dr. Potter."

"I'll stay," I said. "It'll be better for you to tell Jim."

I'm not sure now whether I actually shrank from telling Jim Gould that his wife was dead, or whether it was because in some secret law-abiding place in my heart I felt some obligation to social order. Whether I felt it wasn't safe to leave Alice Gould alone there with Sandra, or whether already I had some deep-seated fear that Jim . . . But that was nonsense, of course. I think Alice Gould understood, however, because as our eyes met across Sandra's body a faint infinitely sad smile moved in hers.

"I'd *rather* go, Grace," she said. "I just didn't like to leave you alone . . . again . . . with death."

She went then, and I went over to the switch by the side door to turn on the overhead light. It seemed odd to me suddenly that neither of us had thought of it before. I squeezed in front of Andy's car and stubbed my toe on something, making noise enough, or so it seemed in the small completely silent segment of night that engulfed me, to wake even Sandra sprawled there. I felt down on the floor to see what it was, and

41

picked up the monkey wrench Jim had had in front of Mr. Toplady's store that morning.

I put it on the shelf and went, feeling my way cautiously, in front of Jim's coupé to the door. I turned on the light. Everything was instantly stark and dismal in the bright glare of the single unshaded bulb set in the middle of the ceiling. A huge moth miller flew in and bashed himself against the bulb; insects of all sorts came suddenly swarming in from the night. I stood alone there with Sandra, waiting.

Outside I thought I could hear someone coming. I moved back in front of Jim's car and between his and Andy's to the door, and looked out. No one was there. I listened a moment, but no one was moving. A dog probably, I said to myself, and looked at my wrist, but I hadn't my watch on. It seemed a long time that I'd stood there, and it was longer still before I heard a door slam and heavy feet dashing down the brick path from the house.

Jim came running around to the back, took one look at me and stopped abruptly.

"Is she dead, Grace?" he asked . . . as impassively as if she were someone he scarcely knew.

I nodded.

Then, more like a man walking in his sleep than anything else, he went inside.

"In Andy's car," I said, because he'd gone straight to his own. He looked bewildered and uncertain, but he turned. I saw him catch the window ledge with both hands to steady himself, and stand there motionless . . . for ages, it seemed. Then he dropped his head down on the back of his hands. I thought he was sobbing—his shoulders moved convulsively once or twice —but when I went over to him and put my arm round his shoulders he raised haggard anguished eyes that had no tears in them. I had no idea what was going on in his mind.

Quite abruptly over our heads we heard a knocking. Old Hawkins's voice came down querulously.

"Mis' Gould, ain' you all never goin' to bed? We got to be out here at seven o'clock, an' you all can sleep till dinnertime."

Sandra's oval face, dyed red with carbon monoxide, stared up at the ceiling. Jim tried to speak, but not a sound came. Outside we heard a car coming along the road from April Harbor, and two long white fingers of light stretched through the night and turned, flattening themselves against us as the car came into the Goulds' drive. Jim's mother appeared then too, in the door, and went to the car to meet Dr. Potter. And then, without the least warning, Colonel Primrose and Sergeant Buck came through the hedge from my garden. Sergeant Buck was dressed. Colonel Primrose had on a striped flannel dressing gown. He looked sleepy; Sergeant Buck did not.

The Colonel came into the garage. His black eyes darted in every corner at once before they fastened themselves on Jim and me, and beyond us where the light from the ceiling struck Sandra's head. He glanced out then at Dr. Potter and another man who were hurrying along the drive, and at me, but he said nothing. He merely backed out of their way and stood near the door, the massive square figure of his sergeant looming portentously behind him.

Jim and I moved back into the narrow space between the fronts of the two cars. I felt his sudden involuntary start as he recognized the man with Dr. Potter. Our Mr. Shryock is something like a turkey buzzard—we see him only at times like this.

"You say she's dead, ma'am?" he inquired of Mrs. Gould. He caught sight of Jim and lowered his voice. "Tragic, tragic," he said. "Tch, tch!"

Mr. Shryock's trouble is that he has to reconcile the difficult roles of local undertaker, wanting private business, on the one side and local coroner doing public duty on the other. We'd seen him work before . . . when Chapin was drowned. We saw him now give Sandra's body a perfunctory glance and look around then at the two men standing silently by the door.

"I'll have to have a jury before the body can be moved," he said. "Will you two gentlemen act? I'll rout out some more."

He stepped briskly out and hailed a man he had left in his car. They disappeared together. In a few moments there was a little circle of our shocked and white-faced neighbors, silent and terribly distressed, standing around outside in the drive, lighting cigarettes, whispering a little among themselves. I looked them over as they came—Ned Bryan, Pinkie Reed, Buzz Dixon. They all lived beyond the Goulds'. I breathed a sigh of relief as I realized that the coroner was headed away from the Bishops'. At least, I thought, they would be spared that embarrassment. But I was wrong. Mr. Shryock came back at last, with him Rodman Bishop, George Barrol and Yancy Holland, the Bishops' caretaker and man of all work.

They made up the twelve. Rodman Bishop nodded to the rest of the group, then moved over to Alice Gould and took his stand beside her. His dressing gown and rumpled gray hair seemed extraordinarily deshabille beside her coat and print dress and properly arranged coiffure. George moved in with

43

the other men, looking about as upset as I've ever seen him, trying to find out what had happened.

Mr. Shryock stepped up on a box in the doorway. "This is a very tragic mission, gentlemen, I've called you on," he said. "I must ask you each, constituting the coroner's jury, to file through the garage here and look at the body. We will then hear what Dr. Potter has to say, and adjourn to Mrs. Latham's house—if she will be so kind as to allow us to do so."

I nodded quite mechanically. It seemed a horribly offhand way of disposing of the awful fact of death.

"You're to look carefully, gentlemen, as you will be called upon to make a decision as to the cause of death and the manner it was come by. You are all men of the world. I will ask you not to omit any fact that seems important to you—such as the odor in the car, for example."

Mr. Shryock went on. It was his hour—he didn't often come into contact with the April Harbor Colony. Most of us died decently in our town homes in the winter of pneumonia or old age. We came to April Harbor for rest and relaxation.

"All right, gentlemen."

Jim Gould stood watching them, white-faced and haggard, as they went in, trying not to look at him, poor dears. They went one by one to the window where Jim had stood, looked in, turned away quickly, blundered back outside and lighted cigarettes again—even Rodman Bishop. George didn't look at her, I'm sure of that. He just got to the door and hurried out, a little green about the gills, and I could hear him protesting in an undertone to the coroner that he oughtn't to have to act, because he had driven home with her. But nobody paid any attention to him, except Colonel Primrose. He stood there quietly, with his head cocked and his sparkling black eyes resting on first one, then another, listening to everything, and rather more like a turkey buzzard than Mr. Shryock, if the truth were told.

That's why I watched him when his turn came. He looked inside the car, and sniffed; bent his head close to Sandra's face and sniffed again, picked up her hands and looked at them. Then he opened the door. A half-empty flask of whisky fell out onto the running board. He picked it up carefully and handed it to Mr. Shryock. Then he touched the back of the seat, and bent down to look at Sandra's slippers. After that he moved away and made room for Sergeant Buck, who did exactly what the Colonel had done and moved away in his turn.

We waited, the twelve men of the jury and myself, for more

than half an hour in my living room before the coroner and Dr. Potter and another man—tall, stooped and dyspeptic—came in.

"This is Mr. Owens Parran, gentlemen," said Mr. Shryock. "He's our State's Attorney. Always on the job, that's his watchword, and you're all going to like his style, I know that. Would you like to say a word at this time, Mr. Parran?"

Mr. Parran shook his head and yawned. "Go ahead," he said. I thought we might be going to like his style, but it was going to be hard to get over his manner. He did, however, shake hands with Rodman Bishop and Colonel Primrose. I suppose it's part of being a good politician to be able to spot the most important men in any group without outside assistance.

"Dr. Potter," the coroner said.

I don't think I've ever seen Adam Potter look as old and completely done in as he did then.

"The cause of death is quite clear," he said in a dry expressionless voice. "The discoloration of the skin that you must all have noticed is due to carbon monoxide poisoning. I think there is no reasonable possibility of doubt that that is the cause of death."

"Thank you, doctor. Now, gentlemen, I understood from Mrs. Gould senior that she and Mrs. Latham here found young Mrs. Gould. I should like to spare the natural feelings of the bereaved as far as is in our power, so I will ask Mrs. Latham to give her account of the situation."

"I heard someone in my garden a few minutes after three," I said. "I got up and came down. It was Mrs. Gould. She was hunting for Sandra—her daughter-in-law."

I don't know why I left out Andy Thorp, but I was quite definitely conscious that I was doing so.

"I thought I heard a motor running and we went into the garage. The engine of the sedan was on. I started to turn it off, thinking somebody had just forgot it. My hand touched a wool coat. I thought it was a man until I switched on the lights and saw Sandra Gould. She had on a man's coat."

"I wished to inquire about that jacket," Mr. Shryock said.

"Mrs. Gould got wet during the evening. I suppose someone gave it to her to wear home so she wouldn't catch cold," I said.

"Undoubtedly got caught in the rain."

I glanced at Colonel Primrose. He was just sitting there.

"Had Mrs. Gould been drinking?" Mr. Shryock continued.

There was no answer from anyone.

"I ask that," he added, "because of the smell in the car, and because it would be extremely simple for a lady under the influence to drop off to sleep without switching off the engine of her car."

A voice spoke up nervously.

"But it wasn't her car in the first place, and she'd certainly not been drinking in the second."

We all looked around, rather startled by this sudden contribution from the ranks of the jurors. George Barrol flushed. "I mean . . . you see, I came home with her. I mean, Mr. Thorp drove us both home from the club house, and they let me out at The Magnolias. Then they drove back. Unless they drank a lot after they left me, Mrs. Gould certainly wasn't under the influence, as you say."

The coroner frowned, and so did everybody else except Rodman Bishop. He looked at me and shook his head a little. The thing about George Barrol is that he's always putting his own and other people's feet into things that had best be left quite free of feet.

"Where is Mr. Thorp?"

The coroner looked about.

"Go get him, Frank. Will one of you gentlemen go with him to show him the way?"

Jerry Nolan went—glad to get out, I think, because he'd been quite devoted to Sandra the last two summers before he married Charlotte Putnam.

The rest of us still avoided looking at each other. Even Yancy Holland was lined up on the side of the Colony, trying to keep the matter as casual as possible. Now and then somebody glanced apprehensively at Colonel Primrose and Sergeant Buck. They were the imponderables. The rest of them could be counted on to help old Jim if he needed it. In fact, as it was turning out, the coroner was doing it all for them. Even I could think of forty embarrassing questions that had not been asked or even hinted at. The doors of the garage, for instance. If Sandra had gone to sleep, she couldn't very well have closed the doors and sealed herself in.

Mr. Shryock was examining a piece of folded note paper he'd got somewhere. He had passed it to Mr. Parran, and Mr. Parran had examined it for a considerable time before he passed it back.

I went out to the kitchen to get some glasses and some beer. I didn't feel in the mood to set fifteen men up to Scotch and soda. Moreover, I couldn't in the least understand the coroner's air. Here obviously was a group of people tremendously upset by what had happened, and he was setting about as if it were an all-night oyster roast.

I had just got back when we heard Jerry Nolan's voice outside.

"Buck up, Andy—for God's sake, old man!" he was saying. They came in. Andy Thorp's face was ghastly. His eyes were bloodshot, he looked altogether as if they'd just swept him out from under a counter. There was a dazed and stricken look on his face and he kept muttering crazily and mumbling something about keys. He was six feet three of complete and total incoherence. He sat down, or rather Jerry Nolan pushed him into a chair. Then, to my surprise, Sergeant Buck was at his side handing him a stiff peg of whisky, and taking the empty glass away.

Andy groaned and dropped his head on his hands. He sat there kneading at his head with convulsive fingers.

"Mr. Thorp, I understand you drove Mrs. Gould and Mr. Barrol home from the dance at the club?"

Andy nodded.

"You dropped Mr. Barrol at The Magnolias. Now if you'll tell us what happened next, please?"

Andy looked up. I think he was really nearer the point of collapse than any of us realized.

"I drove home and put the car in the garage. We got out and closed the door, and walked up the path to the house. Halfway up Sandra said she'd left something in the car. I always lock it, even in the garage—it's a habit you get into in New York. I said I'd go back and get it for her, but she said she'd do it, so I gave her the keys and went on home. That's all I know.—That's all I know, I tell you!"

His voice rose almost to a scream in that last sudden outburst. We all stared at him. He dropped his head in his hands again, making curious strangled sobs. Jerry Nolan patted him anxiously on the back.

Mr. Shryock looked at him for an instant. Then he nodded soberly and picked up the note on the table in front of him.

"Is there anyone here who can identify Mrs. Alexandra Gould's handwriting?" he asked.

Jerry Nolan flushed and raised his hand. There were several others, including myself and Andy. Mr. Shryock passed the thin elegant bit of gray note paper to Jerry.

"Do you recognize this as Mrs. Gould's handwriting?"

Jerry nodded. I thought he rather paled too.

"Will you give it to the next gentleman?"

Bailey Fisher took it and handed it quickly to Frank Gerber, nodding his head.

"That's her writing, all right," Frank said. He gave it to me. I looked at it.

"Can you identify that as Mrs. Gould's writing, Mrs. Latham?"

"I can," I said in a low voice. I'd seen it—a childish uneducated scrawl—a thousand times. She was always writing notes about something.

I handed it back. My heart was like a lump of ice in the pit of my stomach.

The coroner put on his horn-rimmed spectacles and surveyed us over them for an instant.

"I have here a letter that you have heard identified as positively as possible under the circumstances. I'm going to read it to you and then I shall ask for your verdict, gentlemen."

He looked down. We waited. I could hear Sheila scratching at the door upstairs. Outside a few early birds were chirping, getting the business of worms under way. The clock on the hall landing struck four-thirty.

My dearest darling Jim,—You must forgive your Sandra and forget her forever. It is wrong and wicked to kill myself, I know, but I have ruined your whole life Jim and you have been so good to me. In my country we are not afraid of death and I am not afraid now. Good-by, Jim. They say it does not hurt very much this way.—
SANDRA.

The coroner stopped. All of us sat mute and horror-stricken. To hear Sandra's childish English in the coroner's flat nasal Maryland whine seemed unbearably incongruous. After a long time he looked up.

"Mrs. Gould senior found that note on her daughter-in-law's dressing table tonight. That is why she was out searching for her. I think we know what happened, gentlemen. I await your verdict."

I waited for it too. And when it came, after the twelve men, ten of us from April Harbor and two outsiders, had adjourned to the dining room, I sat with my head down, my hands shaking so I had to hold them stuck deep down in my pockets to keep them still.

They filed back. Rodman Bishop stood up, white-haired,

square-faced, hard-jawed. "The jury finds that Alexandra Gould met her death at her own hands from inhaling carbon monoxide fumes while of an unsound mind," he said.

Mr. Shryock looked at the State's Attorney. Mr. Parran nodded sleepily.

"Thank you, gentlemen, thank you," Mr. Shryock said. He rubbed his hands together and looked about. "I think that will be all. I'll make my report in longhand, Mr. Parran, my typewriter's being overhauled."

I still sat there, my hands steadied against the seams of my pockets. Suddenly I looked up. Colonel Primrose was looking intently at me. My lips were very dry. I tried to moisten them without his seeing me. Surely there was no way of his knowing what was beating in my brain until it was numb with dread! The coroner's hand stuck down towards me brought me to with a start. I scrambled to my feet and said good night to him and to Mr. Parran. Rodman Bishop patted my shoulder.

"You'd better get a little sleep, Grace," he said. I thought he was telling me something else too.

I closed the door after them, and stood a moment looking out to the bay, silvery calm in the gray dawn. I knew Colonel Primrose was standing in the middle of the room behind me, waiting. At last I turned around and faced him, my hands behind me holding onto the door-knob to steady me.

Our eyes met, his sparkling black and penetrating, mine trying to hide what was in them. Then he smiled, suddenly and kindly.

"It's hardly fair, is it? Especially when you didn't invite me here."

I took a deep breath.

"Maybe you'll want to tell me about it in the morning," he said after a moment. "I don't mind confessing to you that all this worries me.—You'd better go back to bed."

I'm afraid I literally fled upstairs. I don't know what on earth Sergeant Buck thought, because he came in just at that moment—after having put the bottles away and washed up the glasses, I was morally certain. I saw him give the Colonel a pained admonitory look.

"Up to your old tricks, sir!" he said severely, shaking his head.

And I, stupidly, was the one who misunderstood him.

CHAPTER SEVEN

By morning, however, I should never have thought of telling him. In fact, until I saw Lilac's solemn black face above the pink-flowered coffeepot on my breakfast tray, I had almost forgotten Sandra Gould. It's always seemed to me a curious commentary on the human soul that a few hours' sleep and the morning sun can manage to do away with the most horrible forebodings. I thought of that now as I waited for Lilac to prop the pillows behind me.

"Mr. Jim's wife done away with herself las' night, Miss Grace," she said ominously.

"I know," I said, unfolding the morning paper.

"Don' seem lak she'd do that, somehow. Seem lak she was too ornery."

"You can't tell about people," I answered philosophically.

" 'Deed an' that's what Annie says, at church this mornin'."

Annie is the Bishops' cook, and there's a community bus that takes all the colored help into April Harbor to church at six Sunday mornings and at eight Sunday evenings.

"Hawkins says the carryin's on in the garage las' night sumthin' to hear."

"Really?"

"Yas'm."

I was intent on my paper. I didn't want to discuss this business with her . . . not just then. She's been with us fifteen years. There's not very much she doesn't know about my friends, and her judgments are shrewd.

She stood, a black mountain of irresolution, at the foot of my bed a moment, then went to the door. There she stopped and turned round.

"Shall Ah keep the Cunnel's breakfas' hot, or will he get his breakfas' while he's in town?"

I looked up, too startled to conceal anything.

"He done went out, him an' the Sergeant, 'fore me an' Julius got back from church. We passed 'em on the bridge, goin' into town."

With that she went out and closed the door. The inquiry about their breakfast, of course, was merely a gambit with which I really had nothing whatsoever to do.

I put my paper down and drank my orange juice, definitely disturbed by this move on the part of my guest. I knew from my father and my husband—both of them lawyers—that the most difficult thing for people involved in an unlawful conspiracy to do is to do nothing. Nevertheless, I put my hand out half a dozen times and took up the telephone to call Alice Gould, only to put it down each time.

I was considerably more upset, as a matter of fact, than I liked at all to admit, even to myself. What if Colonel Primrose had decided that Sandra's death was not suicide at all, and got the State's Attorney to open an investigation? What, for instance, would I do about the two bits of information that I had that were so damning to people I cared a great deal about—so much that I hardly dared think about them. The fact that they pointed in wholly different directions didn't seem to matter. Rosemary's flower clutched in Sandra's hand—the letter that Alice Gould had found on Sandra's dressing table. What would I do? Would I commit perjury if I had to?

I wiped the excess lipstick off my mouth with a piece of tissue, looking at myself in the mirror. I knew I would—if I had to. In a sense I'd already done it.

I was on the screened front porch when Colonel Primrose and his sergeant appeared coming around the house. That in itself seemed ominous, as none but the most formal callers bother to come in any way except through the kitchen. His greeting was cheery, but it failed to conceal the look on Sergeant Buck's face, even more iron-grim than usual. The Sergeant did not come in. He marched down the lawn, dug out a dandelion that I've been carefully saving for several years, picked up an empty crumpled cigarette package and a couple of butts and went around the house. You could almost see a garbage can in his mind.

"Good morning, Mrs. Latham. I hope you slept—or did you have time?"

The Colonel smiled and sat down, straightening one rheumatic knee into place with a quite shameless grin to acknowledge the liability of years.

"I'm afraid I was up a bit early. I hope I didn't disturb you?"

"Not at all. I only heard about it through the normal domestic channels. Would you like a cup of coffee?"

I got up to ring the bell, but he put up his hand.

"I've breakfasted—wisely but not too well—at the local undertaker's."

"It sounds bad."

"It was. But sit down, Mrs. Latham. I want to talk to you. I want to ask you something, very frankly. I want you to be equally frank—because it's quite a serious matter."

I sat down again, trying to make myself meet his black intent gaze without telling him I was trying.

"I said I'd been to the undertaker's this morning," he went on. "I wanted to make sure that Sandra Gould died of carbon monoxide poisoning."

He looked at me steadily. I waited.

"And she did. There's no doubt of that."

I breathed deeply, almost without knowing that I'd been holding my breath while I waited.

"But that's not all, Mrs. Latham," he said quietly. "There's a bruise on the back of her head. Only a slight abrasion, but the bruise is fairly extensive."

"Still . . . she died of monoxide gas," I said quickly.

"Her legs are scratched too," he said, disregarding my interruption. "But it's the bruise that interests me. It would have knocked her completely unconscious—if she wasn't already dead, and we've been able to rule that out quite definitely. The bruise was made before she died."

I looked at him, not knowing what all this was leading up to.

"In other words, Mrs. Latham, while Sandra Gould was actually killed by carbon monoxide poisoning, her death was not self-inflicted. She did breathe in the fumes that killed her, but she was unconscious while she was doing it. From her own point of view her death was quite unintentional. In other words again, Mrs. Latham . . . Sandra Gould was murdered."

I stared at him, speechless. Now that my own doubts and fears were put squarely in front of me in the form of fact, I fought them off violently.

"That's impossible!" I cried. "You can't know that! The bruises could have been made when she fell against the door handle!"

Colonel Primrose shook his head.

"That's what your coroner amicably suggested. But he's wrong. It's simple to prove. You see, the blood in the bruised tissue has no trace of carbon monoxide. The rest of her blood is saturated with it."

He looked at me very earnestly.

"You see, Mrs. Latham, this sort of thing is my business.

Buck and I make our living at it . . . keeping people from getting away with murder. And that's what I want to talk to you about."

He hesitated a moment, and chuckled a little.

"Frankly, I've already abused your hospitality. I phoned to Washington last night. The Federal Bureau sent down a make-shift sort of laboratory this morning. Dr. Potter and Mr. Shryock helped out. Furthermore, Mrs. Latham, there was no alcohol in the woman's brain . . . not enough, anyway, to account for the odor in that car. I felt the seat last night, as you may have noticed. The whisky had been spilled on it, for the purpose of misdirection."

I took a cigarette out of the box on the table and held it as steadily as I could while he lighted it for me.

"You see, that's the great trouble with murder. Ordinarily, last night would have washed all this up—completely—except that I happened to be here. That's about the only thing that makes me believe there must be some kind of design in the universe—the number of times that what seems mere coincidence steps in to thwart murder; or murderers, rather. We've no way of knowing how many times murder itself is thwarted and doesn't happen."

I looked at him for a moment. "When did you decide it was murder?"

"Last night."

"Why?"

"Why? Perhaps it's because I've got a sort of sixth sense, Mrs. Latham. And that, I suppose, is made up of little frag-ments of intangible evidence—like, for example, the expression on your face when you saw that suicide note, and the liquor spilled on the car seat. And a pretty strong conviction that a girl like Sandra Gould wouldn't just throw her hand in when a beautiful rival sits in on the game. Added, my dear Mrs. La-tham, to that evening at the clubhouse where at least three women had murder in their eyes, and at least four men weren't —well, let's say as detached as they tried to appear."

"Meaning who?" I asked.

"Nobody that you can't identify as easily as I can. But that's not the immediate point, Mrs. Latham. The immediate point is this: what are *you* going to do about it?"

He looked at me, a little amused and at the same time deadly earnest and calculating.

"I mean, would you like me to go somewhere?"

"Very much indeed, I'm afraid," I replied as casually as I

53

could. "Addis Ababa, just offhand. Or Perth, Western Australia."

He smiled.

"I'm sorry. I'm staying in too, you know. I don't like murder. It's just an old-fashioned prejudice, and I'm an old-fashioned man. No, I'm only offering—not wholeheartedly, because you're so extraordinarily central—to go to a hotel if you ask me to. It's not going to be easy, you know. For you, I mean."

"I'm afraid I'm rather prejudiced too," I said. "I shouldn't like to say I approve of murder as a social pastime—but I think it's possible for one to be pretty well justified."

Colonel Primrose shook his head.

"That's the trouble with you moderns. You've got such a hard, polished exterior. Scratch it, and you're like Sergeant Buck—a mass of sentimental jelly. You don't like consequences; you're glad when something comes along and removes them, even if it happens to be a murder. But you're not going to escape a few consequences of your own."

I must have looked most astonished.

"Don't you see, Grace Latham, that you *know too much?*"

He looked so sober that I was a little alarmed in spite of myself.

"Don't you see that that's the bad thing about murder? That's the chief reason we can't just let it ride and say, 'Fair enough and an easy way out.' Because murderers don't rest easy in their own minds—and you, my dear Mrs. Latham, are just the person that this murderer is going to worry about, more and more. How much you know . . . how much you saw . . . how much you guessed."

He shook his head.

"I imagine that's one of the reasons I'd like to stay here in your house, me and Buck. I'd like to keep an eye on you."

He chuckled suddenly. "It's very reassuring in any kind of dustup to have Sergeant Buck's eye on you."

"You don't think, by any chance," I asked, "that *I* murdered Sandra Gould?"

He cocked his black eyes at me for all the world like a wicked old parrot about to take a piece out of my ear. "I shouldn't like to make any broad declaration of the sort just at this time. I think you're undoubtedly a very important person in the case—perhaps even more important than you realize. I've already told you that you know too much about all this—fore and aft. Perhaps we might even work together."

54

"That," I said, "is nothing but the most unmitigated flattery, and I'm not falling for it . . . not at any rate till it's disguised better. But you may stay here—if you will assure your sergeant that it was your own idea, not mine, and that personally I should be much happier if you'd never set foot in April Harbor."

"It would have come out eventually, Mrs. Latham. Shryock would have drunk too much one night and told Parran. Or one of your friends here would have talked over the bridge table one afternoon. It would have been worse then, and more trouble. If, indeed, the Goulds' order to ship the body to Baltimore for cremation hadn't already done the trick."

"What do you mean?"

"Shryock—*qua* undertaker, not coroner—had that order."

"From whom?"

"From the Goulds, I imagine."

I was silent.

"So you see."

I nodded. "I think I see," I said. "When do you start . . . and where?"

"Now and here," said Colonel Primrose cheerfully. "Mr. Parran is starting in the garage. He's going to meet me shortly. I thought I'd speak to you first. Of course, I want to know about Sandra Gould. What's the history?"

"I don't know much about her, except that she married Jim in Shanghai," I said. "They've been coming here ever since Jim got out of the Navy."

"Why did he get out?"

"I suppose he thought he'd rather sell bonds, or something."

He cocked his head and fastened his sparkling black parrot's eyes on me.

"Mrs. Latham—unless you tell me the truth, there's not much use in taking your time or mine," he said reproachfully.

"Is it truth you want, or all the wretched gossip and malicious imaginings of a hundred busybodies?" I demanded hotly.

He smiled a rather wry subrisive smile. "Unfortunately, gossip usually has a large grain of truth in it. It's extremely useful in my business."

"It must be a rather ghastly business."

He smiled again.

"I take it you think the general idea that Jim Gould got out of the Navy because a certain admiral on a certain China station requested that he be detached because of Sandra is malicious imagining?—The Chetwynds told me that to show

55

how much she'd improved under the tutelage of her mother and sister-in-law."

"She did improve," I had to admit. "She wasn't very attractive when she first came. A little too Eurasian Mae West. Very lush—like a ripe passion fruit. Too much make-up, hair curled too much, clothes too fancy, fingernails too red and not too clean, eye too obviously roving. But she *has* changed. You saw her. Sleek straight hair, marvelous make-up, exquisite clothes. Still very gay and all that but oh so toned down, and . . . Westernized. Thanks to a mother-in-law with impeccable taste and a lot of money. I don't think she's any handicap to Jim now."

"She's a very definite one just this minute, Mrs. Latham," Colonel Primrose said. "Well, what about his marriage, and what happened between him and Rosemary Bishop?"

"Their engagement was broken. That's all I know. He married Sandra then—it frequently happens, you know. The old course of true love and the slip 'twixt cup and lip."

"And the fish in the sea that haven't been caught?"

"Precisely. That's Paul Dikranov. Loads of money—which Jim hasn't any more."

"I see."

"No . . . you don't. Because I don't mean it that way at all. That might just possibly be in Rodman Bishop's mind. It certainly wouldn't ever be in Rosemary's."

He smiled. "Then perhaps I do see, after all," he said.

We heard a car coming in my back drive. Colonel Primrose got up.

He looked at me seriously.

"I think I ought to tell you," he said slowly, "that Parran is going to arrest him. Jim Gould, of course."

I stared at him stupidly. "What for?"

"For the murder of Sandra Gould."

"Nonsense!"

"I wish it were. I'm afraid it's not, Mrs. Latham. Just on the face of it even, there's a powerful case against him. Motive, opportunity . . . all the rest."

I tried frantically to find something for Jim in all this mess.

"What about the letter, Colonel Primrose?"

He shook his head soberly. "It's a forgery, Mrs. Latham. It's got to be. Rather a transparent one, I suspect. That woman didn't kill herself."

He looked at me. I'd recovered myself by then and said nothing . . . for which I was thankful a little later.

At that point the wooden face of Sergeant Buck loomed through the screen at the end of the porch. The State's Attorney Mr. Parran was with him, and behind him were two other men, one of them in the summer khaki and helmet of the Maryland State Police.

"Good morning, ma'am," Mr. Parran said. "Ready, Colonel?"

I watched them go across to the opening in the hedge, towards the Goulds'. The thought struck me then that Colonel Primrose had kept me there talking, asking questions whose answers he already knew, so that I couldn't warn Jim. I sat down suddenly, very sick and weak in the knees.

For the second time that day I resisted the impulse to fly to the telephone. I told myself that that was just what Colonel Primrose would be waiting for and watching for, some move of mine or of somebody's to point a direction for him. So I sat there, pretty miserable, trying to picture to myself just what they'd be doing . . . how Jim would take it, what his mother would do. I never thought of Lucy Lee until I heard a sound in the living room and saw her there beckoning to me, white-faced and terribly frightened.

"What's the matter, Grace? What are they doing—why are they in the garage?" she demanded frantically. "Colonel Primrose is there—Bill told Andy he's some sort of private detective. Don't they—"

She stopped short. "Grace . . ."

"They think Sandra didn't kill herself, Lucy Lee," I said quietly.

She stared at me, gradually shrinking until she seemed more like a child herself than a twenty-six-year-old mother of three. Poor little Lucy Lee . . . always the prettiest, most popular girl at the Harbor, with dozens of beaux, married by the age-old process of natural selection to the biggest, handsomest and most heroic of the lot . . . and it just hadn't worked. If we'd been Vikings, Andy Thorp would have been headman; but in Broadway offices where the headman is a very different sort, Andy doesn't seem to fit. Lucy Lee's fiercely loyal, doing without the things she'd always had, doing her own work in town and pretending she liked it!—She stood in the center of my living room staring at me, her pale soft face paler than usual, framed in her mass of soft short chestnut curls, her dark eyes bigger and more bewildered.

"Listen, Lucy Lee. You've got to buck up. This is going to

57

be rotten for everybody . . . but it's going to be terrible for Jim."

She looked at me as if she didn't understand at all.

"For *Jim?*"

It was my turn to stare. The strangest kaleidoscoping of emotion and calculation went through her pretty transparent face. I wasn't sure she even knew what I was talking about.

"I'm afraid they think Jim killed her, darling," I said.

Fond as I am of Lucy Lee, and devoted as I know she is to Jim, I thought I saw an expression of the most extraordinary relief relax her whole body.

"But . . . it wasn't his car! How could he . . ."

She stared at me silently for a moment. Then she seemed rather more like herself. "Oh, no, Grace!" she cried. "That's not fair, he'd never . . . Oh, Grace, will they drag out all the business about China and Rosemary?"

"I'm afraid they will, Lucy Lee. In fact, they've already started."

"But what if nobody tells them. They can't find out, and they can't ever prove it . . . I mean, that he . . . killed her. He wasn't even with her last night . . ."

She rushed on, from one thing to another, not very convincingly. Two red spots had grown in her cheeks, making her look oddly hectic.

"But . . . they won't be after Andy, will they?"

That was what was alarming her, then, making her willing to cast Jim or anyone else to the lions if she had to, to keep Andy clear of it.

I don't know exactly what I would have said to her, because I was pretty angry. Jim is worth so many dozen Andys—if only for the reason that he grew up and didn't stay a halfback when he should have been doing a job. I didn't have a chance to say anything, however. She saw the Bishops coming before I did.

"I'd better get back," she whispered. "Don't tell anybody I was here."

She fled just as George Barrol opened the porch door for Rosemary and her father.

58

CHAPTER EIGHT

They came in, George Barrol with a little the air of a dep-
utation. I looked at Rosemary, rather alarmed. Rodman
Bishop, in an old seersucker suit with the trouser legs a little
shrunk from years of laundering so that his feet looked enormous, went back to the porch door and threw his half-smoked
cigar out onto the lawn, and came back, wiping his flushed
perspiring face with a large red silk handkerchief. George
wiped his forehead too. He was more flustered than hot. And
between the two Rosemary stood as cool and lovely and detached as a lily. Only a shadow in the fringed gray depths of
her eyes as she looked at me indicated that any of this touched
her at all.

Rodman Bishop sat down heavily.

"Jim's in a tight spot, Grace," he said.

I nodded.

"I've just seen this fellow Parran. Saw him on his way out. I
gather it's Primrose has let the cat out of the bag."

Rosemary smiled faintly. George was definitely upset.

"We haven't anything to hide, of course, Uncle Rod," he
said hurriedly.

Rodman Bishop's brows beetled as they did practically every
time anybody but Rosemary opened their mouths.

"I didn't say we had. All I say is that if you'd kept your
mouth shut, there wouldn't have been any question of its not
being suicide."

"I was merely doing my duty as I saw it," George said. It
was just like him.

"That's one trouble with the world. Too damn many people
going around doing their duty as they see it!"

"Well, I'm sure—"

"Shut up, George, and let Dad get on with it," Rosemary
said amiably.

Her father started to beetle at her, but the sight of her standing by the window tapping a cigarette on the back of her hand

59

changed the expression on his old pirate face. He adored her, and he was disturbed about her too.

"This is what I'm getting at, Grace," he said brusquely. "We've got to get together on this. I've sent for Kaufman. It's his sort of thing. We're going to make this suicide thing stick."

"Do you think Jim's going to like that, dad?" Rosemary asked quietly.

"He'll like it unless he'd rather hang."

"But if he had nothing to do with it, darling—he'd probably like to have the person who did it hanged instead."

Rodman Bishop snorted angrily. His old square face was set in extraordinarily determined lines—and I don't know anyone who can look—and be—more determined.

"It's his one defense," he said. "They've got motive enough to hang him a dozen times. I tell you that's Parran's case. He had the motive and the opportunity, so far as anybody knows yet—and he forged that suicide note and then tried to have her body cremated so the blow on the skull wouldn't come to light when the neighbors started talking."

We were all silent a moment.

"What about that note, Grace?" Rosemary asked, turning from the window. "I mean, is it her writing?"

I nodded. "I'm sure it is."

"But what about the blow on the head?" George Barrol asked nervously.

Rodman Bishop looked steadily at him. "That," he said, "is where you come in."

George turned the color of an old warm oyster.

"Me?" he said.

Bishop nodded.

"Parran is a fool," he said quietly. "This Primrose is an able man. I've heard about him."

He looked inquiringly at me. I nodded. "I should say he's a very able man."

He went on, looking steadily at George and speaking in a deliberate tone.

"You were with her on the boat last night. You saw the jib give her a crack on the back of the head."

"Well . . ." George said nervously. He hesitated. "Well, as a matter of fact, it did, you know."

His face brightened.

"It . . . it knocked her flat. It really did. That's when the mast cracked and broke off and the boat capsized. I got hold of her. I nearly died. I couldn't have held her, but the cold water

60

brought her to. I just hung on to her till she could get hold of the boat."

We stared at him in complete astonishment. That was why she hadn't swum back, then—why she'd let Jim bring her in. It was so simple, and so much like Sandra.

"Why the devil didn't you say so before?" Rodman Bishop growled.

"Why, I just remembered it. And anyway, I couldn't go around pretending I'd saved her life when everybody knows I can't do much more than keep afloat. I thought she'd mention it."

"Then she really might . . ."

Rosemary's face was quite pale now. She steadied herself against the back of the chair, swaying a little.

"I think I'll go back home, dad," she said quickly. Before we knew it she was gone. George dashed after her with one look at his uncle.

Rodman Bishop turned to me.

"I told her not to come in the first place," he said gruffly. "I want to talk to you alone."

I sat down again.

Rodman Bishop was nodding his head with grim satisfaction. "I think that will about do it," he said curtly. "We've got a case now. We didn't have before. I'll tell you frankly, Grace, it's not Jim I was worried about. It's Rosemary."

"You didn't by any chance think Rosemary killed her, did you, Mr. Bishop?" I inquired.

"Don't be a fool, Grace. I mean I don't want her name mixed up in it. She's had a bad enough time without being dragged through a murder trial."

He looked at me steadily through his thick shaggy brows.

"You see, Grace, this marriage of hers means a lot to her, now, and I'm frank to tell you that while I'd rather she was marrying an American, Dikranov is a fine chap. He's got plenty of money, and he's tremendously in love with Rosemary."

I didn't say anything. It seemed a reasonable enough attitude.

"There have been several men I would have liked her to marry—that have had money and position—but she couldn't see it. You see, we've been hit pretty hard, Grace. Chapin's money from his aunt went to his male cousins. Rosemary's has shrunk, so has mine."

"So has everybody's."

61

"Not Dikranov's. He sells arms in Africa, Arabia and Turkey."

Rodman Bishop smiled a little and shook his head at the same time.

"But he's all right, and shrewd as they come."

"I'm glad you feel that way."

"Not that it would have made any difference. Rosemary's as headstrong as a mule. The point is, I don't want her dragged through any scandal. I don't want all that Chinese business brought up. She was nineteen and a spoiled little fool. Jim was a fool too."

He got up.

"I can count on you, Grace—about the note being genuine, not a forgery?"

I nodded. "It's Sandra's writing.—Is Rosemary in love with Paul Dikranov, Mr. Bishop?" I asked as we came out on the porch.

"Officially—madly. Between the two of us, she'll never love anybody but Jim."

He shook his head.

"It beats me. Never a word out of her. Just suddenly, every six months or so, 'Jim and I used to go there,' or in Paris, 'Jim liked Paris'—so you know she's always thinking about him. I want this marriage of hers to go through, Grace. It'll kill her, if she doesn't have something to take it off her mind."

"What about waiting now and marrying Jim?"

"He's poor. Alice'll have Lucy Lee's family on her hands. Rosemary can't be poor. Anyway . . ."

He put on his old panama.

"Kaufman will be here tomorrow. I wish to God we'd never come back."

"Why did you?"

I'd been wondering about that.

"Oh, Rosemary was set on it. George and I were both opposed. I told Dikranov it was a mistake, but he backed her up and I was too weak-kneed to hold out. I persuaded myself it might be good for her."

I went over to the Goulds' garage as soon as he'd gone. The bruise on the back of Sandra's head was the bit of tangible evidence that Colonel Primrose was basing his theory of willful murder on, and I thought he would like to know there was a perfectly simple explanation of it.

They were swarming over the place. I never saw five men—another state policeman had joined them—doing so many

62

different things at once. Except Colonel Primrose and Mr. Parran. I couldn't see either of them.

I asked Sergeant Buck. He looked at me and said, "The Colonel's busy, ma'am. He ain't got no time for visiting."

I must have looked annoyed this time, because he added stiffly, "He's upstairs, ma'am."

I looked up. The window of Hawkins's room over the garage was open, and I could hear his voice.

I went on up. Colonel Primrose cocked his head down and glanced around at me as severely as Sergeant Buck had done. Then he smiled.

"This is my assistant, Parran," he said. "Sit down, Mrs. Latham. Now then. Go on, Hawkins. What time was it when you heard them?"

"It was jus' twelve o'clock, suh."

"Sure of that?"

"Absolutely, Cunnel. Ah'm sure of that, 'cause Ah heared the clock strike. Ah heared Mr. Jim say, 'It's exactly midnight,' an' then Ah heared the clock strike twelve times. Ain' no doubt in mah min', an' that's one consolation. Ah knows Mr. Jim's voice when Ah hears it. He was right over there under mah bed, his voice come up right through the flo'."

Mr. Parran listened, nodding.

"They's always goin' on, Sa'dy night. Ah don' mind the young folks, but it seems to me married folks ain' no call to go gallivantin' all night way into Sunday mornin'. The Lawd floods an' the Lawd sends fire, the Lawd ain't got no more patience with foreigners. Ah tol' Mr. Jim that."

Hawkins is a preacher in Baltimore during the winter. In the summer he's the Goulds' butler and chauffeur, and a man of prominence at April Harbor.

Mr. Parran got up. "Well, you see they don't try to make you change your story, Hawkins," he said.

"Ain' nobody make me change mah story. Ah don' get no sleep to speak of in the firs' place, Ah got a bad heart, Ah don' like this business of bein' kep' up all night. Ah tol' Miss Alice that this mornin'."

"All right, Hawkins," Colonel Primrose said. "You can go back to the house now. You won't mind, I suppose, if we use your room for headquarters?"

"No, *suh.*"

The old darkey shambled down the stairs, his white starched coat glistening in the sun. Mr. Parran spat out of the window.

"Well," he said, in his dry nasal accent, "we'll just see what Mr. Bishop's fancy New York lawyer makes with *that*."

I hadn't meant to take him in on it, but I was annoyed at that.

"He'll make plenty of it," I said.

Both of them looked at me. Colonel Primrose smiled. Mr. Parran didn't. I don't think he liked me any more then than he did later.

"Jim Gould was at my house at twelve o'clock Saturday night," I said. "He got there at quarter to twelve. Your sergeant saw him come in with me. And he left just as you came in, Colonel Primrose—at ten minutes to one."

Colonel Primrose cocked his eye down at me.

"You're sure about those times?" he said soberly.

"Absolutely. There's no possible doubt of it. And furthermore . . . you probably haven't heard that Sandra Gould was hit on the head by the jib when her mast cracked and the boat capsized. George Barrol held her up until she came to enough to hang on to the boat. That's why he was so exhausted when they brought him in, and why she didn't swim in herself."

Mr. Parran stared at me with his eyes first wide open and then narrowed angrily. Then he looked a little doubtfully at the Colonel.

Colonel Primrose took off his panama and wiped his forehead.

"She was?" he said.

He nodded slowly. "It might do it. In any case, Parran, I should think Gould's fairly well cleared, if Mrs. Latham is certain of her times and Hawkins is certain of his. He could mistake the voice easier than the words.—Get him back here, Parran."

The old man had not got very far.

"Yas, *suh*," he said. "It was exactly midnight. There ain' no doubt in mah min'."

He shook his snowy kinky head, looking squarely at the State's Attorney through his gold-rimmed spectacles.

"Ah came down here at ten o'clock, an' Ah read mah Sunday-school lesson twice over, an' Ah went to bed. An' Ah woke up. Ah heared Mis' Gould quarrelin', sayin' she was goin' to see anybody what she wanted to, an' it weren't none of nobody's business. She was talkin' loud an' Ah understood what she said, which Ah don't gen'ally do."

"You're quite sure it was Mrs. Sandra Gould?"

"Yas, *suh*, Ah'm sure. She was talkin' to a lady an' she was mad as a hornet."

The torn velvet petals flashed into my mind. I turned away, because Colonel Primrose was looking at me with that uncanny X-ray stare of his, and I knew I'd have to explain what had struck me then as soon as I was alone with him.

"Ah thought they was gone then, 'cause Ah heared the do' run to an' screech lak a baby owl, the way it does jus' 'fore it goes plumb to 'cause they ain' enough grease on it. Then Ah didn' hear no mo' soun' till Ah heared Mis' Gould laugh an' start singin' one of them songs she got. Then Ah didn' hear no mo' till Ah heared 'em in the cah. Ah prayed de Lawd, an' then they was talkin' under they breath, an' mighty soon Ah heared Mr. Jim—'It's exactly midnight'—an' the clock. Then Ah heared the do' of the garage screech again, lak it was closin' or openin', but they must have changed they min's, 'cause the cah didn' go out."

"You heard the engine?"

"Not fo' very long Ah didn'. Ah didn' hear nothin' else till 'bout three o'clock."

"You probably dropped off to sleep?" Colonel Primrose asked.

" 'Deed 'n' Ah didn', suh. Ah ain' got a wink o' sleep all night."

We stood in the tiny little chamber over the garage, listening to him. Below I could hear the men moving about and the deadened tones of their voices through the carpeted floor. I couldn't have distinguished a voice through there for the life of me, unless I knew it awfully well. But, of course, Hawkins did know Jim's voice very well indeed. He's been with them for years.

Colonel Primrose stood there for some time after Hawkins had gone, looking at me with a puzzled expression on his face, blowing his breath between his lips in perplexed little puffs.

"Are you sure he was at your place at twelve?" he said at last.

"Quite sure, Colonel Primrose."

He nodded and turned to the State's Attorney.

"In that case, Parran, we'll have to look a little further."

Mr. Parran shook his head dubiously. "If that letter is O.K., Colonel," he said dryly, "and she did get hit on the head with the jib, I don't see that we've got much of a case."

Colonel Primrose nodded thoughtfully. "I haven't examined the note," he said. "I'll get at it this evening. Well, we've got to

65

find out who the man was who was down there at twelve o'clock, and who the woman was that Mrs. Gould was quarreling with."

He put his panama on the back of his head in an extremely unmilitary fashion and put his hand on the door.

"It may be suicide, Parran. I may be just a nosy old man. But if you don't mind I'll keep looking around."

Mr. Parran nodded his assent. "I'd be much obliged if you can help clear up whatever it is," he said. "I guess I won't need this, however."

He took an official-looking paper out of his pocket and started to tear it in two.

"You might just keep it awhile," Colonel Primrose said. "Look in this evening if you have time."

We went downstairs and stood a moment in the garage doorway. Sergeant Buck joined us, or at least took up his accustomed position directly behind the Colonel. One of the men had turned on the radio in Andy Thorp's car and was having a bit of music as he worked.

"They've fingerprinted the car, sir, but it's not much use. Too many people been getting in and out. About all we'll find is the coroner's jury."

Sergeant Buck obviously did not think much of the way any of this affair was being conducted.

"Found anything?" Colonel Primrose asked.

"I haven't had a chance to look. I'm waiting till these babies go home to dinner, sir."

We headed towards the Goulds' cottage, and found Andy at home, which was odd. He spends Sunday morning playing golf and Sunday afternoon sailing, and Sunday evening he goes back to New York. I don't suppose Lucy Lee or the kids see more than five minutes of him the whole week end.

He was lying on the sofa in the cozy chintz-hung living room of the cottage. There were three empty cigarette packages and a great quantity of butts and ashes all around the glass ash tray on the floor beside the sofa. Andy's jaw was slightly bruised—which I hoped Colonel Primrose wouldn't notice.

Andy was sullen and looked pretty ghastly. Colonel Primrose seemed to ignore both his looks and his manner.

"Thorp," he said, "I'm trying to settle the time that Sandra Gould got here, last night. Could you help me out?"

"I've told you all I know," Andy said curtly. "I brought her and George Barrol home. We were all soaking wet, and getting cold. None of us were doing much sitting around. We went on out and got in the car, left Barrol at The Magnolias, came on home and put the car in the garage. And that's all."

"When did you leave the club?"

"Right after Grace and Jim. Sandra wouldn't come home at first, and then when one of the colored boys came in and said Jim and a lady had left, she decided she wanted to go. I guess it was about half past eleven."

"And when did you leave the garage, after you'd put the car in?"

Andy flushed a dull bronze that made his bruised jaw look positively purple.

"Oh, it was about five minutes to twelve. She didn't want to stick around. She was sort of crazy wild. Not like herself. She wouldn't let me go back to the garage with her."

"Why not? Did she say?"

Andy Thorp shook his head.

"What did you think?"

"I didn't think anything—see?" Andy shouted suddenly. He glared at us across the room. "Anything she wanted to do was all right with me. I don't believe in nagging the daylights out of people."

"And you came directly here to the cottage," Colonel Primrose said imperturbably.

Andy moistened his lips and fished about for another pack of cigarettes.

"What's that got to do with it?" he said sullenly.

"Sandra Gould was heard quarreling with another woman a few minutes after she left the garage the first time," Colonel Primrose said quietly. I saw his bright black eyes resting on Andy's purplish chin. "I thought that if you'd happened to have stayed out for a last smoke—say—you might have seen who it was."

"Yes?" Andy said. "Well, I didn't stay out, and I didn't see anybody in the second place."

Colonel Primrose's eyes twinkled. "And you wouldn't admit it in the third. Am I right?"

"You are—right the first time."

Colonel Primrose nodded good-humoredly.

"Is Mrs. Thorp at home?"

"No, she's not. She's gone to the other end of the beach to get the kids away from all this damn business."

"You know, Thorp," Colonel Primrose said as he got up, "I'm interested in how it happened that you gave Sandra Gould your car keys. She hadn't planned going anywhere, had she?"

67

"I told you she'd left something in the car."

"I remember you did. I wondered if you wanted to change your story?"

"I don't. And if you wouldn't mind getting the hell out of here . . ."

CHAPTER NINE

We went out. Not precipitately . . . but I don't think that either of us was sorry to go. I didn't wonder now that Lucy Lee was so upset.

"I take it Mr. Thorp was pretty much under Sandra's spell," Colonel Primrose said as he went along the crape-myrtle-grown path to the big house where Sandra and Jim had lived with Alice Gould.

I don't know whether Colonel Primrose was surprised at seeing all the Bishop family there in Alice Gould's long cool living room or not. I was. Not to see Rodman Bishop and George so much, because Rodman and Alice had been very good friends—there'd even been some romantic gossip about them when I was young, after Rosemary and Chapin's mother died. But it was strange seeing Rosemary and the tall dark man she was going to marry there. He wasn't saying much, it appeared, but I don't think he was missing much either. He did not seem actually to be watching either Jim or Rosemary, but I noticed that every time Jim reached for a cigarette, even if his back was turned Paul Dikranov seemed to be there with his lighter. Rosemary dropped a snapshot Alice Gould was showing her, and he retrieved it, though I should have said he was entirely engrossed in the story of my life. I was only telling it to him to give Rosemary and Jim a chance to look at each other for a moment in the cold light of day. They must have looked rather different to each other those years ago under an Oriental moon.

Rodman Bishop was annoyed at me, I think, for bringing the Colonel there. He kept beetling at me, regarding it, I suppose, as a form of fence-sitting on my part. But he looked definitely relieved, I thought, when Colonel Primrose got George Barrol off in a corner and started plying him with questions.

I'm afraid my attention kept wandering, although Paul Dikranov was intelligent and widely traveled and was certainly putting himself out to be entertaining, now that it was his turn.

69

Nevertheless the conversation died—in all parts of the room—and we found ourselves listening intently to what George was saying.

"It hit her squarely on the back of the head. She tried to catch herself. I'm not much good, you know, at that sort of thing, but I caught hold of her. It was a job, I'll tell you, because she was heavy, and I was . . . I was pretty scared. I couldn't have hung on to her much longer, so it was lucky she came to. In fact—I don't really mind admitting it—just as she caught hold of the side of the boat I collapsed, rather, and she grabbed me. I don't remember anything else until I came to on the dock."

"But she was quite all right after that?"

"After she'd got on shore and had a couple of stiff drinks in her," George said. "She was a little wild. I mean, sort of singing and kicking up her heels. But of course I didn't know her well enough to know whether that's the sort of thing she's likely to do."

Colonel Primrose nodded. "Would you have thought it likely that she was planning to take her own life?"

George cast a sideways glance at Rodman Bishop.

"Well . . . I wouldn't like to be awfully positive about it. I . . . I wouldn't be particularly surprised. Not at anything, really."

Colonel Primrose smiled. So did Rosemary. I think it was the first time they had actually looked at each other.

"When they left you at The Magnolias, Mr. Barrol, did Sandra Gould and Mr. Thorp seem to be on good terms?"

George was a little perturbed.

"I wouldn't like to say anything that might be misleading—but I did gather that she wanted to go somewhere or do something that he didn't like, or didn't approve of, or something. I'm not clear about it. You see, they'd given me quite a lot of straight whisky, after I'd got up the hill, and I was awfully sleepy. I wouldn't say I was intoxicated—"

"Nonsense, you were potted when I saw you," Rosemary said.

George flushed.

"I just tripped on the stair rug," he said. "Anyway, you had no business snooping about in the dark."

He said it very stiffly. A sudden startled hush fell on the room for just an instant. Fortunately Colonel Primrose did not know the people there well enough to recognize a storm warning when one was hoisted. He turned to Jim Gould, who was standing there, his face drawn in white ridges, his eyes blood-shot from no sleep and too many cigarettes.

"I think you ought to know, Mr. Gould," he said gently, "that there is still some question about your wife's death. If I might venture a piece of advice, I should like to say that for everyone's peace of mind you ought to let it be definitely settled . . . and permanently settled."

"We want it settled, Colonel Primrose," Jim said quietly. "We haven't any other idea."

"In that case I suggest that each one of you here give me a brief statement of his whereabouts from half past eleven last night until half past twelve. It seems to be fairly definite that Sandra Gould went into the garage at midnight and did not come out again."

Jim's face contorted in a spasm of distress. He turned away and stood a moment with his back to us, pressing out his cigarette against the fireplace.

"I was with Grace Latham, at her house, until a little before one," he said.

Colonel Primrose nodded. "And when you left her—you went directly home?"

"Yes."

"You didn't hear the engine running in the garage as you passed?"

"No."

We had all been looking at Jim, but as I glanced away my eye caught Rosemary's. I don't even now know what it was in her face that made me all at once infinitely more uneasy than I'd ever been in my life. I felt curiously as if all these people here that I'd known so well and so many years had become utterly strange to me—even Rosemary and Jim. Alice Gould, of course, I could never hope to understand intimately, or Rodman Bishop. I felt too, just then, some kind of terrible undercurrent of fear, and something more ghastly than fear— a sense of something present that was suavely pleasant and at the same time selfishly, callously cruel.

Perhaps it doesn't make sense now, but it did to me then. After all, I didn't know Dikranov—what he felt about Jim, or about Sandra, or about anything, really. And even the rest of them . . . I knew, of course, that no one there would take the last piece of cake on the plate; but if it was bread and the last piece in the world—what then? That was nearer to what we were facing. Dikranov wouldn't push me out of his way on the sidewalk—but if I were so seriously in his way that it became his life or mine . . . ? I caught myself from shaking my head abruptly.

A great black and yellow bumblebee buzzed against the copper screen and buzzed away again in the lazy flower-scented afternoon. It was hot and still. From the outside April Harbor would appear as it always had done, lying green and lovely, girdled with blue water where sails nestled gaily like white butterflies in a field of cornflowers. And there was murder here, stealing like a black patch of tar across a white sandy road.

It was then that I had my first vague feeling that we were not yet through with murder here. It was more than a vague feeling. It was almost a sudden primitive instinct, shocked out of the complacent safety of the summer afternoon, that death here was not satisfied . . . and that it was the more ruthless and terrible because it would wear a friendly face.

I looked around at the people there. "But I *know* them," I kept telling myself. I'd known them all my life . . . Jim and little Rosemary, Alice Gould, George and Rodman. Then I remembered that after all Rosemary had been away seven years, and so had George Barrol and Rodman Bishop. Jim had been through hell; Alice had been through hell for him. I had no way of even remotely knowing what was going on underneath the faces they showed to the world. A verse my father used to recite came into my head:

> Since all alone, so heaven has willed, we die,
> Nor even the tenderest heart and next our own
> Knows half the measures why we smile and sigh.

Certainly none knows why we kill.

"And you, Mrs. Gould?" Colonel Primrose asked.

"I got home with my daughter Mrs. Thorp at half past eleven," Alice Gould said quietly. "My son came at a few minutes before one. I didn't hear Sandra come in with him. I glanced in her room. She wasn't there. About half past two, when she still hadn't come in, I went to her room to see if she could have come without my hearing her. That's when I turned on the light and saw the note on her dressing table. I read it. Then I went out to look for her."

"You didn't wake your son?"

"No . . . for a number of reasons. My daughter-in-law was given to melodrama, a little. I thought I'd find her somewhere

72

in the grounds, waiting for my son to take a gun out of her hands in the nick of time. I'd planned to give her a piece of my mind."

"Did you hear the car when you passed the garage?"

Alice Gould paused.

"I didn't pass the garage, Colonel Primrose. I went down past my daughter's cottage and around that way. I thought I heard someone in Mrs. Latham's garden, and I rather thought it might be Sandra. She wasn't always as careful of appearances as I might have liked. I thought possibly she'd gone back to the clubhouse to dance, and just returned. They dance till three."

She pleated the hem of her handkerchief with delicate jeweled fingers.

"When I didn't see anyone in the garden, I called up at Grace Latham's window. I was a little worried by that time. I thought she might help me find Sandra. I've come to depend a great deal on Grace."

She smiled charmingly at me. There was too much underlying significance in that gracious tribute to make me altogether happy, but I smiled as well as I could.

"She happened to be up already. It was she who heard the engine. My hearing isn't as keen as it once was."

Colonel Primrose turned to me.

"What were you doing up then, Mrs. Latham? You presumably went to bed at one o'clock."

"Sheila, my dog, heard someone in the garden and woke me up," I said.

"Did you see anyone?"

"I'm afraid I did," I said with a wry smile. "I'm sorry, but it was you I thought I saw, Mr. Dikranov."

If I'd shot off a cannon I couldn't have surprised them more. Except Mr. Dikranov.

He bowed.

"I wondered if you had seen me, Mrs. Latham," he said calmly. "Please don't look so alarmed, my friends. I was out—walking—because I could not sleep. I mistook Mrs. Latham's house for Mr. Bishop's from the lane, and did not see my mistake until I was close to it. I should have spoken to Mrs. Latham but I wasn't sure that she had seen me, and I did not want to alarm her."

He bowed to me again. The story seemed to me certainly to have a ring of very suave truth. I looked at Colonel Primrose. His head was cocked down and his black eyes contracted intently. He was not looking at Paul Dikranov or at me, but at Rosemary.

Her face had suddenly turned as white as a sheet, her gray eyes were fixed on her fiancé. Rosemary was afraid—that was all I could think of just then. She was white with fear. Jim Gould took a sudden step forward, his face flushed. I don't know what might have happened if there had not been a sudden diversion, so startling in its implication that we forgot Rosemary and Paul Dikranov and Jim.

Sergeant Buck's iron visage appeared in the door.

"Excuse me, sir," he said.

Colonel Primrose got up quickly. "What is it, Buck?"

"I found this, sir."

He held out something wrapped in a brightly colored comic section. Colonel Primrose took it gingerly and opened it.

It was the new monkey wrench that Jim Gould had bought the morning before at Mr. Toplady's general store, and that I had seen in his hand there.

Sergeant Buck pointed down at the end with a large thumb.

"That's what she was hit with, sir. It's got blood and hair on it. I found it stuck up on a shelf under some paper. It's got a woman's fingerprints on it."

I stared at it, horror-stricken. And I knew, of course, that the fingerprints were mine.

Colonel Primrose stood staring a long time at the brown matted blur on the bright iron. Everyone's eyes were glued there in the hushed room. I tried to open my mouth to say, "Those prints are mine," but my throat was too dry. It was as if somebody had written the single word "Murder" in glaring red letters across the white plaster wall of Alice Gould's room.

"We've compared the hair, and the size of the wound, sir," Sergeant Buck said.

Colonel Primrose looked around the room. He said later that each face there stood out quite apart from bodies or clothes—seven separate and complete portraits—and in not one of them was there surprise, or anything like it. "I knew very well you all knew Sandra Gould had been murdered . . . and that you'd all known it from the first."

The thought, I suppose, that was uppermost in each mind at that moment was that the best card in the game we were playing against the plump little man and his granite-faced bodyguard—his guard, philosopher and friend, he once called him, though Sergeant Buck spoke of himself as the Colonel's functotum—had been played, and trumped.

74

Rodman Bishop drew his eyes away from that wrench. He stared stubbornly at the Colonel.

"You still can't explain away Sandra's own statement that she was determined to end her life, and was going to do so, Colonel Primrose," he said doggedly. "Also, I think practically everybody who might conceivably have a motive for murdering Sandra Gould has a perfectly satisfactory alibi."

He turned to his daughter.

"I'm right in saying you went to your room when you came in at half past twelve?"

Rosemary nodded mechanically.

"I had a nightcap with Dikranov," Mr. Bishop went on, "and left him at his door about a quarter to one. That's the lot," he added. "And there you are."

It wasn't the lot, of course, as I thought instantly. It didn't include Andy Thorp or Lucy Lee Thorp. It didn't include a dozen other people who might have murdered Sandra Gould.

But there was another thing about it that was still worse. And Colonel Primrose saw it at once.

He wrapped the comic section around the wrench and handed it to Sergeant Buck.

"I'm interested to hear you speak of the people who might have conceivably had a motive for killing Mrs. Sandra Gould," he said slowly, "and so tacitly include all of yourselves here. May I ask what motive you yourself—for example—could have? Or Dikranov, for instance?"

Rodman Bishop's square face flushed angrily. He was silent, and Colonel Primrose did not press his advantage. He got up, shook hands with Alice Gould and Jim, and went out with his sergeant. I would have gone with him, but Sergeant Buck's square, large and impassive back was not encouraging.

I did go, however, soon after that. Rosemary left with me. Neither of us said anything as we went slowly down the path towards the gap in the hedge. It's hard to talk to anyone you've known very well when you aren't sure any more how they feel about important things. Women must grow apart more quickly than men. Not that Rosemary was very different. It was merely, I think, that someone I'd always connected with Jim was pointed towards another man—and a definitely unusual man at that. I couldn't believe she cared deeply for Paul Dikranov. Yet she was fascinated by him . . . and she was afraid of him. I was sure of that; I didn't see how Rodman Bishop could help seeing it either.

As a matter of fact, if I could only have asked Rosemary

about the crumpled petals Sandra had torn from her dress, I think the invisible barrier between us would have disappeared. But I couldn't, of course. Not any more than I could have spoken to Alice Gould about the suicide note that Sandra had written.

Rosemary caught my arm suddenly.

We had just come in sight of the garage. Sergeant Buck was there with Hawkins. The old man was protesting volubly as he preceded Buck up the outside stairs that led to his room over the garage. At the same moment Colonel Primrose came out. He saw us and beckoned.

"Would you mind going upstairs, Mrs. Latham? I'm trying a little experiment. You might go too, Miss Bishop. Hurry, will you?"

He looked at his watch. "Quickly, please."

We ran upstairs. Buck opened the door.

"Hurry if you're coming," he said impassively.

We went in. Almost immediately, from below at a point just under Hawkins's iron bed, came the muffled sound of a man's voice. "It is exactly five o'clock," it said, perfectly audibly. "This is Station WFBO, Columbus. Jim Sanderson your announcer. It is five o'clock, Central Standard Time." And then a clock chimed: one, two, three, four, five.

Old Hawkins's face turned the color of putty.

"Fo' the love of Gawd!" he quavered. "That's Mr. Jim, that's him . . . he gone crazy!"

Even before he spoke the little clock on his bureau struck the hour . . . except, of course, that the hour it struck was not five. It was six o'clock, Eastern Standard Time.

Colonel Primrose stood in the door. He looked gravely at Rosemary Bishop, shaking his head a little. The two of us stood there utterly silent.

"I thought there was something odd about a man's announcing the time he's committing a murder," he said. "He knew he'd have a witness upstairs here—if he made enough noise—and he knew he would have an alibi for twelve o'clock. Well—it's his one-o'clock alibi we want now."

He hesitated a moment. "You said Mr. Jim Gould left your house at ten minutes to one, Mrs. Latham?"

I felt Rosemary's fingers tighten on my arm.

"Jim was with me at one o'clock, Colonel Primrose," she said. Her voice was perfectly cool.

CHAPTER TEN

A bluebottle buzzed in through the open window of Hawkins's little room under the roof over the Goulds' two-car garage, and out through the door. I stood there, staring from Rosemary Bishop to the plump little man with the sparkling black eyes. Whether Rosemary expected that her simple statement that she had been with Jim Gould at one o'clock would be sufficient to clear him of the murder of his wife I don't know. I do know that the only person in the hot stuffy little room over the garage who was particularly surprised was Sergeant Buck. He made an audible "Tch, tch!"

Colonel Primrose looked rather as if he had been expecting just something of the sort.

"Then . . . you both perjured yourselves?" he inquired casually.

"If you want to call it that."

Colonel Primrose shook his head with a sort of kindly impatience.

"It isn't what *I* want to *call* it, Miss Bishop," he said. "It's what the State's Attorney will instantly see it *is*. You see, that makes it right up his alley."

He hesitated a moment, looking at her queerly, and went on.

"Not so much that Jim Gould was with you when his wife was murdered—but that you both were with her. If you can't prove most satisfactorily that you weren't with her, I'm very much afraid you'll be charged with murder."

Rosemary's fingers tightened on my arm.

"You sure got yourself out on a limb, miss!" Sergeant Buck's harsh worried voice before he snapped back to rigid attention was curiously comforting. I didn't look at Colonel Primrose. He'd already said that Sergeant Buck under his granite lantern-jawed exterior was a sentimental jelly that only needed a beautiful maiden in distress to make him fairly quiver. There was certainly no comfort or sympathy in his own voice. "It's always a good plan, Miss Bishop, either to tell the truth in the beginning, or keep it to yourself to the very end. It depends on your position—in relation to the crime, of course. As it is now, I'm afraid Buck's quite right. You're definitely out on a limb, and Jim Gould's out there with you."

77

"In which case I'd better climb back before somebody saws it off," Rosemary replied coolly.

"By all means, if you can, Miss Bishop," Colonel Primrose said.

I didn't look back at the window over the closed garage doors as Rosemary and I crossed through the hedge to my garden. I knew nevertheless that both men were watching us and that so far as Rosemary was concerned the limb they were on was already as good as crashing to the ground. I wondered, too, what Colonel Primrose thought when we didn't go to the house but walked on slowly, down to the lane running along the top of the bank above the beach. Both of us, Rosemary and I, I think, wanted to be somewhere where nobody could listen through walls or from behind closed doors . . . and neither of us trusted Colonel Primrose or Mr. Parran the State's Attorney further than we could see them, if indeed so far.

"I'm afraid I'm not very bright," Rosemary said.

Her face was set and she was looking straight ahead of her, walking automatically, quite unaware, I think, of where she was going.

"As if it wasn't foul enough for Jim already.—And it was me that made him swear he'd never tell anybody . . . just because I was . . ."

She didn't finish. She stopped suddenly. "Oh, I've got to see him!" she broke out. "I've got to, Grace—now!"

Her dark eyes were almost wild with all sorts of mixed-up passionate emotions that I couldn't begin to make out. But I did know very well that she couldn't see Jim, just then; not without cutting off the limb with her own hands, so to speak.

"Look here, my dear," I said. "From all I can see you've made a bad enough mess as it is without rushing to Jim and making it worse. If he goes off the deep end, you'll sink—both of you. I take it you *were* with him last night."

She nodded.

"I—"

But this time I stopped her myself.

"Look, darling. If you don't tell me, I won't know anything. And therefore I won't have to tell Colonel Primrose anything. Because if I do know it, he'll get it out of me whether I want to tell it or not."

I suppose I was thinking all the time about the petals clutched in Sandra Gould's dead fingers.

She shook her head. "Then he'll figure out that the reason I

78

didn't tell you is that I'm trying to hide something. I think I'd rather tell you, so . . . so you *can* tell him."

We had reached the white rail fence at the end of my land and were leaning against it, looking out over the blue Chesapeake. Suddenly Rosemary turned away.

"I don't know why we came back . . . this place is so full of ghosts."

I realized then what I'd forgotten through years of being so close to it. We were looking down at the inlet where they'd found Chapin Bishop one Sunday morning seven years before.

"I might be dead, walking back through all my life that's worth remembering," Rosemary said.

I saw then that it wasn't Chapin she'd been thinking of, but something else that I wouldn't know about. Something connected with Jim, and days of lost ecstasy.

"Just wait till George blurts out that last night I said I'd probably kill Sandra before I left here," she said suddenly. Then she smiled a little. I stared at her. "I don't know what it is about George that won't let him keep his mouth shut. If it was just other people he got into a mess, you could understand it, but it's mostly himself."

I started to ask her if she had really said that, and changed my mind. If Rosemary didn't want to talk about Sandra and Jim, I was glad enough—in spite of a certain natural curiosity.

"He hasn't changed much, has he?" I asked.

"No. We thought after he got enough to live on he'd set up a bachelor establishment, but he didn't. You know, he's not very well. He's got something that ought to come out, appendix or something—but somebody told him people act frightfully odd when they're under ether or avertin and he actually won't risk it. Now if that were Paul . . ."

She laughed, not very convincingly, and I realized that this was the point we were finally getting at.

"Do you suppose that if we gave Paul ether he'd tell us what he knows about Sandra?"

"Why don't you just ask him?" I said.

Rosemary stared at the small white handkerchief she'd tied into a string of hard knots. "I did," she said shortly.

"And what did he say?"

"He said he didn't know her. That was yesterday when we were coming back from the club before dinner. I was going to let it go at that, because . . . well, after all, I couldn't say, 'That's odd, because she certainly recognized you.' But George could, of course. And did."

79

"Really?"

She nodded, smiling a little in spite of herself.

"He said, 'Isn't that funny, because I could have sworn she recognized you when you first came in—don't you remember, Paul?"

"What did Paul do?"

"Paul looked like a war cloud over the Bosporus. And George, having put his foot in it beautifully, tried to get it out."

"And made it worse?"

"Much. He giggled and said but of course Sandra wasn't the sort of girl a man would be likely to forget if he'd once even seen her, and Paul said, on the contrary, she was an extremely common type in the East, you saw them in every café and Palais de Danse in Asia. And so George, to help matters again, said wasn't that funny, because that's where Jim met her."

Rosemary smiled, trying to hide the sudden tears in her eyes.

"I suppose it would have gone on indefinitely if Dad hadn't told him to shut up."

"But I don't quite see what all that's got to do with Paul."

"Don't you?"

She looked full at me for a moment, and looked away again.

"I suppose nobody would—but me," she said after a long time. "Only, you see, he *did* know her. He must have, because later, you remember, she came up to him and said something about his going out with her for old times' sake. Don't you remember?"

"I remember he looked rather blank," I said, but she shook her head.

"That's it. It must have been something he doesn't want to remember. And . . . well, I wouldn't want to marry him, because I couldn't ever forget. And . . . I've *got* to forget all about her, Grace—all about there ever having been anybody like her . . . if I'm going on living at all."

She looked out across the water.

"It's been pretty rotten. I don't seem to have . . . managed things very well. And if . . . if she's been in Paul's life too—well, it looks as if she's sort of an albatross round my neck."

"You haven't forgotten she's dead, by any chance, have you, darling?"

"I guess a dead albatross is harder to get rid of than a live one," she said. "You see, I asked him again on the way home about her. I suppose I was crazy, but . . . I can't help it. He didn't say anything at first. Then he said he thought he had known her, but he also thought we'd be a lot happier if we didn't pry into each other's past lives, or something of the sort. Let the dead past bury its dead, that sort of thing. Except, of course, that they don't stay buried."

We stood looking over the bay. It was almost deserted, the last straggling sailboats heading for the basin.

"She called him up while we were at dinner. Pearl recognized her voice. He came back from the phone quite angry. And, Grace, there's no use beating about the bush. If she was murdered—and I guess that's settled—then somebody must have done it."

I looked at her, wondering. "Jim seems to be the favorite."

I was sorry, because she drew back almost as if I'd struck her.

"Or do you really think it was Paul?"

"Oh, I don't know, Grace. I'm terribly frightened. Because —well—Paul doesn't have a Western notion about the sanctity of human life. They don't in the East. There are such billions of people—one more or less doesn't matter, especially if he isn't in the ruling class, or . . . or happens to be a woman. I don't mean he's not . . . well, almost overcivilized He's marvelous, and all that, Grace. But I'd be a fool if I didn't see that he could be perfectly ruthless if . . . if he had to be. And if he'd come here, knowing her before, not expecting to see her . . . oh, don't you see?"

I didn't, quite. That is, I didn't see whether she was desperately worried for fear it was Paul, or whether deep in her subconscious mind she wanted it to be Paul—so that it couldn't be Jim. Whether she was like Lucy Lee, willing to toss one man to the wolves to save another.

"You aren't seriously accusing the man you're going to marry of murder, are you, darling?" I inquired as casually as I could. "Or *are* you going to marry him?"

She didn't answer for so long that I thought she wasn't going to.

"Last night I told him I wouldn't marry him unless I knew about Sandra," she said finally, with a twisted little smile. "I'm afraid he'll tell me the same thing—after he sees the morning papers. I don't think he's the sort that'll like the idea of my being out with Jim till half past one. Not when I've told the police I went to bed at half past twelve."

I don't know how long we would have stood there in the gradually lowering dusk, going over and over the same ground, Rosemary telling me nothing, and not knowing that I knew anything but what she had told me. As it turned out, she knew a great deal that she'd never tell. I'm not sure that it would have done much good, because the things she did let slip meant nothing to me, and didn't later—not until I saw them neatly spliced together with others, and knotted and woven into one of the most deadly nets that ever trapped a jungle beast.

Because that was what Colonel Primrose had insisted that he was after from the beginning, no matter how fair-seeming and pleasingly gentle its face or how velvet his claws. It seemed a bit fanciful when he said it. It wouldn't seem so now, when we know how terribly bloody those claws were, how narrow the road that some of us had walked with death.

While we were still standing there, looking out over the bay, a strange thing happened. We both heard someone coming along the lane from our left. That in itself wasn't startling, although the lane isn't used very much. The startling thing was that the man coming was obviously moving in an extremely stealthy fashion, coming on a little ways, stopping to give an elaborate pantomime of just standing there enjoying the evening mosquitoes and not really looking behind him at all.

He was doing that for the second time when we recognized Andy Thorp and saw that he had something inside his gray flannel jacket, pinioned under his arm by the simple act of having one hand in his trousers pocket and his elbow against his side. He stopped before he got as far as my gate and looked around again. Then he dived with extraordinary speed down the bank towards the beach. We heard a few rocks fall, and after a moment Andy appeared again. He brushed the dirt off his legs, emptied the sand and gravel out of his sneakers— using both hands—and strolled back the way he had come. He had not looked our way once, though I discovered later that we had been pretty well concealed behind the tall bunches of Queen Anne's lace that grew along the lane and along the Goulds' fence.

"What does that mean?" Rosemary whispered. It showed how furtive an air Andy Thorp had had, in spite of his nonchalance. Neither of us had spoken. In fact we'd practically held our breath.

"It means that he got rid of whatever he had under his arm," I said.

Rosemary shivered.

"It's getting cold. Let's go up to the house," she said, slipping her arm into mine. It was trembling. She glanced behind us several times on our way up the path, and when a large square figure loomed quite suddenly in front of us she started violently and gave a sharp frightened gasp before she saw who it was. I hadn't realized what a highly nervous state she was in till then—although as a matter of fact the appearance of Sergeant Buck, standing at a sort of modified attention in the shadow of the crape myrtle hedge, had been a little abrupt.

"The Colonel ordered me to tell you ladies you're not to stay out in the dark alone, ma'am," he reported stiffly. Then he added, to Rosemary, "It ain't safe, miss, not when a killer's loose. Take it from me, the Colonel knows what he's talking about. I been with him twenty-eight years, and he ain't never been wrong yet."

Then, with an almost imperceptible coming to present arms, he waited for us to pass, and fell in as a rear rank, and marched us up to the house in a sort of squads right. There was something very comic about it, but there was also something definitely reassuring, though it wasn't at all dark yet. Rosemary had quit trembling, and she didn't look back again.

"I guess I've got the jitters," she said as we came up on the porch into what I erroneously had regarded as the privacy of my own home.

I had not counted on my guest. He was in the living room. More than that, Mr. Parran was with him, and also a hot-looking young man obviously from the city. They were around a table, bending over a small gray sheet of note paper. I didn't have to get a very close look at it to see that it was Sandra's suicide note. They had two other pieces of paper that they were apparently comparing it with.

"I hope we're not intruding," I said.

Colonel Primrose cocked his head down and peered up at me. He grinned.

"Not at all, Mrs. Latham. Come right in."

He said it as cordially as later he invited me into his own yellow brick house on P Street in Georgetown.

"Awfully kind of you," I said.

The quick amused flicker in the snapping black eyes disappeared instantly as he looked past me to Rosemary. She was just inside the door. Her face was like wax, and I had a sudden feeling that it had just turned that way, from something she had seen as we came in. I glanced around as unobtrusively as I could, but I couldn't see through the large bulk of Law—so that whatever was on the table by the fireplace was out of my view. I hesitated, with Colonel Primrose watching me, to step deliberately around to where I could see.

Furthermore, it was perfectly apparent that they would be

glad when we left. So we went—as far as the kitchen. Nobody has servants Sunday nights in April Harbor—they all go to church and we get our own suppers, usually everybody at somebody else's house. I got Rosemary a glass of water. She drank some of it and put the glass down, staring at it on the table in front of her, opening and closing her fingers around it, watching the warm prints of her hot fingers against the cold surface fade out and disappear as the glass cooled.

"It's funny to think they're still there . . . and that they could make them come out again," she said abstractedly, nodding towards the living room door.

"Is this an amateur lecture on fingerprints, Miss Bishop?" I asked. I was a little worried.

She didn't pay any attention to me, just kept on making the prints on the frosty glass and watching them go out.

"Can they find them on cloth?" she asked.

"I think so."

She emptied the glass into the sink and started to set it down when she stopped, listening.

Outside there was a faint scrabbling sound coming towards the door. It didn't sound like an animal. We waited, a little breathless probably, until there emerged out of the dusk the stocky sober little figure of young Andy Thorp junior. His face was streaked where two big tears had been wiped resolutely towards his ears with dirty little fists. He blinked at us for a moment.

"Hello, Aunt Grace. Is Juyus here?" he said sturdily.

"No, Andy. He's at church. Can I do something for you?"

He stood there irresolute, his four years weighing heavily on his blond little brow, determined not to cry.

"Juyus helped me find Daddy once, and I fought he'd help me again," he said.

We stared at him for an instant. Then Rosemary sprang up and went over to him and picked him up in her arms.

"Oh, you lamb!" she said. "I'll help you find him!"

She was weeping, but young Andy wasn't.

"Don't cry. Men don't like people that cry all the time. That's why Daddy doesn't like . . ."

Some sixth sense propelled Rosemary out with him . . . or perhaps she'd seen the pantry door move. She and young Andy were gone just as Colonel Primrose cocked his head into the kitchen and followed it immediately.

"I wish you'd go away," I said.

"I know you do."

84

He smiled and shook his head sympathetically.

"But if I did, you'd be out hunting Andy too, and it isn't safe."

"Then you'd better send your sergeant after Rosemary."

"No," he said. "Rosemary's safe enough."

I stared at him, my mouth slightly open, I'm afraid. He grinned.

"Do you know, Mrs. Latham, you seem to me a curious example of a bright woman being almost abysmally stupid—or perhaps obtuse is a better word?"

"Meaning?"

He sat down and looked at me intently.

"Meaning that—like Gaul—all people who are around in an affair like this are divided into three parts. Those who are trying to find the murderer. The murderer himself, who is trying to hide. And thirdly, those well-intentioned—or not well-intentioned—people who are trying to hinder the investigation. So far, we've got Parran and myself in the first group. The second group is X—still unknown."

"And . . . the third?"

"The third group is enormous, Mrs. Latham."

His eyes sharpened, the amused twinkle in them quite gone. He leaned forward.

"In fact, Mrs. Latham, it includes—besides all the Goulds and the Bishops—such oddly assorted people as yourself and my Sergeant Buck."

"Sergeant—"

"Exactly. I told you he had a heart of jelly. He also has a deep and abiding conviction that women are the root of all evil —and I've never seen him anything but a complete fool when he meets a pretty one in trouble. Now, *I* have a great weakness for Woman . . ."

"But not individual woman?"

He chuckled.

"Perhaps that's putting it a little strong. I—"

There was a sudden elaborate clearing of a throat just outside, and the harshly disapproving face of Sergeant Buck appeared in the open window over the sink. I felt pretty silly, and also definitely annoyed, because it was perfectly obvious that Sergeant Buck was convinced I had the basest designs on his wretched colonel.

CHAPTER ELEVEN

It was after nine when I ran across the garden to the Bishops'. I hadn't intended going out alone after what Colonel Primrose had said, but when I saw him and Mr. Parran and their small cohort leaving the place I changed my mind.

Rosemary and George Barrol were on the screened front porch. I spotted them by the two small red dots of their cigarettes. George got up and opened the door.

"Come in—we were just going over. Your Hawkshaw's got Paul on the carpet," he said. "What'll you have? Scotch?"

"Nothing."

I sat down on the foot of the wicker chaise longue where Rosemary was sitting.

"Did you find Andy?"

"He was home—said he hadn't been out," she answered. "He said Lucy Lee had taken the kids over to her mother's and he guessed young Andy had decided he'd stick with him, and probably had got scared and so on. Children aren't particularly reliable."

"They make up things," I said, understanding by the little pressure of her foot against my knee that the less said about Andy's strange antics in the lane the better. Unless we wanted George to blurt it out suddenly at the most inopportune moment.

"I wonder what he's saying to Paul?" Rosemary said.

"I wonder what he was saying to old Potter?" George put in.

I looked at him in complete astonishment. *"Dr. Potter?"*

"Didn't you know he was at your place this evening? I went over to find Rosemary, and Potter was coming out, wiping the perspiration off. I said hello and he jumped a foot. What about that rumor that Sandra Gould had him going six ways for Sunday?"

"Dr. Potter?" I gasped.

George looked at me, surprised and a little chagrined.

"Don't tell me I've put my foot in it again," he said sheepishly. "I thought everybody knew about it. Elsie Carter told me yesterday afternoon that he was just another one of the dubs. Anyway, he was looking like a pickled oyster when I saw him coming out of your place. I'm sorry, but I didn't know—"

"Of course you didn't . . . but, darling, if you could only keep what you don't know to yourself," Rosemary said patiently.

It's lucky she had eyes in the back of her head, because I should never myself have noticed that Paul Dikranov was coming. She caught my look of surprise as she turned suddenly. "It's his cigarette," she said softly. "They're something special from the Balkans."

I caught the pleasant fragrance of Eastern tobacco as he came out . . . tall and slender and dark, and always polite and a little elegant.

"Good evening, Mrs. Latham. Your colonel's gone. He is a very shrewd man."

He stood in the doorway, towering above all of us, the dim light of the living room behind him making him still taller and darker.

None of us spoke for a moment. I suppose it was my nerves that made me suddenly intensely uneasy. Or maybe it was the slightly sibilant emphasis with which he said, "He is a very shrewd man." George Barrol must have felt something too. He laughed nervously, and would no doubt have said something unwise if Rosemary had not stepped in.

"Why don't we have a rubber of bridge?"

George jumped up. "Good idea—I'll get the table."

Paul Dikranov moved aside for him to pass. Then he did a rather odd thing. He stepped to Rosemary's side, took her hand and raised it to his lips.

George, still in the door, laughed nervously again. "Oh, dear," he said. "Rosemary, I'll bet the Colonel's told him all."

Dikranov shook his head.

"On the contrary, George. The Colonel can tell me nothing. I merely salute the lady I love."

Somewhere in the house the telephone jangled noisily: one long, three short.

"That's yours, Grace," George said. "I'll answer for you."

He went on in while I waited. We're all on one rural line, so that you can answer your phone at anybody's house.

When George came back he had the bridge table and the cards.

"It's your colonel, Grace," he said. "He's bellowing 'Hello, hello,' and nobody's on the line. They must have hung up."

He set up the table, Paul Dikranov helping. Our bridge wasn't very successful. Dikranov and I collected $1.80 from Rosemary and George at 11:30, and I went home. George went with me—at least to the hedge. I didn't expect him to go farther, because he doesn't like being out alone in the dark and I've never minded.

Colonel Primrose was in the living room when I came in. He'd pulled a table out into the middle of the room and was sitting there meditatively with his back to the door. He glanced up when I came in, nodded and pushed back his chair. I looked at the table, and my heart sank to my boots.

In the middle of it, on a piece of white note paper that had been taken from my desk, were two crumpled blue velvet petals.

I stared at them while he looked calmly at me.

"Sit down, Mrs. Latham," he said. "I want to ask you some questions."

As he spoke he reached for a leather envelope and pulled the zipper around to open it. I sat down with a pretty sickening sense that he was putting it up to me, and that I'd have to decide quite definitely whether I was hunting with the hounds or running with the foxes.

He reached into the leather case and brought out the gray sheet of note paper that Alice Gould had found on Sandra's dressing table, and laid it carefully on the table by the blue petals. He took another piece of paper, folded oblong in a narrow strip, and put it on the table too. Then he looked at me and said, surprisingly, "I want you to tell me about your telephone."

"My telephone?"

He nodded soberly.

"Well, it's a rural phone, with a bell attachment," I said. "There are a dozen or so of us on the line. In fact there's only one single-party line in the place, and that's at the club. It's arranged so the men can have a private wire for business. The other system's always been here, and we get along with it. You complain a lot when you can't ever get the line, and when you know somebody like Elsie Carter's listening in. But that's the country phone. Why?"

He looked at me for an instant, his black eyes gleaming a little.

"It's just that that interests me," he said slowly. "The listening in. There's somebody on your line that listens in nearly every time I answer your phone. I want to know who it is."

"I'm afraid I don't know how you'll find out, Colonel Primrose," I said. "The operator in the village doesn t get a signal unless you crank."

He nodded.

"I guessed that," he said. "No, I can't find out But you can find out for me—if you will. Will you?"

I hesitated.

"You're afraid, aren't you? Afraid of—"

"Afraid of spying on my friends? Yes. I suppose I am. After all, Sandra Gould caused enough trouble when she was alive—"

He shook his head again, looking at me queerly.

"Hasn't it occurred to you, Mrs. Latham, that the person who murdered Sandra Gould may just conceivably *not* be a friend of yours?"

"What do you mean?" I said.

He chuckled suddenly. "The determination with which all you people calmly assume that whoever killed her was one of you is a little . . amusing. However, I've got to have some inside help."

He stopped, thinking intently a moment.

"Let's put it this way, Mrs. Latham. You get me the information I want. If it involves someone you don't want involved, then you can keep it to yourself—on the condition that you *do* keep it to yourself. That you don't, in that case, give *me* away either. Will you do that?"

I nodded—not very happily; and he nodded with some satisfaction.

"All right then. There's one other point about your phone, Mrs. Latham."

His eyes were fastened on mine in a sharpened sort of calculation, as if he was trying to decide whether to trust me a little further. I moved uneasily. All things being equal, I'd just as soon he didn't.

"You haven't been as close to your phone as Lilac and I have the last few days."

I looked rather surprised, I suppose. He went on.

"Someone has been calling you up, and then hanging up without speaking. Now, whether they've expected you to answer and didn't care to talk to me or your cook, and have rung off for that reason, I don't know. It might simply be that."

"You mean that after you answer the phone they hang up without speaking?"

He nodded.

89

"It's happened a number of times. Once while you were out earlier today, and three times while you and Rosemary were down at the lane this evening."

"While Dr. Potter was here?" I asked—rather craftily, I thought. He shot me a quick glance.

"And after he left," he said calmly. "But what interests me most is that they called last night about 3:15, when you were out of the house. That's what woke me up, and that's how I knew you were out Because I waited quite a while before I answered it."

"But you were sure they'd not hung up—because you did wait so long?"

He shook his head.

"No, I traced that call. This morning, after I had breakfasted with your undertaker."

I waited for him to go on, quite unconsciously holding my breath.

"It came from the pay box at the foot of Church Street in the village. The operator didn't know whether it was a man or a woman."

"In the village . . . at a quarter past three?" I demanded. "That's ridiculous!"

"Why?"

"Well, I mean people don't go about calling you up at quarter past three and hanging up Not unless they're very tight.'

"Or are under a great strain, Mrs. Latham. The strain of having murdered somebody, for instance. Or of thinking perhaps that they know who did murder somebody."

All this left me completely in the fog "You mean that the murderer is calling me up?"

Colonel Primrose hesitated. "I've also traced this afternoon's calls," he said

"Where do they come from?"

"The operator can't tell me definitely It's a two-party line. One of the parties is the vestry room of St. John's Church in the village. I suppose that's a semi-public phone."

"I wouldn't know about that."

He nodded.

"You see, Mrs. Latham, this is a fairly common psychological phenomenon. Someone has something weighing on his mind. He's projecting himself by means of the telephone into the heart of this wretched business for a number of possible reasons. He might want to talk and decide to talk, then back

90

down when he gets his party. He might just want to see that we're still here; he might be keeping tab on you. However, that's not the point."

"What is it, then?" I said meekly.

"It's this. Every time this phone of yours rings—whether it's a genuine call or your mysterious caller who hangs up immediately I answer—someone is listening in. The presumption is that it's not our shy friend at any time—for a reason that I'm about to tell you. It's some one of your neighbors, in other words, Mrs. Latham. Now . . . will you find out which one?"

"My dear man," I said, "don't be silly! How can I?"

He chuckled, and then became instantly serious.

"I'll tell you," he said. "It's quite simple. The person who's listening in betrays himself, unconsciously, every time he does it. He has a clock, close to his phone and quite audible."

I thought quickly of all my neighbors' telephones. The Goulds' clock is on the mantel, their downstairs phone in the hall, the upstairs one in Alice Gould's room by her bed.

It's odd how perfectly simple things escape you. I couldn't possibly remember, try as I would, where Lucy Lee's phone was or whether there was a clock by it.

"It isn't unusual for a clock to be by the phone," I said. "A dozen people could have one there."

Colonel Primrose nodded. "I know. This is a rather special clock. It has a very odd little hippity-hop in the tick. You'll notice it the first thing. Furthermore, it's not a big clock, I should think. Not likely to be in the living room or the hall."

He looked at me steadily. "Suggest anything to you already?"

"No," I said. "It doesn't. And you mean you'd like me to go snooping about people's bedrooms listening to the ticking of their clocks."

He nodded calmly.

"Something of the sort. And remembering always, if you want to, that if you find out something, and find you can't tell me, that you won't tell anybody else."

He looked at me with a queer little chuckle.

"Well, that's settled, then. Now—about this."

He picked up the piece of gray note paper that Alice Gould had got from Sandra's dressing table and handed it to me. I took it, trying to keep my hand from trembling as I did.

"Mrs. Latham," he said, very earnestly. "Are you sure, beyond any doubt, that that's Sandra Gould's writing?"

I couldn't trust myself to speak, so I nodded as calmly as I could.

He took it back, laid it carefully down on the table in front of him and looked down at it with a puzzled scowl.

"This mystifies me," he said. "I can't understand it. I was sure this was a forgery. Because this woman was murdered, Mrs. Latham—and what's more, there's not one of you here that has the least doubt of it. And yet—she'd just written a plain, definite suicide note."

He shook his head, staring down at the little gray oblong.

"Is this at all like Mrs. Gould's writing, Mrs. Latham?"

I smiled, thinking of Alice's delicate precise little script, and the naïve childish flamboyant scrawl in front of him.

"Not in the least, Colonel Primrose, I should say. No, I'm certain that's Sandra's writing."

His sparkling black eyes, shrewd and sharp and bright as an old parrot's, looked steadily into mine.

"It's absurd, isn't it," he said slowly, "to think for a minute that that woman, in such a situation, would be so obliging as to kill herself—or even that the idea of threatening to would enter her mind. Especially just before she was murdered."

"Are you sure she was murdered, Colonel Primrose?"

"Very sure, Mrs. Latham. So are you. So is everybody here."

"You don't think she was hit over the head by the jib?"

He nodded. "Probably. Also by Mr. Jim Gould's monkey wrench."

He hesitated a moment, and added—quite unnecessarily, I thought, "Which has your fingerprints all over it."

I probably flushed a little. "I told you I picked it up when I stumbled over it on the garage floor."

He nodded absently. "I know."

We were silent for a moment. "Do you think she knew Paul Dikranov?" I asked.

"Certainly."

"Does he admit it?"

"No. But he's a very shrewd fellow."

"That's just what he said about you, a few minutes ago," I said.

Colonel Primrose's eyes brightened humorously.

"That's bad. I was just going to add that shrewd fellows often come pretty hard croppers."

"He also told Rosemary he didn't know Sandra."

"I know. His story is that she's a common type in the East— which is quite true, of course."

"Where does he come from?"

"He's a Georgian. Money from oil concessions—and also, I take it, from supplying arms to natives in one place and another."

"Has he explained what he was doing barging about in my garden at three o'clock in the morning?"

Colonel Primrose cocked his head down and gave me an amused sideways glance.

"Can you have any possible doubt, Mrs. Latham, that he was interviewing—or planning to interview—the late Mrs. Gould?"

I stared at him. "Do you believe that?"

"I don't know, Mrs. Latham. Besides, I thought it was more important to get explanations from all the people who were barging about the Goulds' garage at one o'clock."

"Oh. And did you?"

"Not very satisfactory ones," he admitted cheerfully. "No. For instance—I still don't know who the woman was that Hawkins heard quarreling with Sandra. Whether it was Rosemary—"

He paused an instant. I tried mightily not to look at the blue petals on the table. They loomed up at me as big as a peony.

"Or Lucy Lee. Jealousy is one of the most powerful irritants. Or—"

He looked at me steadily a second before he added, "—Mrs. Alice Gould."

"I suppose," I said, "there *was* a woman there? Hawkins didn't just make it all up?"

Colonel Primrose nodded. "That'll be the defense stand, certainly. However, so far there's no reason to believe Hawkins has misled us."

"Are you sure?" I said. "He hated Sandra. Like everybody else he was convinced she ruined Jim's life. He always called her a foreign devil. Anyway, couldn't he have heard a quarrel over the radio, the way he did Jim announcing the time?"

"Are you the official Devil's Advocate, Mrs. Latham?" Colonel Primrose asked with a chuckle.

"I'd just like to save you from making a mistake. I understand from your sergeant that so far you've never been known to make one."

He laughed.

"I believe in Hawkins's woman, myself. You know, of course, that the whole business looks definitely on the womanish side."

I looked at him aghast at that.

"It was all easy for a woman to do. Nothing mannish required. The spilt whisky, the crack on the head with the wrench—a slight blow, Mrs. Latham; you'd have thought a strong person would have struck harder than that. Then this telephone nonsense. Also the motive. From the so-called a priori evidence, I should say more women would have cause to hate Sandra Gould than men—always excepting her husband."

"You mean you haven't excepted him?"

"We examine all sides of the business, Mrs. Latham—with a view to forestalling Nathan Kaufman when he comes tomorrow. He's a good criminal lawyer—"

Colonel Primrose stopped a little suddenly.

"But . . ." I said.

"But people don't usually hire him unless they're guilty as the devil, Mrs. Latham."

"Jim Gould didn't hire him."

Colonel Primrose smiled so that his black eyes were lost for an instant in a network of humorous wrinkles.

"No—but Rodman Bishop did."

For a moment I didn't get the possible significance of that—and when I did the chance had passed.

CHAPTER TWELVE

Suddenly my telephone jangled, eerily in the silent house. One long ring, three short, sounding in every house in our end of the estate. I looked at Colonel Primrose. There was something definitely ominous about it—about going to the phone and finding no one there . . . no sound but a ticking clock.

He nodded to me. I got up slowly.

"You'll listen for the clock, won't you," he said quietly.

Suddenly I wanted to scream, and say no, no, I wouldn't, I couldn't—but his eyes were fixed on me steadily, and there was something horribly like a command under the suave reminder. I went towards the door. The telephone jangled again. It's strange, I thought, how an inanimate object can take on a sudden startling malevolence. My hands were icy cold as I took down the receiver and held it to my ear, listening a moment before I said "Hello."

Colonel Primrose was right. It was there; I could hear it distinctly. Tickety-tick, tickety-tock; tickety-tick, tickety-tock.

"Hello," I said, making my voice sound as natural as I could.

Instantly there came a frantic, perfectly familiar voice.

"Oh, Grace, they've stopped Andy, on the plane up. They wouldn't let him go! What are they doing? Grace, you've got to find out for me!"

It was Lucy Lee's voice . . . and beyond it the tickety-tick, tickety-tock.

"I'll ask Colonel Primrose, darling," I said, a great deal more calmly than I felt with that tickety-tick, tickety-tock beating in my ears—barely perceptible actually if I hadn't been so morbidly aware of it. "They probably wanted him to be here tomorrow just in case they open the inquest again."

And then I did something that made me feel like a snake in the grass.

I said, "Where are you, Lucy?"

It suddenly came to me that I *had* to know where that tickety-tick, tickety-tock came from.

"I'm at home—at Mother's. But, Grace—tell Colonel Primrose Andy was in the house at twelve, last night! He was, Grace, really!"

"I'll tell him, Lucy Lee. You go to bed. It'll be all right."

Tickety-tick, tickety-tock; tickety-tick, tickety-tock.

I could hear it sounding in my ears when Lucy hung up, and after I hung up. I tried to get it out before I went back into the living room to Colonel Primrose. The idea came to me at first that I couldn't let him know I'd heard it too. But he knew it without my telling him, although he didn't mention it.

"Why have they stopped Andy?"

He glanced up inquiringly.

"Was it Lucy Lee?"

I nodded.

"He was boarding the plane."

He looked blank. I explained that a lot of the men at April Harbor had jobs in Philadelphia and New York and chartered a plane every summer. It picked them up Saturday noon or Friday night sometimes and debouched them in the landing field that was actually the first hole of the golf course, and picked them up again Sunday at midnight.

"I gather Andy was boarding it to go back to New York when Parran's men stopped him," I said. "Don't say you didn't know anything about it."

"I knew they had an eye on him. I shouldn't have supposed he would have gone back."

"I don't suppose Andy's boss takes much interest in his family affairs," I said.

Colonel Primrose got up and went to the door. I think he was rather more disturbed than he cared to have seen. He started abruptly when the phone rang again. One long, three short. We looked at each other, I suppose both wondering whether there would be anybody there or not.

"If you hear that clock again, and anybody answers you," he said, "will you please say that I've left April Harbor on the night plane?"

I looked blank myself. The phone rang again.

"Theirs not to reason why," said Colonel Primrose politely.

"Sorry," I said. I went through the swinging door to the inner hall. If I had known he'd cut up to my room and was listening in himself, I should have been pretty sore. But I didn't. I had not yet realized what the business of having a detective in the home was actually like.

I took down the phone. It was Jim Gould.

96

"Grace," he said hurriedly. "Listen!"

I *was* listening—for the tickety-tick, tickety-tock, and I heard it . . . in the background, Jim's voice urgent against it

"Tell Rosemary they've set the time at one o'clock—not twelve."

I could have wept.

"She knows it already, Jim. And she's told Colonel Primrose she was with you then."

There was a long silence in which I heard nothing but the odd ticking of that ghastly clock. Then Jim Gould groaned. "O God!" he said. I knew then for the first time since the dreadful thing happened that Jim was really feeling something besides shock and anger and humiliation.

"And listen, Jim, *carefully.* Colonel Primrose told me to say that he'd gone on the night plane."

There was another pause. The clock beat its tiny rhythmic noise.

"Yes?" Jim said "Good-by. I'll be seeing you."

We hung up. I stood there a few seconds, wondering suddenly if Colonel Primrose had made all that up about the mysterious caller. It came to me then that I hadn't seen Sergeant Buck, not since I'd come back from the Bishops'. I looked into the kitchen, thinking Lilac and Julius must be back from church. But they weren't. The outside door was shut and probably locked. Nevertheless I went over and tried it. I had a vague uneasy feeling that wouldn't down.

I went back into the living room. Colonel Primrose was not there, and he had moved the exhibits of the prosecution. I remembered then that he hadn't shown me either the petals of blue velvet or the second piece of paper, the one folded into a pleated spill, the sort of thing that an Englishman keeps in a jar on the mantel to light his pipe with.

I don't suppose, actually, that it would have made any difference if I'd known about it, but I've thought several times it might have. It certainly wouldn't have made any difference in what happened that night, as it turned out.

Sheila, my Irish setter, was lying on the cool stone hearth where she'd been asleep all evening. She got up while I stood hesitating in the middle of the room. I didn't know whether to turn the lights out and go upstairs or not—having, as I said, little notion of the house habits of detectives. It was hot, and I was pretty miserable about all this.

Sheila licked my hand and went over to the door, looking back, inviting me to come out with her. I went out on the porch. The stars were out, and the night perfectly still. I forgot Colonel Primrose's repeated injunctions—at least I didn't think of them as I opened the porch door and went down the brick walk to the cluster of white Gibson Island chairs stationed there like sentinel ghosts in the middle of the lawn under the big sycamore tree

Sheila sniffed and growled. I felt her long red body stiffen. I caught hold of her collar. She growled again. Then I heard someone moving very softly on the grass I couldn't have told the direction that the sound came from except that Sheila was looking past the tree towards the Bishops' place, but not towards their house.

And then, as softly and undeniably as any sensory evidence can be felt, I knew that it was Paul Dikranov, somewhere in the line of shrubbery that divides my place from theirs. The faint unmistakable odor of Turkish tobacco came gently through the warm soft air. For a moment I thought of calling out, but Sheila's deep bass growl seemed warning enough, probably, that I was not alone. I turned back to the house, and then I stopped as abruptly as I had ever stopped in my life.

Somewhere behind me there was a sharp crack that split the air, and simultaneously a hot streak zip-whizzed past my ear. A sudden instinct, or maybe it was the Wild West tales I'd read to my children, made me first duck and then flatten myself out on the grass. Or maybe it was sheer blue funk Anyway, I did, and I was glad I had, because there was a second crack and another shot screamed through the air about where my shoulder blades had been. Sheila, who's gun-shy, scuttled to the house whimpering.

It all happened in an instant, and in another instant I heard heavy feet pounding across the grass, and saw Sergeant Buck coming with amazing speed. He took one look at me, still lying there on the grass in the starlight. At first I thought he said, "Thank God, you're not hurt," but he didn't; he said, "Thank God, you're not the Colonel," and dashed off toward the direction of the shots.

I sat up, took a trial breath—rather the way Goerge Barrol had done after he was nearly drowned—got up gingerly and made a bolt for it to the door.

I don't think I was ever so completely and utterly scared in my life. I didn't wait for Buck to come back or for Colonel Primrose to appear from somewhere; I went upstairs and locked my door behind me. I should very much have liked to crawl under the bed with Sheila. I turned out my light and lay there pretty shaken, trying to figure out just why Paul Dikra-nov wanted to shoot me, of all people under the sun

The sudden jangle of the phone on my bedside table made me jump almost out of my skin.

"Hello, Grace!"

It was Alice Gould.

"Are you all right? The Sergeant was here, looking for Jim He says you were shot at?"

"I'm all right," I said. "I was shot at, and missed Tell Jim—"

"But, darling, that's the point—Jim isn't here "

"Isn't there?"

"No. He's not "

I thought what that might mean to Sergeant Buck—and to the Colonel. "Oh, dear!" I said.

And then for the first time I realized that I was not hearing the tickety-tick, tickety-tock of the unknown clock

"Alice," I almost shouted into the phone, "where are you?"

"Where am I? '

The gentle worried voice was puzzled.

"At home, of course, dear. We must find Jim, Grace, don't you see?"

I'm afraid I did see, clearly. In fact a number of things. One of them was that the clock that I'd heard when both Lucy Lee and Jim had spoken was not near the phone their mother was using. Which meant one of two things, of course. Either Alice Gould was not at her own phone, or whoever had been listening in on my two previous conversations had not been listening to this one. And that in turn implied enough to make me even more uneasy than I'd been before. For my own sake, now, I saw the genuine necessity for finding whose phone the clock was near.

I turned out the light. Colonel Primrose's remark that Sergeant Buck was a good man to have around in case of trouble went through my head, or I doubt if I'd have gone to sleep as promptly as I did. I turned out the light. But I didn't go to sleep. Every time I closed my eyes I could hear footsteps and creeping sounds—on the paths outside, in the hall, downstairs. My reason knew they were nonexistent, but my nerves didn't. Nor was Colonel Primrose's remark that Sergeant Buck was a good man to have around in case of trouble entirely reassuring. I couldn't feel that he would take my removal as a great personal tragedy in any sense.

If I were a logical person I suppose I should have quietly put

every event of the last two days into a neat little category . . .
and come to a perfectly erroneous conclusion. I certainly
couldn't have got anywhere near the truth, not without being a
lot brighter than I am—though I must admit it was all there,
even then, for anyone who was logical to see. However, I'm
not; and furthermore I was a lot nervier than I like to admit
even now. There's something definitely upsetting about being
shot at like a rabbit on your own front lawn.

So I lay there, not thinking it out so much as just seeing it in
a jumble of sudden vivid pictures, such as Sandra saying to
Dikranov, "Just for old times' sake, hein?" and Dikranov's lean
expressionless face. With that picture came the instant question, Why did he deny knowing her? And why was he in my
garden? Why should he of all people shoot at me of all people?
What connection did he really have with Sandra, what did he
mean when he told Rosemary that the less they inquired into
each other's previous lives the better off they'd be?

I thought of Lucy Lee then, with a sudden picture of her
crouching miserably on the stone steps with the lightning
flashing above her, and again in my house willing to hand over
Jim's head on a charger to save her husband's. And what about
Andy? Why had he been in such a ghastly state at the inquest?
What had he stowed away under the bank? Why had they kept
him from going to New York? And I could see Jim Gould,
with Sandra wilting against his arm, and then with his white set
face in front of my fireplace, utterly silent. Why had he gone
directly to his own car to find Sandra, instead of to Andy's?
Why had his mother still been dressed at half past three in the
morning? Why had she insisted on going to the garage? Did
she know Sandra was there, was she definitely preparing me,
when she told me Sandra had tried to kill herself, for what she
had decided I must find?

And that note . . . What would Colonel Primrose say
when he learned it really wasn't a forgery?

But above all, and the thing that was definitely terrifying,
was the business of the telephone. Who could conceivably have
phoned from the pay station in the village at 3:15 on the
morning Sandra was killed, and what could he have wanted?
And who was it whose clock sounded on the line with that
sinister little tickety-tick, tickety-tock . . . and what did *he*
want?

I must have gone to sleep thinking of that, because I came to
suddenly and sat bolt upright in bed. The clock on the table
said 3:28. It was dark and perfectly still. For a moment I

100

wasn't quite sure what had waked me. Then I reached for the phone.

"Hello," I said. I waited. Then I spoke again, and suddenly remembered. There was no sound at the other end of the wire —that is, no sound of a voice; only a steady ticking of a clock tickety-tick, tickety-tock; tickety-tick, tickety-tock.

I had a strange panicky feeling, and I rattled the rod up and down frantically. The ticking went on. Tickety-tick, tickety-tock; tickety-tick, tickety-tock. For a fleeting moment I wondered if I couldn't hear someone breathing. Then I did hear a definite sound. It came from the telephone in my own guest room, and it came quite sharply.

"Would you mind hanging up, Mrs. Latham? I'm trying to put a call through."

I gasped, but I hung up, the idea that I would certainly be glad when my guests had departed running through my mind. I turned over to sleep again, not even trying to figure out what this was all about. And when I woke up again it was the telephone that woke me, and I reached for it quite cheerfully. A thing that is a terror by night can be a diverting game in the broad light of day.

But it was Alice Gould this time.

"Grace," she said, "would you come over as soon as you're dressed? I'd like to see you a moment before I go to the village."

Her voice was cool and unhurried. A quick memory of the two shots the night before and the soft persistent tickety-tick, tickety-tock in my ear again were all that made the request seem an urgent one. I got up and was dressed when Lilac came in with my tray.

The idea of Alice Gould creeping about, listening in on other people's telephone conversations, seemed pretty absurd, I thought as I took a spoonful of fragrant yellow melon. But when I came to think of it, anybody I knew doing it was equally absurd. Leaving out Elsie Carter, of course, who's a born snooper, or Maggie Potter, who hasn't anything else to do, but who, as it happens, isn't on our line. I couldn't have told why her name came to my mind just then. Perhaps it was because what George had said about Sandra and Dr. Potter had slipped into my mind the way things do without any apparent reason.

Colonel Primrose and Sergeant Buck were not in sight when I came down, but Julius intercepted me as I was slipping out.

"The Colonel, Mis' Grace, he says he wants to see you as soon as it's convenient."

"You tell him it'll be convenient a little later, Julius."

"Yas'm. Ah'll tell him that mahself."

I cut through the hedge to the Goulds' and saw him. He and Sergeant Buck and Mr. Parran, with four or five other men, were standing in front of the garage, talking earnestly. Colonel Primrose was giving directions, or so it looked from the way he was pointing this way and that.

I slipped back and went farther down towards the lane. I didn't want to be seen just then, and there was another opening in the hedge, one that led directly into Andy and Lucy Lee's side garden where the children's swing and ladder set stands. It isn't used much any more, not by grownups, and the children are too busy on the beach to play on their trapeze. I parted the branches of the crape myrtle and started to duck my head to go through when I saw something that made me hesitate.

Someone else had been there quite recently. Twigs were broken off, and one spear of red blossom was purple and dead where it was hanging. I glanced back to see whether Colonel Primrose had seen me, but no one was in sight. I pushed the branches farther apart and looked at the ground. Heavy feet had gone through there. The longish grass was trampled noticeably in one spot, as if someone had stood there quite a long time. The cold sensation down my spine was enough to tell me that this was undoubtedly where the person had stood before he began taking pot shots at me the night before. I didn't need the little brass case that I saw shining in the grass a yard or so away.

I bent down to pick it up, and for some reason changed my mind. I had an odd notion that someone was watching me in spite of the fact that nobody was in sight.

I felt a curious reluctance to going on through the hedge to the Goulds'. It seemed to me now that it couldn't possibly have been Paul Dikranov shooting at me . . . if, indeed, I hadn't simply imagined the whole business. The morning sun and a cup of coffee work wonders with the terrors of the night. But if I hadn't imagined it, how could a strange person find one of the very special intimate spots in my hedge—one that, furthermore, a lot of other people knew quite well? And if it wasn't Paul Dikranov, who was it, and why?

CHAPTER THIRTEEN

I went through the hedge nevertheless. The windows of Lucy Lee's cottage were open, the brightly printed curtains showing dimly through the shining copper screens under the drawn shades. It seemed the most utter nonsense to think of anyone behind any of those windows peering out at me. I shook off the idea and went around in front. There was no sign of life about the house, no clatter of dishes and yelling children, no Lucy Lee singing as she banged her pots and pans about. The whole place was as quiet as the grave.

Through the trees I could see Mrs. Gould's house—large and white, with its wide lawn running down to the lane along the beach. I hurried along the flagstone walk and went in through the side door. Hawkins was there in his white coat with a coffee service balanced on one pink palm. He looked at me like a great black owl and said, "Mis' Alice she's in the dinin' room, Mis' Grace."

He held open the swinging door for me, muttering something perfectly unintelligible about the general goings-on.

Alice Gould was at the head of a long table pretty well littered with the remains of children's breakfasts. The children were gone, but Lucy Lee was there, looking ill and drawn and with more rouge on her face than had ever been there in all her life before.

Alice raised one delicate purple-veined hand, heavy with the jewels she always wore, and smiled at her daughter. "If you don't mind, Lucy Lee, I'd like to talk to Grace alone. If I were you, darling, I'd go get Andy and go down the beach for a swim. He oughtn't to be over there by himself."

Lucy Lee shook her head as she got up.

"I've got some things to do," she said.

Her mother watched her with a troubled face.

"I wish you'd tell me what to do with those two," she said. "When I was young, people didn't just get up and walk out on their husbands—with or without their children—no matter how bad they were."

103

"I can't blame Lucy Lee very much," I said.

"My dear, I'm not blaming her. Andy's been a terrible fool. But I'm just old-fashioned enough, Grace, to believe that this sort of thing is largely the woman's fault."

She smiled gently.

"You see, I couldn't be so frightfully sorry for Jim, if I didn't think that."

She stirred her coffee and gazed a long time into the cup before she looked up at me.

"Grace, it's about Jim that I want to talk to you," she said quietly. "I gather from something he said that he and Rosemary were pretty indiscreet. He says it was his fault.

She smiled again, faintly, and shook her head.

"You think it was Rosemary's?"

"That's the mother in me. I'm afraid I do. I think Jim would have died before he did anything dishonorable."

"Oh, my dear," I said. "You don't think one last meeting before she goes off to marry and live abroad is dishonorable?"

"Perhaps not—unless you go into the whole dismal past, and realize that Jim still loves her, and that the whole Sandra business was just a ghastly tragic thing. Like a terrible illness—if you get away from it, or get over it, you forget it, and it has no meaning for you."

She looked away, her hands pleating the edge of her napkin.

"I've seen Jim—so many times—leave in the morning, and the minute he was out of the house he was like himself again . . . and in the evening I could see it all back on him the minute he got in the house and saw her there. It almost broke my heart. I never knew how it all happened, Grace, until one of his classmates drank too much one night."

She laughed mirthlessly.

"He insisted on talking about it. How Jim had a week's leave —he got it because Rosemary was in Shanghai and they were going to be married. Then they had their quarrel. Heaven knows what about—they've probably forgotten themselves. Rosemary gave him back his ring and left him cold there, and he went out and got roaring drunk . . . at the place where Sandra danced. And then when he came to, days later, he was married to her. I suppose he did the decent thing. He got drunk again and they loaded him on board ship and the captain tried to do something about it. Jim's a stubborn fool . . . if he couldn't marry Rosemary he didn't care whom he married."

104

She stirred her coffee monotonously

"You know the rest of it. He had to resign—the Navy can't have that sort of thing, not the sort of person Sandra was I think she improved a lot. But they couldn't wait for that, in the Service."

She looked at me steadily.

"It's a terrible thing to say, Grace, but I'm glad she's gone. I'm sorry it had to be this way. I tried to get her to divorce him, but she just laughed at me. You know Jim never used to drink. He's drunk much too much these last two years, while she was making a fool of every man that came within sight of her."

She got up and went to the window, and looked out a long time. Then she came back to the table suddenly

"Colonel Primrose is coming up the walk," she said quickly. "You'd better go. I just told you, Grace, because I want you to know that I feel there's nothing .   . no wrong done to her .   . that equals the wrong she's done to Jim. And that no sacrifice of   convention—"

She shrugged her fragile shoulders

"I think you know what I mean I just wanted to tell you. Now run along, out the back."

Which was a mistake, because Colonel Primrose, dispensing with the formality of a proper entrance, was coming in the back.

"Oh, good morning," he said cheerfully. "I've been hunting for you everywhere "

He smiled, but his black eyes weren't involved in the smile at all. They were sharp and probing He took my arm. "Come back inside. I want to talk to you.'

Mrs. Gould rose from the table as we came in. Nothing in her manner or her face showed that she was the least surprised at the failure of her plan to get me out.

"Good morning, Colonel Primrose," she said, extending her hand to him with a simple dignity that matched his own. They were the same generation and the same sort of people. They seemed to be meeting on common ground even if they were in opposite camps.

"Let's go in there," she said. She led the way into the large white living room. The Venetian blinds were drawn. The sun through the open slats made gay little ladders along the thick grass rugs. Alice Gould sat down in one corner of the deep sofa, folded her hands in her lap, and motioned me down

105

beside her. Colonel Primrose pulled up a hard chair and sat down, straightening out his rheumatic knee with a deprecatory smile. Then he looked at me.

"I wasn't sure I'd find you alive this morning," he said soberly. "She was shot at twice last night, you know."

He turned to Alice.

"Oh, it was obviously a mistake," she said earnestly. "I can't think anyone would want to . . . to hurt you, Grace."

"My boy scout training came in handy," I said.

"What were you doing, Mrs. Latham?"

"Nothing. I answered the telephone and came back to the living room. You had gone. Sheila wanted to go out and I went with her. I forgot all the things you'd said—I'm so used to being perfectly safe here. Then I walked down the path as far as the white chairs under the sycamore tree. Sheila growled, and I . . . well, I began to get a little uneasy. I started back to the house, and—well, that's all."

"It came very close to being quite all, Mrs. Latham," Colonel Primrose said. He shook his head seriously. "You must see now that what I told you is true—that you know too much for somebody's peace of mind . . . and that one murder makes another seem simple—and necessary."

He turned back to Alice Gould. She was sitting perfectly still. Even her fingers that usually pleated and unpleated her handkerchief were still, almost as if she dreaded something that must come and was bracing herself for it.

"This is getting to be a very serious matter, Mrs. Gould," he said. "I'd like you to tell me about Saturday night again, please."

"Gladly, Colonel Primrose."

I thought there was a subtle note of relief in her voice.

"I'm very happy to do so, if it will help. Of course it does involve a certain amount of public linen washing, but I have the utmost confidence in your kindness and discretion."

I looked at Colonel Primrose and shook my head. I hadn't. From all I could make out, he would hang his grandmother with the greatest urbanity, if the necessity arose.

"You were at the clubhouse when the business about taking the boat out in the storm came up?" Alice asked. "Andy was supposed to have taken Lucy Lee home early. One of the children has a cold. But in the excitement at the dock he forgot all about that. I brought Lucy Lee home. We sat here waiting for Jim and Andy to come. Lucy Lee is a silly little goose, and like a great many wives who aren't awfully interested in sports she feels that Andy's week ends are too much taken up with sailing and golf and all that. Saturday night, after I'd got her back here, she worked herself into a fury. She'd been looking forward to the dance, and the orchestra was late and so on. So when Andy came in extremely early—it was a little before midnight, as a matter of fact—they had a good old-fashioned family row."

Mrs. Gould shook her head in mock despair.

"It lasted until half past twelve. I put them both out then and told them to go home and stay there."

"That was at half past twelve?" Colonel Primrose said politely.

Alice nodded her snow-white curly head and raised her serious unlined face.

"Yes, you see Jim hadn't come in yet and I knew he'd left the club. Andy had told me that. He didn't say he'd brought Sandra home. But under the circumstances I think that was more than wise. Considering the state Lucy Lee was in."

I glanced uneasily at Colonel Primrose. If there was only some way I could head Alice off! She seemed absolutely bent on putting a noose round her own daughter's neck, drawing it tighter then with every word she spoke. Then quite suddenly I realized the dreadful situation. Alice Gould still thought that Sandra was murdered at midnight . . . She did not know that her twelve o'clock alibi for her daughter and son-in-law was utterly worthless.

I opened my mouth to say something, but Colonel Primrose looked at me steadily and I closed it again.

"Where did they go, do you know, when they left here, Mrs. Gould?"

"Home. I watched them from the porch. I saw them turn on the lights in the cottage."

"And when did you find out that Andy had brought Sandra home?"

"When Lucy Lee came back to the house a few minutes later."

"After she'd gone home," Colonel Primrose said.

Alice Gould nodded. There was obviously something wrong here, and I could see that Colonel Primrose saw it too.

"She came back later. I gathered the quarrel hadn't ended and she was coming home to Mother. In fact, she's still here. She moved the children over the next morning."

"She stayed in this house Saturday night then?"

Alice Gould nodded again.

"And when did she get here, that last time?"

"About one-thirty, I think, Colonel Primrose."

There was no change in the expression of polite interest on Colonel Primrose's face.

"And Jim?"

"He came in about one o'clock, and went to his room."

"Did you tell him his wife wasn't in, Mrs. Gould?"

"Oh, dear, no!" Alice exclaimed. "I shouldn't have thought of it. Not for an instant. You see, Sandra frequently stayed on to dance long after Jim was worn out. Some friend usually brought her home. Both she and Jim belong to the modern school that thinks husbands and wives cleaving together is nonsense. I'm afraid Lucy Lee is the only old-fashioned member of my family."

"And you, Mrs. Gould—didn't you wonder about her?"

"Oh, of course. But I've wondered about Sandra a good deal in the last seven years."

There was a slightly sardonic note in Alice's voice.

"I did glance in her room when I came in with Lucy Lee, and later Jim had gone to bed. That's when I found her note."

She looked up, as guileless as a kitten, meeting those sharpened black eyes without a quiver. I forced myself not to look at Colonel Primrose.

"I see," he said. "About that note—I wonder if you would be good enough to show me just where you found it."

"With pleasure."

Alice led us up the wide white-paneled staircase, down a sunny hall to a room overlooking the walk to the garage. She opened the door. I think, strangely enough, it was one of the very few times I'd been in that room since it was Sandra's. It looked more like a stage dressing room than a lady's bedroom . . . all the superimposed bits that were Sandra's anyway. The basic decoration of pink sateen was not unlike her, but it was the sort of thing a decorator would do.

Around the mirror were snapshots, mostly of men about the Harbor taken with Sandra. There weren't many of Jim—one taken several years before, another of him in a group on the club veranda, including, oddly enough, both Andy and Dr. Potter. Other bits of local interest hung about the room—a broken canoe paddle with a lot of names scribbled on it, invitations to cocktail parties, programs of the Harbor yacht races, the horse show and the dog show—and literally dozens of pictures of Sandra herself, at all hours of the day and night.

Alice Gould picked her way through the room with a sort of humorous resignation. It wasn't, you could see, her idea of a daughter-in-law's room.

"I found it just here."

She pointed to the dressing table with its profusion of cosmetic boxes and bottles and mirrors.

"Was the light on?"

"No. I turned it on. I could see from the hall light that she wasn't here. She leaves her things strewed about when she comes in, and there was nothing on that chair. So I turned on the light."

"Why did you do that?"

"I don't know. It seems a natural thing to do. And, of course, she might possibly have got in and laid down, without taking off her things."

Colonel Primrose nodded. "Did she drink?"

"More at times than I approved of. Though I'm an old-fashioned woman, as I think I've said before."

"What did you do when you saw the note, Mrs. Gould?"

"I read it, and I went out to hunt for her. As I told you before, I thought it was all part of the heroic nonsense that began with the boat episode. I never for an instant thought it was anything but a grandstand play for Jim—to make him more wretched than he already was. You see, Sandra was intensely a woman. She knew all the old tricks about appealing to a man's sense of honor and so on."

Colonel Primrose hesitated a moment.

"And you went to Mrs. Latham's—"

"Because I think Grace is one of the few people who know Sandra as well as I do. And—well, I wanted some moral support when I'd found Sandra about to slay herself, or even just pretending to be about to."

Alice shrugged, her face a little drawn, as if the strain of being casual about the things that really meant a lot to her was telling on her at last.

"I don't think it's strange. I've come to depend a lot on Grace."

I tried to smile back at her, but I saw too clearly the bog she was getting both of us into to be very cheerful about it.

We left Sandra's room. Colonel Primrose, a little ahead of us, was looking back, talking, and he went past the stairs and blundered on in the wrong direction, into Alice's bedroom. He jumped back.

"I'm *so* sorry!"

"Quite all right," Alice said. "I don't suppose the beds are made yet."

I wondered if she would have thought it was all right if she'd suspected that Colonel Primrose was not blundering, but very coolly looking to see if she had a telephone—and a clock—in her room. I was only surprised that he didn't inspect the rest of the house while he was at it.

Lucy Lee was in the living room when we came down the stairs. She was standing in front of the fireplace. She turned as we came, obviously expecting to see only her mother and me, and the plain fear on her face when she saw Colonel Primrose was a little shocking.

"Oh!" she said. "I'm sorry, I thought you—"

"Colonel Primrose was asking about Saturday night, Lucy Lee," Alice Gould said quietly. "I'm afraid I had to tell him about the row you and Andy had here."

Lucy Lee stared at her mother, her face chalk-white, her lips parted stupidly.

Alice gave me a quick alarmed glance and hurried to where Lucy Lee stood. "Child—what's the matter!"

"Nothing, Mother," she said. She brushed the short chestnut curls from her forehead, trying desperately to smile. "I just heard, Mother, that it was one o'clock that Sandra was . . . killed, not twelve. He found it out."

She nodded towards Colonel Primrose.

"Grace knew too—they all knew! Only they wouldn't tell us! Oh, Mother!"

She flung herself into her mother's arms in a passion of tears. Alice Gould's face above the dark soft head of her sobbing child was a mask of conflict—doubt, fear and anger.

"I thought you knew it, until just a moment ago, Alice," I said weakly. "Jim knew it last night. It never occurred to me he hadn't told you."

"I'm afraid I prevented her from telling you, Mrs. Gould," Colonel Primrose said quickly. "You see, I not only know that, I know a number of other things. One of them is that so far none of you has told the truth. If I may say so, I think you're all pretty much at cross purposes . . . because you haven't told each other the truth either."

A flush deepened in Alice's face. Her lips tightened ever so faintly. Lucy Lee raised her head and stood there, face tear-stained, staring dully at the carpet, her mother's arm round her slim shoulders.

110

"For instance which one of you met Sandra as she was leaving the garage and quarreled with her, so violently that it woke Hawkins?"

He smiled at Alice Gould. Whoever it was, I thought, it plainly wasn't she. I don't think Alice had ever raised her voice in her life.

"I think your husband could answer that if he would, Mrs Thorp."

Lucy Lee flushed.

"Why don't you go and ask him?" she said in a low voice

"I think I shall—unless you'd send Hawkins for him, Mrs Gould."

CHAPTER FOURTEEN

And when Andy Thorp came he wasn't yet any more like himself than he had been the day before. He ignored Lucy Lee completely, barely nodded to his mother-in-law and me, and turned to Colonel Primrose.

"I can thank you for muffing a big deal for me."

He almost snarled it.

"You can thank yourself, Thorp," Colonel Primrose said curtly. "When you begin to give right answers to the questions that are asked you, and quit telling the most childish falsehoods, you'll be allowed to go about your business."

Andy reddened under his sun-tanned hide.

"It would be rather pleasant for everybody if you'd stop being an idiot, Andy," Alice said gently. "No one thinks you had anything to do with Sandra's death."

Andy looked at her an instant, said nothing, dug into his pocket and brought out a battered pack of cigarettes.

"I'd just like to hear again what happened after you left the club, Thorp," Colonel Primrose said. He spoke quietly, but there was an iron undertone in his voice. It must have been like hearing the head coach again. Andy answered almost civilly, still without even a glance at Lucy Lee.

"Sandra dried out in front of the fire," he said. "I guess she didn't have much on but an evening dress. She borrowed somebody's coat and was waiting for Jim. One of the colored boys came in and said Jim had gone with Grace."

He looked around at me.

"Sandra wanted to go home then and said she'd join me and Barrol in the car. We waited about ten minutes for her, I guess. George was cold, he didn't dry out as quick as Sandra, but neither of us had anything to drink on us. I started back to get a pint when she showed up. She was high as a kite."

He tossed his cigarette into the fireplace and lighted another.

"She'd been drinking, inside?" Colonel Primrose suggested.

"Not while I was there, except a toddy they made her. I

112

don't know what she was doing that ten minutes George and I waited in the car."

. Colonel Primrose nodded, looking at him steadily and I thought rather oddly.

"We started off and dropped George. He was about half-tight with all the rye they'd poured into him at the club He staggered up the steps, and we came home."

Andy looked down at the carpet, his face a dull crimson

"I wanted her to take a ride, but she wouldn't So we put the car in the garage and started up to the house. Halfway up she asked me for my keys. We had an argument, but I gave 'em to her. She started back to the garage I went on a little way and looked back. She was talking . .   to a woman."

"Yes," Colonel Primrose said briskly. "Who was it?"

"I don't know, I tell you."

"You didn't recognize her at all?"

"I didn't recognize her at all. That's English, isn't it?"

"Yes," Colonel Primrose said, almost cheerfully. His old black eyes were shining, for some reason that I at least did not understand. "Yes, that's English. It was no one you knew?"

"I tell you it wasn't."

"Was it light?"

Andy nodded. "It was pretty light."

"You probably could have told, for instance, if it had been Mrs. Latham, say?"

Colonel Primrose smiled at me. I tried to smile back, but I don't think my attempt amounted to much.

Andy looked at me an instant. "I should think so."

"Or .   . Mrs. Gould, for instance?"

"It wasn't. I tell you again, and I hope to God for the last time, I didn't know her."

Colonel Primrose nodded absently, as if he were thinking hard about something else

Then he looked at Andy very queerly.

"It's rather strange, isn't it," he said slowly, "that you should have looked back there and seen Sandra talking to a strange woman . . . a woman that you'd never seen before?"

He shook his head a little.

"I guess it is," Andy said. "That's what happened just the same."

"All right," Colonel Primrose said. "What did you do?"

"I started back. Sandra ran up to me and said to go on, she'd take care of it. I asked her who it was. She said, 'Oh, a poor

113

crazy woman.' I didn't pay any more attention to it. There are plenty of crazy women around. I came on up."

"She said just those words?"

Andy nodded. "Just them."

"Have you got any idea of what the woman looked like?"

There was silence for a moment. Then Andy spoke rather hesitatingly. "I got the idea she was sort of old, from what I could see. I just looked at her for a second. She was standing outside the light at the side of the door there."

"And that was just before midnight?"

Andy nodded.

"Sandra didn't tell you what she wanted with the car?"

Lucy Lee moved a little, and Andy's face flushed still darker.

"I thought she had a date she wanted to keep."

He kept his eyes fixed on the floor.

"You don't know who with?"

"I guess you could ask Rosemary's dago friend if you wanted to find out. Personally I wouldn't know."

Colonel Primrose nodded politely. "And you didn't see her again . . . after you left this house at half past twelve?"

"I didn't."

"Sure about it?"

'Why?" Andy said. He stared at Colonel Primrose aggressively, his chin out a little. "Aren't you?"

Colonel Primrose got up. "Thank you," he said suavely.

The telephone out in the hall rang: one long, three short. Colonel Primrose glanced at me.

"That's mine," I said. I felt a queer little sensation along my spine. "May I answer it, Alice?"

"If you don't mind," Colonel Primrose said calmly, "I'll answer it myself."

He hesitated a moment, standing there, looking from one of us to the other, and added, "I've got an idea it's the woman Mr. Thorp saw Saturday night."

He chuckled a little at the expressions on our faces and went out.

The door closed behind him. But when he came back his face was a dead giveaway.

"It wasn't?" I asked.

"It was Sergeant Buck. He's back from the village. I think we might be getting along, Mrs. Latham?"

I glanced at Alice Gould, trying to let her know I'd do my best. She nodded imperceptibly. I followed Colonel Primrose out. We walked down the flagstone path past the Thorps' cottage, and stopped in front of the door.

"There's a path to your place from here," he said with a smile. "Where is it?"

"How do you know?" I asked.

"Because one of my men lost you somewhere in here this morning."

"Lost me?"

"Yes. You're being escorted places, after last night. I don't want you killed, you know. After all, my hostess . . ."

He chuckled. I was quite touched—until he added, "You're much too good a decoy."

He chuckled again. I took him down to the break in the hedge. There was obviously no point in not doing it. I saw his eyes sharpen as he spotted the broken spear of crape myrtle. On my side I glanced down at the plantain leaf that concealed the brass jacket of the shell, and started in spite of myself. It was gone. It had been there less than an hour before.

"There's another matter, Mrs. Latham," Colonel Primrose was saying, just behind me. "When young Andy was hunting his father, and his father denied being out of the house, he was seen by one of the colored boys from the club. He was going to the Bishops', along the lane from the club. The boy says Mr. Thorp looked as if he didn't want to be seen. He told Buck that this morning."

He looked at me and smiled.

"Buck has a great way of getting information," he said. "I can't say I always approve of his methods. The queer thing here is that the boy also says he saw you and Miss Bishop leaning on the fence there. So it would seem you'd seen Andy too."

"Is that why we're going down this way?" I asked.

"Don't tell me you thought we were taking a morning stroll."

"No," I said. "I thought maybe you were turning my house inside out, and wanted me out of the way for a while."

I was thinking, desperately fast. Andy had hidden something under the bank. I didn't know what it was, but I knew that it was something that connected him very closely with the death of Sandra Gould.

"I don't suppose," Colonel Primrose said placidly, "that your duty as a citizen . . ."

"Rodman Bishop says the trouble with the world is that too

115

many people are dashing about doing their duty—and getting everybody else in trouble," I said.

"May be something in it," he admitted cheerfully. "In this case it just happens you don't have to do yours. There's Buck. I've no doubt he's done it for you."

The Sergeant's massive figure was there ahead of us in the lane. He had taken off his coat and was in his vest, with two fancy pink ribbon armbands holding up his shirt sleeves. He was peering over the bank, not far from where Andy had gone down. It must have looked as if an army had gone over, I thought, remembering the rocks we had heard crashing to the beach. I took a deep breath, hoping for the best. It was about all there was left to do.

I followed the Colonel through the wicket into the lane, and peered over the edge. Sergeant Buck was leaning forward, burrowing into the bank like an otter with his great hands. His face hadn't the slightest expression, not even when he abruptly stopped burrowing and reached into the hole he'd made. Colonel Primrose and I watched him pull out—of all things under the sun—a pair of tiny stained rose-satin slippers.

He held them up towards Colonel Primrose. Then he peered inside them, and pulled out of the toe of one of them a crumpled bunch of blue velvet flowers.

I stared. The slippers were Lucy Lee's . . . but why should Andy have hidden them, and still more why should he have hidden Rosemary's flowers? It was beyond me. I think it even puzzled Colonel Primrose. He took them from Buck, who scaled the bank with the most astonishing agility, and turned them over in his hand.

The slippers were a mess. The thin soles were sodden as if they had tramped miles in wet grass, and the brown stain covered the scratched torn toes.

Colonel Primrose examined them intently. The thing that seemed to hold him longest was the black grease spotted on the toes and heels. Finally, without saying a word, he handed them to Sergeant Buck and took the bunch of blue posies. After a moment he gave that to the Sergeant too, and smiled at me. He shook his head a little.

"I think that cleans up one little matter," he said calmly.

He turned to Buck. "You can run me into the village. Have you got the car?"

"It's along at the clubhouse, sir."

"You can pick me up at Mrs. Latham's."

"Yes, sir."

Sergeant Buck passed me with a fish-eyed stare, giving at the same time the general appearance of a snappy salute, and turned on his large heel. I haven't the slightest doubt that he wished the bullet or bullets—one or both—had got me squarely in the back Indeed I wasn't at all sure, now that I came to think of it, that it wasn't Sergeant Buck firing them

Colonel Primrose held the wicket and I went through

"You probably thought I was extremely rude last night, by the way," he said

"Last night?"

He chuckled.

"In the middle of the night, when you were on the phone I just wanted you to hang up I didn't want our listener to sus·pect we knew he was there. And the caller had already hung up."

"Oh," I said. "Then they *are* different."

"Yes. They are."

We walked on a moment. Then he said, "The call last night came from the same place. The same party line."

"You mean the St John's vestry room?"

"That's one party."

"Who's the other?"

"The other," he said deliberately, and looking queerly at me, "I think is the 'crazy woman' Sandra Gould talked to—and of course later had her quarrel with."

I stared at him in perfect astonishment.

"It's quite impossible," he said soberly. "However, as Sherlock Holmes says, when all the possible things have failed, the impossible must be true That's where I am now, Mrs. Latham. I'm going to the village to try to prove it By the way, this gossip about Dr. Potter—did you know the village is full of it? He and Jim Gould had a sort of mild run-in in the club bar just before dinner Saturday night."

"Oh, that's nonsense!" I said warmly. "Though I don't see how you could blame Adam Potter really, with Sandra always acting like Circe on her pillar."

"Island," Colonel Primrose said. There was a little twinkle in his eyes. "Not a pillar. Aeaea, it was called. Nice name."

"Island, then. And poor Maggie!"

"I know," he said. "An invalid, isn't she. For a long time?"

"Years. It's perfectly foul."

We had come the length of the garden, and stopped there a moment, looking back.

Colonel Primrose pointed to the hedge.

"Someone shot at you from there last night, Mrs. Latham," he said very seriously. "Will you stay indoors till I get back?"

I shook my head. "No. But I'll go over to the Bishops'."

"All right."

He hesitated a moment.

"While you're there you might tell Rosemary that if she lures Jim Gould out again when there happens to be trouble brewing, just about once more, she'll succeed in hanging him where Parran may fail."

A horn sounded in the back drive as I nodded.

"There's Buck. We'll take you as far as the Bishops'."

We went around the side walk and Julius, seeing me through the window over the sink, called out: "Mis' Grace! Oh, Mis' Grace! They's a lady here to see you. She's in the livin' room. She wants to see somebody, Ah couldn't quite make out."

"Maybe it's you, Colonel," I said. "Come and see."

Sergeant Buck had jumped out of the car and was standing at attention on the other side.

"Just a minute, Buck."

"Yes, sir."

We went in through the kitchen. Lilac was making watermelon pickles and singing about a sycamine tree and the River Jordan. I got a drink of water at the sink and gave Colonel Primrose one. We went through the pantry into the hall.

It seems odd to me now that I had no intuition about the other side of the living room door. It hardly seems possible. There was no preparation, no foreshadowing, nothing to let us know, in any way, of what was there waiting quietly for us.

I pushed the door open, as I do a thousand times a day, and walked in . . . and stopped, utterly and horribly aghast.

On the sofa in front of the fireplace was a woman I had not seen for years. She had on old-fashioned clothes, and her face was sallow and drawn and unlovely.

My hand dropped slowly to my side and my head swirled. Colonel Primrose steadied me quickly with an arm around my shoulders. We stood there, silent, stupefied, for one terrible instant.

"Who is it?" Colonel Primrose said.

"It's Maggie Potter!" I whispered.

"Good God!" he said.

Maggie Potter was dead. Even from there I could see the crushed and blackened, blood-and-hair-matted spot on the base of her skull where she had been murderously struck.

I caught myself with a terrible effort.

"But she can't walk!" I said. "She hasn t been out of the house for seven years!"

Colonel Primrose shook his head.

"She was out Saturday night," he said quietly. "And she's been trying to tell us about it ever since."

"Over the phone?" I whispered.

He nodded, and looked at me steadily.

"We've got to find that clock soon, Mrs. Latham," he said "It belongs to a murderer."

CHAPTER FIFTEEN

Colonel Primrose stepped quickly across the room and touched the painted doorstop lightly with the tip of his brown and white shoes. I kept my gaze riveted to it, trying not to see the lumpy protruding feet in their house-worn black strap slippers, the bony legs in streaked gunmetal stockings, that ghastly head. It was all so unbearably, hideously grotesque. The gaunt sallow figure in the mousy old-fashioned clothes that hadn't been in the sun for seven years—and on the floor in its usual place the white-painted iron basket full of gay red and blue and yellow and white iron posies . . . splotched and splattered with blood.

I stared at it, trying desperately to keep from being sick. It was Colonel Primrose who saved me. He shook my arm, and I came to sharply, out of the dark swirling fog.

"Mrs. Latham! Get Buck, send him in here; phone Parran, and watch that telephone! And get hold of a doctor! Is there anyone else in town—any other doctor?"

I shook my head mechanically.

"Get him then. Poor devil! But hurry—don't just stand there!"

I went back through the door into the hall and called Julius.

"Wha's the matter with you, Mis' Grace?" he exclaimed.

"Nothing, Julius. Just tell Sergeant Buck to come quickly, and you stay in the kitchen," I said.

I let the door swing to and took down the telephone. For an instant I almost heard the tickety-tick, tickety-tock, tickety-tick, tickety-tock, but it must have been in my own head, because what I really heard was Elsie Carter's voice saying, "Creamed chicken and peas in patty shells is always nice, and the men enjoy it."

A thousand church suppers rolled over my head. I gripped myself firmly to keep from screaming.

"Elsie," I said. "This is Grace Latham. Would you mind letting me have the line? I have to get Dr. Potter, immediately."

120

There was an instant's startled silence, then Elsie's avid voice. "Is somebody sick, Grace?"

"No," I said. "*Please*, darling."

"I'll call you later, Mary.—If there's anything I can do, Grace . . ."

"Thanks."

I hung up the phone and cranked to signal the operator.

"Mr. Parran, please."

"Yes, Mrs. Latham—he's just gone to his office," the operator said, with the friendly helpfulness of the village exchange. Which was also the reason that I just told Mr. Parran, when I'd got him, that there had been an accident and Colonel Primrose wanted him immediately.

Then I tried to get Dr. Potter. He was out. I could hear the phone ring again and again.

"Mrs. Potter must be upstairs, Mrs. Latham," the operator said. She's a village girl whose mother mends for me. "I'll keep on ringing."

"Don't bother, Mabel," I said. "But if you hear where he is, tell him to come to my house as quick as ever he can."

I hung up, knowing she would find him before I could. Then I took down the phone again and listened to see if I'd missed the tickety-tick, tickety-tock, or if it really had not been there. But it wasn't. Only Elsie, saying, "Are you through, Grace? I just saw Dr. Potter leaving the Goulds'—he's gone in to see Annie Kellogg now, she cut her knee on an oyster shell. Shall I tell him you want him?"

"Please—and tell him it's urgent," I said. I knew she'd break her neck to do it, and anyway she wouldn't let me have the wire in peace again.

I went back to the living room. Colonel Primrose and Sergeant Buck were standing at the door. Buck was more like a piece of artillery than a human being, or so I'd imagine, having only the faintest notion of what artillery is. All I mean is that he seemed ready to go into instant action when his chief gave the word.

He said, "It's all in the cards, sir, but who'd have guessed it."

"I should have guessed something, anyway," Colonel Primrose said shortly. "When Potter left here."

He looked around at me.

"Mr. Parran's coming," I reported. "Mrs. Carter said she just saw Dr. Potter leaving the Goulds'. He's at the Kelloggs' now. She's getting him."

121

If I had dropped a minor bomb shell, or even a major one, into the middle of my living room, I don't think Colonel Primrose would have jerked about so quickly.

"Just left the Goulds'!" he repeated.

I didn't even then see what to them was the appalling significance of the fact, because it would never have occurred to me—even if I'd not been very well acquainted with Adam Potter for many years—that a doctor would kill his wife that way with so many other easier ways at hand. I forgot entirely Elsie Carter's theory that he'd been killing her by degrees for seven long years. It wasn't till later even that I remembered the Saturday morning in Church Street in front of Mr. Toplady's store.

"No telling what they'll do when they're jealous," Sergeant Buck said. It occurred to me suddenly and incongruously that one of his gifts I'd not yet noticed was the gift of sententious remark.

"I wish to God I'd used my head," Colonel Primrose said bitterly.

Sergeant Buck shook his, with the utmost conviction. "It wouldn't have done no good if you had, sir," he said. He drew his wide hard mouth down at the corners, shaking his head back and forth like one of those loose-headed toy policemen children have. I don't know why the two of them—Sergeant Buck about a foot behind, and towering at least a foot above and projecting a good deal to each side of the stocky gray-haired man in the tan poplin suit—should have seemed so utterly incongruous just then. They looked much more as if they should be inspecting the beer at the canteen than viewing the ghastly figure of Maggie Potter, sprawled feet out and dreadfully motionless on the sofa in front of them.

"Neat at that, sir," Sergeant Buck said.

I could see that it was. I knew that room so well—and except for Maggie Potter and the blood-spattered iron pot of painted flowers, there was nothing out of place that I could see, and nothing that wasn't always there. No convenient bits of upholsterer's twine or ends of cigarettes with orange lipstick on them.

Colonel Primrose nodded slowly.

"That's the confounded part of it," he said. "Somebody walked in, and walked out again. A hundred to one nobody would ever notice him."

As if to prove his theory the Thorp children and their nurse straggled across the garden not twenty feet from the porch,

122

and young Andy came to the screen door, banged once or twice and called, "Juyus, Juyus!"

I started out to head him off, but his nurse called and he ran along after her.

"You see. Anyone else could do the same and come on in," Colonel Primrose said.

He bent down to examine the doorstop.

"However, we may be a bit forrarder. There's no doubt that Mrs. Potter knew something, and was on her way here to tell it, after trying to say it on the phone and being afraid to. And I suppose there's no doubt it was something that happened Saturday night."

He stared down at the doorstop, then cocked his head around and peered up at me.

"I take it Andy Thorp wouldn't recognize Mrs. Potter, in the dark?"

I shook my head.

"He used to know her, of course, but he hasn't seen her for . . . oh, I suppose seven years, or more. She used to be around a lot. She played bridge every afternoon with the older women at the club. Andy knew her casually. I don't think he'd recognize her. You're thinking she was the woman Sandra was with at the garage?"

He nodded. "Probably."

"Of course it was dark there too."

"Not very, Mrs. Latham," he said. "That light over the side door of the garage is pretty bright."

"Andy said she wasn't in the light."

"I know."

"And above all," I said, "how on earth did she get there?"

Colonel Primrose shook his head. "Your guess is as good as mine. However—she even got here."

He looked down at her and shook his head again. "Not a very amiable sort, was she?"

I didn't need to look at her again. I knew what he meant. The querulous face of a childless and selfish woman, with nothing to occupy her mind or her heart but herself and her ills, petty and resentful, envious of other people and suspicious of them. For years her husband had quit even dropping in at the club bar for a highball at night. He'd only begun again the last few years—after Sandra came, as Elsie Carter was to point out significantly.

We heard a car in the drive at the back of the house. Colonel Primrose moved back a step or so into the corner where he could watch the door without being seen. I should have connected that up with Dr. Potter, but I didn't. Anyway, it wasn't Dr. Potter, it was Mr. Parran, the State's Attorney. He pushed the door open and came briskly and inquiringly into the room, and stopped dead in his tracks, staring blankly in utter horror.

"Good God!" he said. "Maggie Potter!"

Then he looked at the square granite figure of Sergeant Buck, and his eyes moved on to the Colonel.

"It was Maggie trying to phone?" he said.

Colonel Primrose nodded. "She was the other party on the line."

"And it was her quarreling with Mrs. Gould."

"Probably."

Mr. Parran's head moved back and forth. He was still staring down at Maggie Potter there on the sofa, his face a little white.

"And when they told me young Mrs. Gould was carryin' on with old Potter, I laughed. The old—"

Sergeant Buck cleared his throat violently, and jerked his head towards me. Mr. Parran gulped his words back with an effort.

"Beg your pardon, ma'am," he muttered, very red in the face. Which showed one reason for his not being invited to mixed parties on the Estate. I never heard Jim or Andy or Rodman Bishop swallow anything in my life, in the line of words—or any of their friends. Nevertheless, I knew now that I'd rather underestimated Mr. Parran.

"We've sent for him," Colonel Primrose said. "He ought to be here any minute. He was at the Goulds', apparently, when it happened."

Mr. Parran's lean jaw tightened. Colonel Primrose turned to the Sergeant.

"Go over to the Goulds' and see if he was there. Mrs. Latham, would you mind asking Julius to step in here?"

When I went out into the hall Julius peered in from the pantry saucer-eyed and putty-faced, sensing easily that something had happened.

"No one's going to hurt you," I said.

He stuck his head out of his starched white coat collar like a sand turtle stretching his neck.

" 'Deed an' Ah know that, Mis' Grace.—Was that there lady Mis' Potter?"

I nodded.

124

" 'Deed an' Ah thought Ah knew her. She used to come here, didn' she?"

I nodded again.

"What time did she come this morning?" Colonel Primrose asked.

"She come about a quarter of 'leven, while Ah was sweepin' the back walk. Booths's taxi stopped, an' she got out. She told him not to wait, an' she wanted to know if you was home, Mis' Grace. Ah said no, an' she said is the man here that's a detective. Ah said you was both on the place, an' would she wait, an' she said yes. She kep' lookin' around like she was scared somebody'd see her."

"Did anybody see her?"

"Not that Ah know of, suh."

"Did anybody pass in a car?"

Julius craned his neck around slowly.

"There was *cars* passin'," he said. " 'Course, Ah didn' notice who was in 'em."

"Try to think, Julius," I said. "Didn't you notice anybody you know?"

His face brightened.

"There was Charlie Bates."

Charlie Bates drives his father's grocery truck.

"Ah didn' see nobody else, 'cept, o' course, Dr. Potter."

We stared at him standing there, ashy-pale and shaking. And my head kept whirling. Was it conceivable that Colonel Primrose really thought Adam Potter had killed his wife, here, in this living room? Because to me it was not conceivable, it was utterly fantastic and impossible. But, I kept thinking desperately, the idea that any of us—that someone from my own little group there—could have done such a thing was just as impossible.

"An' o' course there was the regular people . . . nobody that ain't always flyin' up an' down like the devil was after 'em."

Mr. Parran looked at Colonel Primrose in patient disgust.

"Well, just who were they, Julius?" Colonel Primrose said.

" 'Deed, Colonel, an' Ah don' recall jus' which. You see, Ah had other mattuhs to attend to."

They might as well have stopped there, because the fact that Julius had other matters to attend to is final. In the fifteen years he's been with me it has definitely explained everything, from burnt biscuit to frozen radiators.

"You don't recall anyone except Dr. Potter?"

"No, suh. Ah only recalls him 'cause Ah thought to mahself that there lady looks powerful like Mis' Potter, but if he don' know her, an' if she cain't walk, like they say, then Ah mus' be mistaken. So Ah ast her who she was, an' she says it didn' make no difference, she'd wait. So she jus' walked in an' set herself down in a chair."

"You just left her there?"

Julius craned his neck out and wet his lips. He looked at me.

"Ah didn' feel exac'ly *comfo'table*," he said. "She didn' look jus' right in her mind."

I could see exactly what he meant. Maggie was perfectly sane, of course.

"She is rather odd-looking," I said.

Colonel Primrose nodded. "Didn't Lilac know her?"

"Ah don' think Lilac even *seen* her," Julius said. "She was talkin' to Hawkins, an' she wasn't payin' no attention to the outside."

"What about Dr. Potter? Did he speak to you when he went by?"

Julius shook his head.

"He waved his hand, suh, like he always does. Ah guess he didn' see her 'cause she was facin' the house."

Colonel Primrose looked at me. "All right, Julius," he said. He nodded to Sergeant Buck, who departed for the Goulds'. When he went on errands he set out on a sort of double-quick, and you half expected to see a line of khaki-clad men materialize out of the empty air and file along—either that or little Mercury wings sprout suddenly at his heels and ears, like the florists' emblem.

Colonel Primrose and Mr. Parran set to work. If the Sergeant's line of men hadn't appeared, the State's Attorney's had. I retired to the dining room. I could hear Colonel Primrose's terse clipped instructions, the men moving about, the clicking of the camera, Mr. Parran's nasal Maryland drawl. I felt curiously helpless and at loose ends, not knowing at all what to do. It's an odd sensation, having the corpse of somebody you know quite well but have no emotion about appear suddenly on your living-room sofa. But I suppose any corpse would be much the same. I opened the screen, brushed out a wasp and closed it again.

"I'm going over to the Bishops'. Will you come along?"

I turned. Colonel Primrose had come back from the living room and was standing there regarding me with an eye cocked in a manner definitely and disturbingly speculative. At least he can't think I had a hand in this, I thought. But it was impossible to tell what he was thinking, actually.

"Are you all right?" he said.

"Oh, yes."

I was all right, after that first terrible shock. There was no point in being anything else.

We went out through the kitchen, leaving Julius and Lilac pretty ashen and saucer-eyed.

"You ain' goin' *away*, is you, Mis' Grace?" Lilac said desperately.

"Just over to the Bishops'. Mr. Parran's here."

"Ah *knows* he's here," Julius said, very pointedly.

"If he bothers you, phone me," I said. "Anyway, Sergeant Buck will be back in a minute."

Julius looked very unhappy.

"I wish," I said as we went out, "there was some way of going at police work without first terrorizing all the servants."

"Hawkins doesn't seem particularly terrorized."

"He has the consolations of religion," I said. "Anyway, he's no doubt delighted that another Jezebel has bit the dust."

Colonel Primrose looked at me, startled.

"Mrs. Potter?"

"O Lord, no. Sandra. Mrs. Potter is Julius and Lilac's problem. He can enjoy that at a distance. And furthermore—while I'm complaining about the law—why do you go off and leave that man in charge? Julius is probably perfectly correct in suspecting that the minute we get out of the house Mr. Parran'll arrest him and Lilac. Just to be doing something satisfying in a big way."

Colonel Primrose shook his head.

"No point sitting around in the barn after the horse has left," he said. "You have to take a bridle and go after him."

"Is he over at the Bishops'?"

His face sobered abruptly.

"I wouldn't be sure. He's not awfully far away."

We went along.

"I'm sick of this!" I cried suddenly.

"I dare say," he said. "It won't be long now."

"What do you mean?"

He cocked his head down and looked up at me with his black sparkling eyes.

"I mean that our murderer is getting panicky, Mrs. Latham."

CHAPTER SIXTEEN

We went on across the garden.

"Isn't that a bit on the locking-the-barn-door side, Colonel?" I asked.

"Oh, definitely," he admitted. "Well, anybody but a complete ass would have seen, knowing what I knew—or what I'd guessed—about Mrs. Potter, that she was in danger."

"You really think it was she at the garage?"

"I can't figure it as any of the rest of you, Mrs. Latham, someway."

He held up a straggling trailer of trumpet vine for me to go under through the wicket between my place and the Bishops'.

"Who, for example? Lucy Lee?"

He smiled soberly.

"I'm afraid Lucy Lee is pretty transparent. Frankly, it's really your Rosemary that interests me now. It doesn't seem credible, does it?—Look at her now."

We were crossing the lawn up to the great screened and pillared veranda of The Magnolias, hidden from the people there for the moment by the two gigantic shiny-leaved trees that helped give the place its name.

"You wouldn't think, to look at her, that she's practically tying a noose—they hang people in a shed in the penitentiary yard, here in the Free State of Maryland—round the neck of the man she was and is popularly supposed to be pretty mad about . . . or her own neck?"

I stared at him open-mouthed. "You don't still think—"

"My dear young woman," he said quietly, "Mr. Parran is the State's Attorney—not I."

We went along across the grass.

"You know, Mrs. Latham—you have a charming but decidedly naïve streak in you that makes you assume everybody is exactly what he or she appears to be. Which means—all these people being your friends—just what you want them to be. Now I, and still more Mr. Parran—having no illusions or preconceptions about these people, or about character in general—can see clearly that—just to take one point—the mainspring of human conduct, even in nice humans, isn't always love."

He shook his head. "I haven't time to go into it. We've got to find out what these people up on the porch have been doing with themselves this morning."

We came out from behind the magnolia trees. George Barrol came to meet us. I remember wondering fleetingly, as he came, why with his share of his aunt's money he still acted as the household secretary—or general functotum, as Sergeant Buck called him. The Sergeant called himself that also, so the word hadn't any derisive significance.

"They tell me you were shot at last night, Grace!" he said. "Dear me, it was lucky I didn't go home with you. They might have got me too!"

George giggled in his nervous way, but it was perfectly obvious that he meant every word of it. That's one of the nice things about George; he's frank.

"It happened they didn't get me," I said. "And it was long after I left here, so you'd have got home safe."

"If Grace keeps such odd company, she'll have to expect to get shot at," Rosemary said.

She came down from the porch, almost breath-takingly lovely, with her warm golden skin and dull gold hair and serious wide-set gray eyes above a simple high-throated earth-brown cotton frock. I glanced back and saw that Colonel Primrose thought about her as I did; his interest had quickened perceptibly.

Behind her, not very far away, giving the impression that he was not going to be far away for a moment, was Paul Dikranov. I wondered if he had come to some decision to keep an eye on her, and why. Since Colonel Primrose had said she wasn't in any danger I had been wondering. Since the night before I had wondered still more. For granted no one would want to hurt Rosemary, who could there be who felt strongly enough about me to shoot me . . . and at the same time hadn't hesitated at the brutal murder of a perfectly harmless hypochondriac?

As Paul Dikranov greeted us in a friendly way I wondered a little, too, if George's constant presence didn't annoy him. Rodman Bishop seemed to keep out of the way diligently, but so far I couldn't remember having seen Dikranov and Rosemary together once without George. Except that unfortunate period Saturday night, and that was hardly George's fault.

The matter was settled conclusively before long, however, and in George's inimitable way.

"Is your father here, Miss Bishop?" Colonel Primrose asked.

Rosemary nodded. "Come on in," she said. "He's in the library with Nathan Kaufman."

"I'll tell him you want him, shall I?" George said helpfully. His face fell, and then brightened instantly. "It'll be all right if I go, now that Grace and the Colonel have come."

Then George turned brick-red, and well he might, for the look Rosemary gave him would have charred a hide only slightly less tough.

"Oh, dear!" he said.

Dikranov's face darkened. George departed uneasily. Rosemary smiled with remarkable self-possession.

"Let's go up on the porch, shall we? Dad'll be out in a minute."

"I'd like to see him now, if you don't mind," Colonel Primrose said.

Rosemary glanced at Paul Dikranov. "He's engaged at the moment," she said reluctantly.

At just that moment a querulous, slightly pompous voice came out of the hall.

"Well, bring him in, bring him in. We want to see him, we want to get the *facts!*"

The owner of the voice came out onto the porch—a short small slightly paunchy man with thick black hair going white at the temples, bloodshot eyes that looked as if they had never had an illusion to lose, and a red choleric face. As Rosemary said later, he had the consistency of a persimmon, ripe and just ready to burst. Mr. Nathan Kaufman looked as if he drank too much, and I dare say he did. He certainly drank a lot.

"Let him come in here," he was saying. "Nobody's going to lynch him."

I assumed, unraveling this, that the first "him" was Colonel Primrose. The second, surprisingly enough, was Jim Gould.

"This is Colonel Primrose, Mr. Kaufman," Rosemary said. Mr. Kaufman made some sound not in ordinary usage, and they shook hands. Rodman Bishop came out, still dressed in the ancient shrunk seersucker suit, towering over everybody, beetling his black shaggy brows right and left except when his gaze happened to rest on his daughter. Then a proud satisfied smile lighted his leathery piratical old face . . . though now, when he looked at her as he came out of the cool hall, his eyes were worried too. It seemed almost as if he were avoiding

130

meeting her, and when he sat down and she came over and sat beside him on the arm of his chair, he gripped her hand and patted it clumsily, his jaw working savagely.

It was Jim Gould that Colonel Primrose looked at. Something had obviously been going on inside Jim. His eyes were narrowed a bit and his jaw and lips tight. He stood there tall and erect, the sort of person who would knock you down and throw you overboard if necessary, but who certainly—to my mind—wouldn't hit a sick old woman over the head if he'd wanted to kill her.

"Well, we're all friends here," Kaufman said, darting a quick look about. Then he laughed a pursy little "Heh, heh, heh!— Or are we?"

George giggled—or started to until he caught Rodman Bishop's beetling glance and the giggle died into a cough.

"Of course!" Rosemary said. She included everybody in a cool definitely wicked half-smile. I shook my head uneasily. We weren't, of course. Far from it.

"Now then, Colonel," Mr. Kaufman went on briskly. "We're on the side of law and order, and if my client—though so far I'm damned if I can make out just who my client is—"

"It's all of us, isn't it, Colonel Primrose?" Rosemary asked.

Colonel Primrose smiled politely. Why he sat there without so much as mentioning the ghastly business that was going on over at my house, I couldn't make out. It seemed to me that he was deliberately wasting the most valuable time.

"Perhaps it wouldn't do any harm, Mr. Kaufman," he said, "if I told you just what the police know about this case, so far."

Mr. Kaufman flipped a piece of paper out of his pocket and unscrewed his pen. "Now we're getting somewhere," he said.

"Mr. Parran knows," Colonel Primrose said deliberately, "that Sandra Gould was upset and definitely excited when she went to the club Saturday evening. That's what, in his mind, gives credence to the suicide note Mrs. Gould found on her dressing table."

"You any idea about that note, other than it *is* a suicide note?" Mr. Kaufman asked sharply.

"So far . . . no," said Colonel Primrose. I thought he was a little annoyed. Kaufman grunted.

"Here's another point, Colonel. The lady didn't die by that blow on the back of the head. I've seen your medical reports. Now, even if you could establish who struck her . . ."

His finger pointed arrestingly at the Colonel. Colonel Primrose smiled.

"I'm aware of that."

"Even if my client—whoever the devil he is—should *confess* to striking her, that's not murder, Colonel."

Colonel Primrose shook his head suavely. "Oh, no, no. Not as such."

I looked at him in horror. "Maggie Potter, Maggie Potter!" I wanted to scream out. But he was saying nothing about it. He was, as Lilac says, as smooth as owl's grease.

George Barrol was staring, almost fascinated, at Jim. Indeed, I think everybody was, except Rodman Bishop and myself.

"I haven't confessed anything of the sort," Jim said angrily.

Mr. Kaufman waved his hands in the air helplessly. "Oh, my God!" he said. "Of course you haven't. Of course you haven't. You keep still."

He looked expectantly at Colonel Primrose.

"After the incident of the capsized boat," Colonel Primrose went on slowly, "she came up to the clubhouse and dried out in front of the fire. She was apparently waiting for her husband."

He looked at Jim, who'd sat down and was staring down at the floor between his feet.

"He didn't come. He went home with Mrs. Latham, and sat there till ten minutes of one, when he left. Well, it so happens that the period between then—or, to go back a little, from twelve-thirty, say—and one-thirty is the period that we've got to find out about. So far we know this:

"1. Sandra Gould quarreled with a certain woman after midnight.

"2. Between that time—after twelve, when Andy Thorp says he saw her last—and one o'clock, we haven't much idea.

"3. At one o'clock, on Hawkins's testimony, there's not much doubt she was put unconscious in Thorp's car with the motor running.

"4. Hawkins says someone closed the door of the garage just after one o'clock. He thought it was twelve, but it was twelve Columbus time, not Eastern Standard.

"5. Of course whoever did it waited until it was time to announce the hour, turned the radio on, turned it off and left. That's the person we want."

He paused a moment.

"Mr. Andy Thorp, looking back towards the garage when Sandra Gould had left him to go back there, saw her talking with a woman, whom he didn't recognize. There's no question that this woman was also there later, and saw all that went on that led to Sandra's murder."

There was a strange silence on the porch. I think all of us must have looked guilty. All except Paul Dikranov, who looked interested but intensely unconcerned. If it hadn't been for the scene at the club, I should have thought he didn't even know whom we were talking about.

"Now then," Colonel Primrose said. "We know that between eleven-thirty, when some of you left the club, and three-fifteen, when Mrs. Gould and Mrs. Latham found Sandra Gould's body, a good many of you—namely, Mrs. Gould, Mr. Dikranov, Mr. Gould, Miss Bishop, the woman whom Sandra quarreled with, and both Mr. and Mrs. Thorp—were out of your houses within easy calling distance of the garage. And we know this also: that for some reason there's been a strong disinclination on the part of all these people, or virtually all, to tell the truth. In fact, most of them, excepting Mr. Dikranov probably, have deliberately lied. Mr. Gould and Miss Rosemary are the two most conspicuous examples of what I'm saying."

Nathan Kaufman grunted.

"If you've got an eyewitness, I think you ought to bring her forward without delay and pettifogging," he said angrily.

"I should be glad to," Colonel Primrose said quietly. He looked round at each face in the group. "Unfortunately, she has been killed."

There was no sound on the porch.

"She was murdered . . . this morning. An hour ago."

Murdered.

The word went like a shadow compounded of sound and moving lips around the stunned circle.

Then a dreadful thing happened. Jim Gould staggered to his feet, his face as gray as death. Rodman Bishop's big hand tightened on his daughter's, checking her sudden impulse to rise. George Barrol said, "Isn't it awful!" and looked from one to the other of us and back at Jim. I don't suppose he meant to be heartless; everything disturbs him equally—a mislaid pack of cigarettes, death, a slump in sugar.

Colonel Primrose spoke quickly, looking steadily at Jim.

"Not your mother, Mr. Gould," he said quietly.

The color surged back into Jim's face as he realized, I suppose, what an awful thing he had done. He steadied himself against the back of his chair a moment, then sat down and took out a cigarette without a word.

I suppose we all stared at him, George especially. He started to speak and closed his mouth, flushing a little. It was obvious to everybody that he was going to point out what everybody must have realized, that Jim thought it was Alice Gould who'd had the scene with Sandra at the garage Saturday night before she was killed. Rodman Bishop glared at him furiously.

Jim said nothing at all. He had never had a ready line of snappy comebacks even in his best moments, and there's no doubt anyway that keeping one's mouth shut, whether it's judicious or merely because you can't think of anything to say, has its points. The effect of what he had done was stunning enough.

Only Paul Dikranov seemed sufficiently detached to keep to the point.

"Who was it, Colonel Primrose?" he asked easily.

Colonel Primrose looked from face to face again.

"Mrs. Potter," he said.

"*Who?*" Rosemary cried.

"Maggie Potter," I said. "In my living room."

Rodman Bishop leaned forward. "That's . . . why, it's preposterous," he said, glaring at me. "The woman's bedridden! She hasn't been out of her house for seven years!"

"Not since Chapin—"

George Barrol caught himself again at a swift warning glance from Rosemary. Rodman Bishop's face darkened. He has never been the same since Chapin Bishop was found dead in the inlet below my place. It had made Rosemary too much the center of his life, in some way. I remember then, even at such a moment, thinking that it would have been so much better if he'd married Alice Gould.

"There's no doubt Mrs. Potter had heard some of the rumors that have been fairly rife this summer," Colonel Primrose went on gravely. "You all know what I mean—that her husband was interested in Sandra Gould."

Jim's eyes stayed on the floor. He flushed a dull hot red.

Nathan Kaufman, I could see, was watching him out of the tail of one eye. The other, if possible, he had fixed on Rosemary. I suppose he would conceal all that when it came to the trial, but it was plain that at the moment he had quite obviously a strong suspicion in his mind. He glanced up, caught my eye, stared at me coldly a moment and turned away. After all, a husband in love with a girl like Rosemary, saddled with a wife who carried on with country doctors who had invalid

134

wives—it wasn't a pretty picture. Moreover—even leaving out the fact that Jim was in love with Rosemary—it was a picture that a jury could easily understand. You could almost hear Jim's life story being unfolded in court.

"Jealousy is a powerful tonic," Nathan Kaufman said professionally.

Colonel Primrose nodded.

"The woods are full of it," George Barrol said flippantly.

Colonel Primrose looked soberly at him for an instant.

"You see," he said quietly, "in spite of that suicide note, and whatever it may represent—"

I could feel his eyes on me for a bare instant.

"—there is no possible doubt, after what has happened to Mrs. Potter, that Sandra Gould was murdered. The immediate point concerns Mrs. Potter. I must find out where every person here—except Mrs. Latham, who was with me, and Mr. Kaufman—was from approximately quarter of eleven, when Mrs. Potter arrived in a taxi from the village, until a quarter past eleven, when Mrs. Latham and I found her dead in Mrs. Latham's living room."

His voice was moving quietly against a background of utter silence. When it stopped there was nothing there. Even George had no word to say. Colonel Primrose looked around with a smile.

"Good God, Colonel," Nathan Kaufman said suddenly. "People can't just offhand say where they were at any hour of the day."

"An hour ago?" said Colonel Primrose, still more quietly.

Kaufman shook his head. "Not even then, sometimes. I got here a few minutes after eleven. You were here then?"

He looked at Rodman Bishop. Mr. Bishop beetled his heavy brows at George Barrol, as if poor George was responsible, somehow, for the whole situation. I suppose that's the penalty for being a secretarial doormat and a relative at the same time. Not that Rodman Bishop wasn't awfully decent to George always, and very fond of him, but he did demand more constant service than anyone would have stood for who was less dependent. Socially dependent, not financially, because George has a very superior income. Just why he did stand for it no one could ever figure out, except that he had no other family and liked the life that Rosemary and her father led. Being with them was convenient, in a way, too, for it allowed him to go everywhere and at the same time protected him from designing mothers. No one else would ever think of him as marriageable —being as he is the old-fashioned semi-hardy variety of perennial bachelor.

When Rodman Bishop beetles at him he always gets flustered and blows his nose quickly. He did so now.

"George and I were down in the cellar," Rodman said emphatically. "Bottling the blackberry wine my son and I made when we were here before. It's been in an old sherry keg."

"Didn't know bottle could Barrol wine," Mr. Kaufman said, and laughed "Heh, heh, heh, heh" until we all thought he wouldn't stop at all.

"And you, Miss Bishop?" Colonel Primrose asked gently.

Rodman Bishop looked at that instant about like a man sentenced to death.

"I'm very much afraid I can't tell you without consulting Mr. Kaufman privately," Rosemary Bishop said.

Her cool gray eyes met Colonel Primrose's steadily.

"Because it just happens that I was at Grace's house from about half past ten until after Mrs. Potter came. In fact, I left *after* she came."

CHAPTER SEVENTEEN

We stared at Rosemary—or most of us did—in complete horror. A little self-possessed smile deepened in the corners of her mouth.

"You see," she said calmly, "it's rather awful, being in love with a man whose wife's just been murdered, so that if you speak to him even it looks like collusion."

I caught my breath sharply. I suppose for a moment we all thought she'd lost her mind completely. Only Colonel Primrose looked at her with perfect calm. Jim Gould stared at her, half rising for an instant from his seat, his face suddenly white, then dark red as the color rushed to his cheeks. Then he smiled suddenly, still staring at her. It was the first time he had smiled, I imagine, for some time. For just an instant he looked like the old Jim of the pre-Sandra days. But not for more than that.

The silence was more than awkward. George Barrol tittered, as he would, for all the world like the village postmistress, and Nathan Kaufman raised one eyebrow with a sort of and-what-in-God's-name-do-they-expect-me-to-do air. I glanced sideways at Dikranov. He was perfectly unmoved. Rodman Bishop was mopping his forehead.

"And I had to see him," Rosemary went on. "So I asked him to meet me at Grace's. I knew she wouldn't mind."

Colonel Primrose nodded politely.

"And did he come?"

Rosemary nodded. "Yes. He came."

She smiled across at Jim.

"Not very willingly. He's got old-fashioned notions about propriety. He doesn't want people to talk."

"I don't want them to talk about you," Jim said simply.

"He didn't stay very long."

"How long?" Colonel Primrose asked.

"Just long enough to tell me not to be silly."

"My God," said Nathan Kaufman. He stopped abruptly and looked at Rodman Bishop. Colonel Primrose smiled a little. He turned abruptly to George.

137

"And you, Barrol?"

George jumped. "Me? Oh, I was down in the cellar with Uncle Rod, barroling the wine. I mean bottling it."

He blushed and glanced anxiously at Rodman Bishop.

"I see," Colonel Primrose said.

He got up. I felt a little silly following him, but he seemed to expect it.

We'd got as far as the hedge when I looked back. Jim Gould was coming out. He didn't follow us. He went around to the road and out that way. He was whistling.

We crossed the tennis court and the lawn to the porch just as Adam Potter's car drove in the back gate. Sergeant Buck was on the porch. He came to meet us.

"All there except the husband," he said, in a loud whisper. "This Potter had been there but he'd left."

Sergeant Buck glanced around over his shoulder at the man getting out of the car.

"They said he was feeling the heat. I went to the club. He'd had two whiskies neat which he never done before that the bartender can recollect. Said he'd never been known to take a drink during hours."

He drew off a little and stood at an informal attention as Dr. Potter came up. He looked definitely haggard.

"Elsie Carter said you wanted me," he said, taking off his new panama and wiping his forehead. He looked from me to Colonel Primrose inquiringly. "It sure is a scorcher."

Sergeant Buck really needn't have gone to the club bar. The man's breath was appallingly eloquent.

"I wanted you, doctor," Colonel Primrose said.

Even if he had not known it, one glance at Sergeant Buck's granite physiognomy should have been warning enough—or no doubt one glance at my face should have been—that something unusual was in store for him.

"Inside, if you please."

Colonel Primrose led the way. I knew he was watching Adam Potter like a hawk, seeing every hesitating nervous twitch in his face and hands. If I'd dared I would have cried out that she was in there, dead. But I didn't. And I couldn't help thinking that he knew it, even though that was impossible.

He went along with them. I stayed behind, watching their painful progress to the porch steps and through the screen door that Sergeant Buck held open. He'd have to see her in two or three more steps, through the French windows, lying there!

I turned away. I couldn't bear to have it all happening in my house.

Then there was a shout and confused steps and a hysterical babble, and when I turned around Dr. Potter was trying to pull away, with Sergeant Buck holding him, and Mr. Parran and two of his men on the porch. Then abruptly there was no more confusion, only Adam Potter slumped down there in a porch chair, his head in his hands, Mr. Parran standing over him.

I went up to the porch. Adam Potter's face was ghastly.

"I didn't do it, I swear to God I didn't do it," he was saying. He shook like a leaf.

"You passed here and saw her. You came back and murdered her."

"I didn't. I swear to God I didn't."

"You struck her with the doorstop."

"No, no!"

"When did you kill her?"

"I didn't, I didn't! I tell you I didn't!"

Mr. Parran bent his thin face down towards him. "Before you had a drink, Potter, or after?"

I glanced angrily at Colonel Primrose. The man was in no shape for this.

"Listen, Dr. Potter," he said gently. "We know you went by in your car while she was out in back talking to Julius."

Dr. Potter raised his head. He nodded dumbly.

"I thought I was crazy," he muttered. "I thought I was crazy."

Parran looked significantly at Colonel Primrose, who shook his head a little.

"You knew it was she?"

Dr. Potter nodded. "But it couldn't have been, she couldn't walk! She hasn't gone out for years! I thought I was having hallucinations."

"You realized she'd been out before?"

Dr. Potter stared at the State's Attorney. "No, no!"

"That she'd been spying on you, Saturday night? When you killed Sandra Gould?"

Dr. Potter shook his head dumbly.

"Didn't you kill Sandra Gould?"

He shook his head back and forth.

"All right," Colonel Primrose said. "All right. Take your time."

Dr. Potter seemed like a man coming out of a stupor. He

passed his hand across his wet forehead and moistened his lips.

"No, no," he said. "I tell you, I saw her, but I didn't believe it was her. I thought I was ill. I . . . I haven't been sleeping nights."

Mr. Parran leaned forward again. "Something on your mind?" he drawled.

Adam Potter looked at him more quietly with a little of his normal self showing in his face. He even smiled a little. "No," he said. "My customers have been having babies."

"Where were you Saturday night, Dr. Potter?" Colonel Primrose said. "After the boat episode at the club? When your wife was undoubtedly out of the house?"

Dr. Potter stared at him for an instant. A light dawned slowly in his haggard face.

"So that's it," he said, half to himself. He looked directly at Colonel Primrose.

"I got a call at the clubhouse just after the orchestra came, Saturday night—some people up at Nag's Head. Their first baby, and they called me in hours before they needed me. I phoned Maggie from the club, then I tried to get her from Nag's Head about one, to tell her I probably wouldn't be in till morning. I couldn't get her. I was worried about it, but I couldn't leave. When I got back, around three-thirty, she said the phone hadn't rung. I put it down to the fact that she must have been asleep and didn't hear it."

"You said no more about it?"

"No, no. I . . . anything else was impossible, I tell you!"

Dr. Potter shuddered, motioning towards the living room. "But why that—for Maggie? I don't understand . . ."

"She was out having an eye on you, Potter," the State's Attorney drawled. "She thought you were keeping a late date with Sandra Gould. She was seen quarreling with Sandra at the garage, just about the time the murder took place. Were you there too?"

Adam Potter's face, lean and sallow and hot, flushed a sudden angry red. He controlled himself with a painful effort, and shook his head.

"I don't understand it at all," he said to Colonel Primrose. "I still can't understand it. I've seen a lot of Sandra Gould professionally and around the Colony. Maggie never acted as if she'd . . . heard any gossip. God knows there's always enough of it around, about anything. Maggie only complained because nobody ever told her any."

"You never noticed anything unusual about her manner, lately?"

He shook his head wearily.

"I suppose I'd quit noticing anything. I see so much sickness, real and imagined. I get used to it, I guess. Maggie wasn't sick, she'd just gone under. Neurotic, nothing to do, good way to get sympathy—dramatizing herself. Oh, I guess she'd have been different if I'd been a successful practitioner in Baltimore—instead of a country hack."

He gave me a tired smile.

"I guess that's why Sandra Gould appealed to me. Just a healthy animal, lively and gay. No history of her ills to drive you crazy with."

He ran a disillusioned hand over his damp forehead, took a deep breath and got to his feet.

"That's all I can tell you about it, Colonel Primrose.—Do you want me to . . . look at her?"

They went inside. After a while Colonel Primrose came out, with the Sergeant and Mr. Parran.

He sat down and shook his head soberly.

"It's an odd thing," he said. "He saw her, standing out there talking to Julius when he went by, but he knew she wasn't there, couldn't be. So he analyzed himself and decided he was getting pathological. I imagine Mrs. Gould probably was on his mind—more than he'd admit to us. Well, my next move is the clubhouse. I leave this end to you, Parran. Will you come with me, Mrs. Latham?"

I wanted so much to get away from there that I would have gone to China with him. I said, "I'd love to," and picked up my hat.

Sergeant Buck, standing at a sort of sentry post by the door, cleared his throat abruptly, and said, quite out of an empty sky, "There's no fool like an old fool."

We all looked at him, planted there, a solid mountain of disapproval; and I'm sure Colonel Primrose reddened a little.

"I was referring back to Dr. Potter," Sergeant Buck added stiffly.

"Oh," Colonel Primrose said. He gave me a sideways grin, and I felt definitely like a fool myself. "Well, in that case let's go along, Mrs. Latham."

CHAPTER EIGHTEEN

We didn't stop at the clubhouse. We went down the stone steps to the dock. It was a gorgeous sunny day. A few men who hadn't had to get back to town for business were there in old slacks and sweat shirts or in bathing trunks, puttering about their boats or getting blistered in the sun. They would glance up as we came to them, say "Hi, Grace," and nod to the Colonel, and then, as we passed, I could hear the uneasy silence settle down, feel it behind me. I knew they were looking and wondering, as well they might.

"I'm afraid I'm ruining your reputation, Mrs. Latham," Colonel Primrose said as we came to Andy's boat with the broken mast tied to the dock.

"Nobody will ever trust me with a secret again, certainly," I said.

He had passed that and was down on one knee, looking into the shallow boat rocking there gently on the little waves.

"They brought them in here?"

"Farther down," I said. "Both Jim and Andy dived in. Somebody else must have got the boat."

"Sandra was a good swimmer?"

"She was a marvelous swimmer. Her parents were undoubtedly amphibian."

"And George Barrol?"

"George's parents dwelt on a mountaintop," I said. "He's terrified of water."

Colonel Primrose shook his head. "Dreadful experience for him," he said. "That woman had a powerful attraction, to get him out.—It's odd, though, isn't it?"

I looked at him, puzzled.

"I mean, odd that he held her up, till Jim got there?"

"That's *his* story," I said. "She was struck by the jib and knocked out. He hung on to her till his strength gave out. She came to—it couldn't have taken very long, either for her to come to or for George's strength to give out—and held him up. She had him by the collar when Jim got out there."

Colonel Primrose nodded. "It's reasonable," he said. "She was certainly entirely recovered from the crack on the head when she came up to the clubhouse."

He pulled the jib out from under a pile of white sail and looked carefully at it. He shook his head. "It went overboard, of course. Raining hard anyway."

He got painfully to his feet and brushed off his knee.

"She was so perfectly herself," he went on, "that that's why I couldn't think she'd been hit very hard with this thing."

"Did you see them when they came up?" I asked. I don't know why I'd just assumed he hadn't.

"Oh, yes. There was a great to-do about getting them dry, and borrowing a blazer from somebody's locker to put on Sandra, and so on. She was quite the heroine of the occasion. I take it, of course, she'd be delighted to be the center of attention. George looked like a drowned rat. She was exactly herself, just as if she'd been out for a plunge."

He stood there a moment, thinking. "You and Jim Gould didn't go up with them?"

"No. Jim was pretty sore. He thought Sandra was putting on an act. I don't think he really believes yet that she was in any danger—just scaring the wits out of George for the fun of it. So she'd manage to get the spotlight away from Rosemary too, of course. They'd been out there five minutes, you see, before they capsized. I think Jim still thinks she did it on purpose—it was one of her favorite tricks. She'd love it, and the rougher the better. Poor George! It must be a pretty sickening feeling if you can't swim."

Colonel Primrose nodded absently. "It must be that," he said.

We went back up the steps and across the lawn, parched brown in spots with the summer heat, to the broad cool veranda of the old mansion. A few children were playing there; hardly anybody comes out, as a rule, until afternoon. Alec, the colored houseboy, was polishing the brass knocker on the big front door. We went on into the hall. A few people were in the lounge having early cocktails, talking about Sandra, I suppose, because they stopped abruptly when we looked in. I don't know what else they could be expected to be talking about.

"Is there a maid in the ladies' powder room?" Colonel Primrose asked.

"Not ordinarily. Clara's around all the time. She was there, Saturday night, to take care of people's wraps, if that's what you mean."

He nodded. "See if she's there now, will you?"

I crossed the lounge to the door in the corner and looked in. Clara was there with a dust mop in one hand and a fly swatter in the other, a sun-tan silk stocking pulled toboggan-fashion over her kinky old head. She peered at me through her gold-rimmed spectacles.

"Mo'nin', Mis' Grace. How's those boys?"

"Fine, Clara. Look here—Colonel Primrose wants to ask you some questions."

Her old lips drew into a thin line.

"I ain' tellin' that man nothin'," she said.

"Can I bring him in?"

"Ah don' know—"

We didn't need to argue. He was already in. I saw that in the scared look in her eyes as the door opened behind me.

"I want to ask you about last Saturday night," he said, after I'd formally introduced him. Clara has a strong sense of the proprieties, and having an Army gentleman in the ladies' dressing room obviously was a gross infringement of them.

"Ah don' know nothin' 'bout Sa'day night," Clara said. "First Ah heard 'bout Mis' Gould's carryin's-on was when Miss Rosemary tol' me 'bout it."

"Oh?" Colonel Primrose said. "When was that?"

"When they was out in the bay."

"Miss Rosemary came in here?"

"She come in lookin' lak a ghost, an' Ah says, 'Honey, what's the matter?' She says, 'Nothin', Clara.' Then Ah heard a lot of shriekin' an' yellin'. Ah didn' know whether Ah could go out or whether Ah best stay with her. She says, 'Go on, Clara, it's a good show, go an' watch it.'"

Clara wagged her old head, and Colonel Primrose nodded his, with apparently a good deal of interest.

"She did?" he said. "What did you do?"

"Ah didn' lak her looks, an' Ah tol' her so, an' she jus' laughed."

"What did you think was—"

It wasn't necessary for him to finish his question. Like so many of these old colored folk who can't read or write, Clara is as bright as a whip.

"Ah couldn' say 'zactly, Colonel Primrose. She was settin' by the fireplace, jus' starin' at the grate, jus' studyin' like. She says, 'Go on, Clara, Ah'm O.K.' So Ah went, but they was all acomin' up the hill. Ah come back an' Ah says, 'Thank God, they's safe.' Miss Rosemary she got up, throwed her cigarette

144

in the fireplace, an' says, 'Well, that's that.' Ah declare Ah was s'prised at Miss Rosemary. 'Deed Ah was—ain' nobody sweeter round here."

Colonel Primrose nodded. "Did anybody else come in?"

"Nobody but Mis' Alice. She come in an' didn' say nothin', she jus' walks over to Miss Rosemary an' kisses her on the forehaid an' goes out again, an' Miss Rosemary she didn' say nothin' either. After a while Miss Rosemary goes over to the lookin' glass, powders her nose an' goes out herself. 'Deed Ah ain' never seen people act lak that in all mah days."

"Then Miss Sandra came in later?"

"You mean Mis' Gould?" Clara inquired. The colored people around the place have been there, most of them, for a long time. We knew some of them when we were children. They called Mrs. Gould 'Mis' Alice,' but Sandra was always 'Mis' Gould.' It was curiously effective, of course, in emphasizing the fact that she really didn't belong.

"Mis' Gould? Yas, suh. She come in. She never looked lak she even been scared. She come in dancin' on her toes, singin' a foreign song. An' she never said nothin' either, she jus' went over to the lookin' glass, grinnin' an' makin' pretty faces at herself. Then she come over to the writin' table."

The old woman pointed to the desk against the wall under the window.

I listened to her with a sort of measured interest. It's often occurred to me later that it was strange I didn't realize the tremendous importance of what she was telling us. I don't think Colonel Primrose did either—not just at the moment, while we were both standing there in the powder room. But, as I saw in just a moment, he had far more excuse for not realizing it than I had.

"She sat down an' wrote."

"She *wrote?*" Colonel Primrose asked.

"Yas, suh. Look lak she couldn' make up her min' 'bout what she want to write, 'cause she kep' writin' a little an' then pullin' out a fresh piece of paper an' writin' some more."

"What did she do with the old ones?"

"When she got all through she picked 'em all up an' took 'em over to the fireplace, an' she set a match to 'em," Clara said. "An' then out she traipses, never sayin' a word an' lookin' almighty pleased with herself."

Colonel Primrose smiled a little. He looked over at me again. "I suppose she knew it was a good show," he said.

He took an envelope out of his pocket and opened it. I

145

watched him with increasing interest. He took out the folded creased piece of paper I'd seen on the table in my living room the night before, next to Sandra's suicide note and the blue petals.

"Could this be the piece of paper?"

Clara looked at it and nodded.

"That there's *one* paper—Ah cain' say it's the same piece, 'cause they's paper all through the club *lak* it, but it might be, an' she never took no envelope."

Colonel Primrose handed the paper to me. "That's her writing, isn't it, Mrs. Latham?"

I could only suppose he intended me to read it. I did. It said:

I think I must talk to you. I have a proposition. I will forget what *I* know if you will do a *very little easy* thing for *me*. I will meet you in my garage as soon as I can after I go home. Be sure.

That was all. No signature, no salutation; no names to show who had written it or for whom it had been written. I handed it back to Colonel Primrose.

"It's her writing," I said. "You could compare it with the other note."

He looked at me oddly for just a fleeting instant. My heart chilled a little in spite of all I could do.

"I've done that, Mrs. Latham," he said. He put the letter back in his pocket.

When we were outside I asked him about it, but he shook his head.

"You know," he said, "I can't make out Sandra Gould's literary remains. In fact, this whole business gets harder and harder."

He spoke with a sort of resigned humorous petulance.

"You don't believe those two notes are hers?" I inquired sweetly.

"Oh, yes. That's what makes it hard. There seems no doubt they are hers. But why should she write the suicide note at all? And why write this thing at all? And why write all the notes and start off on another, as the maid there says? And why burn all the ones she'd done?"

He looked at me with a puzzled frown.

"It doesn't make sense, Mrs. Latham."

"Well," I said, "Sandra was always scribbling notes. Have you found out who that one was written to?"

146

He nodded.

"This is strictly in the lodge. It was found—I prefer not to say how or by whom—in Dikranov's pocket."

"Oh." I had the feeling, which turned out to be perfectly stupid, that this was beginning to make things clearer to me.

"He says she didn't give it to him and he never saw it before I showed it to him. As a matter of fact, I saw her when she came out of the powder room. He was dummy at the bridge table. I saw her go up to him in the hall before she went out. Andy Thorp had come up and was looking for her. She didn't have time to speak to him, but she certainly had time to thrust that note into his hand—or his jacket pocket."

"Did he meet her?" I asked.

"And did he hit her over the head with a monkey wrench?" he said. "I don't know. I presume he did meet her."

He grinned suddenly.

"All I know about the wrench is that it has your fingerprints on it, Mrs. Latham."

"I picked it up off the floor—" I began patiently, and a little annoyed too.

He smiled again. "I know. The point is that Jim Gould says he left it on the kitchen porch when he came from town. He admits buying it at Toplady's."

I could remember so clearly that Saturday morning. He had it in his hand when he spotted George Barrol coming across the street.

"You see, Mrs. Latham, I know everybody here would perjure himself to hell and back again to save the Goulds. But just think about Jim Gould a minute. What a case the State's Attorney's got against him! He's not himself, to begin with, he's been drinking heavily—more than he ever had in all his life. He and Sandra are quarreling constantly. All the servants say that. He's fed up to the teeth with her. I saw that long before I knew any of the Rosemary business. She'd ruined his career, ruined his life. She was flirting with every stray male she met—even poor old Dr. Potter."

He smiled a little as I shook my head.

"I don't say Potter was having an affair with her. Well, she was ruining Jim's sister's life too. Thorp had obviously lost his head over her. He was acting—still is—like a first-rate jackass. To cap it all, Rosemary comes back quite suddenly. He doesn't know anything about it. Nobody tells him. He sees her cold. The shock sends a mint julep crashing out of his hand onto the floor—in public. Then Sandra puts on a scene that makes him

147

ridiculous and cheap, in front of all his friends. He goes home with you, sore and hurt and desperately unhappy, I'd imagine —and ready to throw in the sponge. Then he goes home, leaving your place at ten minutes to one. He meets her. Maybe he met Rosemary first, which wouldn't help anything certainly. Let's say he met Sandra with Dikranov. He goes to the house. She follows him. You can imagine the state he's in. He hits her over the head with the wrench and goes on inside—or goes along to meet Rosemary, whichever way it happened. It doesn't make much difference."

"And how did she get into Andy's car in the garage?" I asked, a little triumphantly, knowing I had him there.

He shook his head.

"That's so easy, Mrs. Latham," he said, rather reproachfully. "You haven't understood this. She has scratches all over her legs, her shins are skinned, her arms are bruised."

I stared at him in astonishment and horror. He met my gaze steadily.

"There's no remotest doubt, Mrs. Latham," he said soberly, "that somebody carried, or dragged, Sandra Gould to the car. She was hit over the head with that wrench, and *put into the car with the engine running.*"

We were walking back to my place from the clubhouse, along the patch overlooking the bay. I tried not to look at him. It all seemed so devilishly futile to try to hold out against this slow inexorable closing in and weeding out, drawing the net tighter and tighter before he would, one moment, open it and find somebody wriggling helplessly in the toils of it.—And it would be one of my friends!

"A man," he went on deliberately, "could have got her into the car, you'd think, without all those bruises and marks. Unless—just for instance, Mrs. Latham—it was a man coolly and craftily trying to make out that it was done by a woman."

He shook his head.

"Complicates things, doesn't it?"

"It still could have been . . . Andy, for instance, then."

"Andy obviously has ideas on this subject," he said. He smiled a little. "The fact that he buried Lucy Lee's slippers in the bank shows that. Those slippers are interesting. The soles show a frantic search, or chase, or perhaps a vigil, in pretty damp grass. There's car grease on them that somebody's tried to clean off with benzine. They've had whisky on them. In fact, they show pretty conclusively that they've been in a garage, as well as in the wet grass."

I waited with a sick ominous feeling in the pit of my stomach for him to go on to the bunch of blue flowers, but he seemed to have forgotten them.

"We know," he went on deliberately, "that Lucy Lee left her mother and went home at ten-thirty, Saturday night. She came back later. The implications of what she did are obvious. She wouldn't have been out if her husband hadn't been out. He knew Sandra was somewhere with his car—or so he says. Oh, well . . . the question is, Where was he? And where was Lucy Lee? And where was Mrs. Gould senior? And where were Rosemary and Jim, who were meeting at one o'clock? And why, in so small a space, didn't some of them see some of the others? Of course, the answer to that, Mrs. Latham, is that they did. They must have."

I could think of only one thing to say.

"And Paul Dikranov?"

Colonel Primrose smiled. "Oh, yes. Mr. Dikranov. He's an interesting fellow. I doubt if he'd want the Bishops to know just how extremely interesting he is."

"Sandra knew him, of course."

He nodded.

"I'm afraid she did. But I didn't know how to prove it—or, what's more interesting, what difference it makes."

"Then," I said, "you don't really think Jim killed Sandra?"

He looked at me steadily. "If Jim Gould struck Sandra in great anger, with that monkey wrench," he said slowly, "and left her, he didn't kill her. Don't forget it was carbon monoxide that *killed* her."

"How ghastly," I couldn't help but say.

"On the other hand, if someone else struck Sandra with intent to kill, and someone else still, thinking Jim had done it, let's say, and that she was already dead, had put her in the car . . . well, that becomes a horse of a different color, doesn't it?"

"Does it?" I asked stupidly.

"Well, legally perhaps not. But actually, with a jury trial, I should think so. If you and Mrs. Gould had been trying to cover up Jim—"

I gasped in horror.

"Me!" I said. "Oh, dear!"

He looked at me with a sort of sardonic amusement.

"Let's skip it then. I don't want to distress you. But you haven't told me yet why anyone wanted to shoot you."

"Lots of people can't stand the way I comb my hair," I said.

149

It was a feeble attempt to reduce all this to a palpable absurdity.

He shook his head.

"That's where you're making a big mistake. People don't attempt to murder other people for such good reasons as that. No, it's never that simple. Motives for murder are generally definite and commonplace. Take Mrs. Potter and the attempt on you. They're obvious. Someone was trying to cover up. You're both in the way. Whether you know why, and are perjuring yourself to save somebody, I wouldn't know. You're a fool if you are. Mrs. Potter knew and was on the point of telling—and look what happened to her."

It wasn't a pleasant idea. I didn't, furthermore, know how to convince him that I really had not seen Sandra killed. Which apparently he seemed to believe.

"As for Sandra, that's a different matter," he went on thoughtfully. "I'd say the chief motives for murder generally are greed, fear, love—or hate, jealousy or revenge. Those are all pretty fundamental psychological concepts. Mrs. Potter's death was due to fear. That can be a complex business, you know. A cornered rat fights because of fear. I'd say offhand it's a damned sight more powerful and more universal motive for murder than many of the others—than jealousy, for example."

This was a little hard for me to follow.

"Then what have you been saying about these people?" I demanded. "Surely if Rosemary, or Lucy Lee either, had murdered Sandra, that would have been the motive. Jim's, or his mother's—that would be hate, I suppose. But what about the others?"

"The motive that was behind the monkey wrench wasn't necessarily the one that was behind the carbon monoxide," he said.

I thought about that a few moments.

"That was fear, I suppose," I said. "But it wouldn't be fear *of* Sandra so much as fear *for* someone else."

"I said fear was a pretty complex business," Colonel Primrose remarked. "It's one of those things that have long roots—and long arms. It doesn't have to be anything that happened today, or yesterday."

"I see," I said. I knew he was thinking about the note in Paul Dikranov's pocket.

CHAPTER NINETEEN

I suspect Colonel Primrose was as surprised as I was to see Jim Gould and Sergeant Buck sitting on the front steps of my house so deep in conversation that they didn't even see us coming until we were almost up to them. When they did Buck jumped to his feet, giving the Colonel a sharp probing glance—unless I was mistaken—no doubt to see whether I'd proposed to him. Then he came to an abrupt attention.

"Mr. Gould's got an idea, sir," he said stiffly.

"Really?" said Colonel Primrose. "What is it?"

"It's about the foreigner, sir."

"Yes?"

Colonel Primrose gave me a glance.

"Yes, sir. It's his idea that the foreigner knew the missus in Georgia."

He looked over at Jim out of one eye.

Jim grinned. There was something decidedly grim, just the same, about his lean set jaw and steady eyes, fastened, squinting a little against the sun, on the Colonel.

"It sounds cockeyed, Colonel Primrose, I admit," he said easily, shifting his long sinewy frame from one leg to the other. "I didn't pry into my wife's affairs. But I guess anybody'd have been blind if he didn't see she knew him when he first came into the clubhouse."

"I noticed she did," Colonel Primrose said.

"You did? Well, then, I guess I'm not telling you anything."

"That depends, of course."

"She called him up when we were at dinner and talked to him. She was pretty sore when she came back to the table."

"You didn't hear what she said?" Colonel Primrose asked bluntly.

"I heard it, all right, but I don't speak the language."

Colonel Primrose nodded. "Georgian, of course.—You didn't happen to see him, when you were with Miss Bishop, Saturday night?"

Jim shook his head. "No."

"Whom did you see?"

"Nobody but Santa Claus," Jim said cheerfully.

"Did you see Santa Claus this noon too? When Mrs. Potter was killed?"

The smile left Jim's face.

"No. I didn't see anybody. Except Miss Bishop. I saw her, here. I went directly home by the side door. I didn't know Mrs. Potter was in the house."

Colonel Primrose nodded politely. "And Saturday night—where did you meet Miss Bishop, at one o'clock?"

Jim hesitated. Then he nodded down towards the group of white chairs by the tree.

"Down there. I was going for a walk before I went home. We walked down to the lane and back up through their garden. I cut straight across here and home."

"When would that be?"

"Two-fifteen, perhaps, I don't know."

"You're sure you didn't see anybody, except Santa Claus?"

The fraction of an instant that Jim hesitated was imperceptible unless you knew him very well, or so I thought.

"Quite sure."

"Just what was your mother doing, Gould?" Colonel Primrose asked—suavely.

Jim flushed a little. "I didn't see my mother, Colonel Primrose," he said evenly. The two of them looked directly at each other for a long time. I couldn't have said whether it was challenge or merely appraisal.

"That's straight, Colonel," Jim added steadily.

Colonel Primrose nodded again. Jim took a packet of cigarettes out of his pocket. His brown hands were perfectly steady as he held his lighter to his cigarette and snapped it shut.

"I didn't come over for a cross-examination, anyway," he said curtly. "I just came over to tell you I don't think much of the method of hounding women and children, and tell you I'm in on this myself from now on."

"That's fine," said Colonel Primrose cheerfully. He hesitated an instant, looking questioningly at Jim. "Have you . . . learned something?"

Jim hesitated also, a barely perceptible fraction of a moment. He shook his head grimly.

"Well," Colonel Primrose remarked, "you'll find it a little difficult to take much of a part in this if you've just made up your mind about things. And a little dangerous."

"You can leave that to me, Colonel."

152

We watched his long figure move swiftly across the lawn towards the Bishops'. I looked at Colonel Primrose. He was staring after him thoughtfully. He looked at me, shaking his head a little.

"That young man's headed for trouble," he said. "He's found out something, or thinks he has, that's changed the setup for him. What was it, Buck?"

The iron-faced Sergeant shook his head.

"He's had a heart-to-heart talk with his brother-in-law, sir, is all I can get."

Sergeant Buck looked at Jim's disappearing form with some approval. "He's a good boy, sir," he added.

I brightened up considerably at that, for some reason, but I learned later that that was a mistake. It seemed that in all the businesses of this sort that the two of them had been in, the people Sergeant Buck took a fancy to invariably turned out to be monsters of villainy. At least, so Colonel Primrose maintained. I learned later, also, that Sergeant Buck was a man of considerable means, having invested his army pay and army poker winnings in houses on the Coast near naval stations, and actually, what with his retired pay and his rents, doing rather better than his colonel with his retired pay and his nonproductive stocks. There was never any confusion about their relationship, however. The Colonel was still the Colonel and the Sergeant still the Sergeant—though he did often seem a pretty severe manager.

It was apparent now that whatever Jim had said or done while we were away, he had quite definitely sold himself to Sergeant Buck. Personally I suspected it was because the Colonel had left Buck and taken me. Also, of course, here was Jim obviously a fine young fellow done in by a woman, and a foreign woman at that.

I left the two of them a few minutes after Jim had gone and went around the house to get my car. I hadn't been to the village all day, and the family larder was definitely low. I got the car and set out for Church Street with utterly no idea of what an important development in the business of Sandra Gould and Maggie Potter I was about to run into, or how—just as in Mrs. Potter's case—a hitherto quite trivial figure in the whole affair was to take on new proportions. It was, I suppose, nothing short of Fate that when I walked into the tea store Elsie Carter should be there, pressing the cantaloupes and turning the berry boxes upside down.

She abandoned the whole business the instant she spotted me and came across to where I was.

"My dear Grace, this must be simply terrible for you, you poor child!"

She fixed me with a bright predatory eye.

"I'm bearing up wonderfully, Elsie," I said.

"Oh but my dear! What could you expect? I told poor Maggie just last week that I didn't see how she stood it."

I stared at her a horrified instant.

"You did?" I said, and no doubt very bitterly. "Then you can thank yourself for Maggie Potter's death."

Elsie turned a livid green.

"And what's more," I went on furiously, "if you could bring yourself to stop all this nonsense about Rosemary and Jim, we'd all be better off."

I don't really know why I said that, except that I was dreadfully angry all of a sudden at her carrying her wretched gossip to poor Maggie Potter. Certainly I hadn't the faintest notion that it would affect Elsie as it did. She went from green to a dead-white. Her sharp beady eyes fairly burned holes into me.

"You're not the one to talk, Grace Latham!"

She almost spat the words at me.

"Don't think I haven't got eyes in my head. What's Rodman Bishop doing around your house all the time?"

I gaped stupidly at her. She'd got started and under way, and when Elsie once gets that far nobody has ever been known to stop her.

"And what's more, if Rosemary Bishop comes back here, and hasn't the decency to leave Jim alone, you can't *blame* Sandra for fighting for her happiness—and you can't expect *me* to perjure myself when Colonel Primrose asks me about it! Heaven knows I'm merely doing my duty as I see it!"

"Oh dear!" I thought. I could have known that very astute little man with the sparkling black eyes had no doubt been doing lots of things he hadn't told me about. And I thought again that Rodman Bishop was quite right. The trouble with the world is that too many people are barging about doing their duty as they see it. George Barrol wasn't the only one.

"I didn't know Rosemary and Sandra had taken to fighting, or at any rate not in the public streets," I said, as casually as I could manage.

"Then the crowd's wrong in thinking Colonel Primrose takes you into his confidence," Elsie snapped spitefully. "He came to me yesterday afternoon. Obviously realizing that the whole lot of you couldn't be relied on to tell the truth.—Even if you knew it," she added with sharp malice.

I don't know why I felt I had to defend my position as confidante of the Colonel—especially when what she was saying about our unreliability was only too true. But there's something about Elsie's predatory nose and thin lips and prying eyes that would make a cat defend a mouse.

"Colonel Primrose hasn't pretended to take me into his confidence," I said stiffly—and truthfully. I realized also that it was more truthful than I'd thought. And actually it was really more truthful than I realized even then.

Just then somebody reached past her and started to take the largest and crispest head of iceberg lettuce. Elsie turned and grasped it firmly out of her hand. I fled, feeling just as if I'd eaten a large cold pancake.

What must Colonel Primrose have heard from Elsie Carter —or rather, what couldn't he have heard from her? I dreaded to think of it, but I couldn't keep the series of crazy notions Elsie had had for years from rushing like wild horses through my head. Rodman Bishop and Alice Gould had been "carrying on." Dr. Potter was slowly doing poor Maggie to death. Little Andy Thorp was deaf and dumb, because he didn't talk till late. Sandra's baby had been born Chinese, or Malay, or green, or yellow, or something pretty ghastly. As it was also born dead, no one ever knew but the hospital people. The manager of the club had sold the original paneling to the Metropolitan one winter and replaced it with beaverboard and pocketed the money. Rosemary's dull gold hair was peroxide, my auburn hair was henna. Sandra was really from Hoboken, New Jersey; she was really an escaped Georgian aristocrat, misunderstood and nagged to death by Alice Gould. Chapin Bishop's head had been forcibly held in the pool until he'd drowned. The Catholics were building a tunnel to the White House, President Roosevelt was a Jew.

In fact, I couldn't think of any notion that Elsie Carter hadn't had. I shuddered to think of the tale she must have told Colonel Primrose. Especially if, as she'd virtually said, she'd actually seen Rosemary and Sandra quarreling . . .

I opened the door of my car and waited for the boy to put my groceries on the back seat.

"Hello, Grace," somebody said. "How's the charnel house doing?"

155

I turned around. Bill Chetwynd was coming down Mr. Toplady's steps, carrying a can of kerosene with a potato stuck on the spout.

"It's just dandy," I said.

Then I thought of something.

"When did you leave the clubhouse the other night, by the way, Bill?"

"I wouldn't know, Grace." He grinned. "My friends can probably tell you."

"Would you happen to remember when the Carters left?"

Bill Chetwynd wrinkled his forehead and squinted his eyes, trying to think, which is rather hard for him.

"Yeah, now, lessee. You mean the lady that's a cross between an elephant and a hawk, married to the little guy that looks like the stuff they used to give us in the nursery instead of tea."

"That's the people," I said patiently.

"Lord, Grace, you don't think *she* did Sandra in—"

"Shut up," I said quickly. Elsie was coming stalwartly out of the tea store, her lips compressed, not missing anything that was going on, from Bill and me to the Reverend Arrowsmith's daughter in shorts smoking a cigarette with some boy at the popcorn stand.

"Hello, Mrs. Carter!" Bill said. "Lovely day, isn't it? Too hot, though."

He grinned at me as Elsie went on.

"Now, lessee. I *can* tell you, if it's important. What I mean is, I'm not going to all the trouble to think about the Carters unless it's *damn* important. I'd rather think about anteaters, or a nice cool drink of vitriol."

"Please, Bill, don't be an idiot," I pleaded. "I really want to know."

"O.K. Then I was in the bar having a drink."

"I know, darling. It's the Carters—you know, *the Carters*."

"Sure. I was in the bar. Ferney Carter was in the bar too."

"Be serious, Bill—please!"

" 'Struth. Ferney Carter was there having a lemon coke. It was—lessee—it was just when they dragged the foreign gal and Georgie out of the water. I said—"

"*No*, Bill. *The Carters!*"

"I'm getting to 'em. Elsie came to the door and said, 'Ferney dear, we ought to be going home, it's late.' Need I say more? Next thing I knew there was a gap, and then Andy Thorp was filling it by saying a double whisky neat."

"Oh," I said. "Then the Carters left before Andy and Sandra."

"Not so fast, girl. Not so fast. When I went upstairs, Ferney dear was sitting in the hall, hat on his knees. Dame Elsie was gassing with some old girl about whether the men wouldn't prefer creamed chicken and peas at the auxiliary picnic to peas and creamed chicken."

"Bill, *please!*" I said. "This is serious, really!"

"But that's a fact, Grace. I know, because I'd had just enough to make my heart bleed for poor old Ferney. I said, 'Elsie, can't Ferney go have another coke, just one more?' She said, 'Bill, you're a man, which would you rather have, creamed chicken and peas—' and I said 'Yes' and tottered off. I waited to dance with Rose, but she'd gone too. Then I went and fetched Ferney a lemon coke, but I had to water the rubber plant with it. He'd gone."

"You wouldn't know what time that was?"

"It was before one," Bill said earnestly. "Because I don't remember anything after one."

"Well, that's a help," I said. "I wanted to know, because Elsie's going to be an eyewitness to Rosemary slogging Sandra over the head with the monkey wrench, or something, before another day's gone, and I just wondered whether she could possibly have been anywhere in the district."

Bill shook his head. "Couldn't tell you," he said cheerfully. "I can tell you this—I'd like to slog her."

"Wouldn't we all."

I answered rather absently, because it was a sort of academic point anyway. Chiefly, however, because I was just then remembering the crack she'd taken at me about Rodman Bishop, and trying to figure out what she'd meant by it. I should probably have thought about it seriously enough to see its importance if I hadn't had to go on to a Red Cross Board Meeting, and after that out to Mrs. Rowe's to get two country hams she'd been saving for me. As it was I dismissed it—much too lightly. Even Elsie Carter has to be right once in a while.

CHAPTER TWENTY

It was after five when I got home. No one was around, and the Bishops had phoned for me to come over for a cocktail when I got back.

"Where are the Colonel and Sergeant Buck, Julius?" I asked.

" 'Deed, Mis' Grace, an' Ah couldn' say," Julius said serenely. "A boy come clear out with a telegram fo' the Colonel, 'stead of phonin' it, an' they got in the cab an' drove off. 'Deed an' Ah don' know which way they went."

It didn't take very long for me to find out where they'd got to. I saw Colonel Primrose the minute I passed the magnolia trees and came towards the porch. He was there, very much at his ease, and oddly enough the Goulds were there too, all of them except Andy. If it hadn't been for the haunted look in Lucy Lee's eyes, and the constant cigarettes she smoked, and George's uneasy titter, I should never have guessed from the group on the porch that the heavy dreadful somber cloud of murder hung over them, like a French funeral pall première classe.

Jim especially was more jubilantly himself than I'd seen him for years. The sun, filtering through the leaves, made a moving arabesque of light and shade on Rosemary's gold hair and warm peach-tan skin, and played on her yellow sun-backed frock and bare brown arms and legs. She looked extraordinarily lovely and detached too—only her long gray eyes were warm and alive and intensely present.

Dikranov watched her, I thought, with an almost wistful quality of worship in his dark face. Rodman Bishop watched her too, more quietly, less obviously worried about her than he'd been in the morning. Now and then he and Alice Gould exchanged a half-humorous, half-despairing glance, as if they'd both given up completely. Nathan Kaufman sat on the side lines, as it were, giving in some way the impression that he was holding a rather vague watching brief tightly by the scruff of the neck.

"Where's Andy?" I said cheerfully, before I'd remembered

about the funeral pall. My house guest gave me an amused little half-smile.

"Sulking in his tent," Jim said.

George Barrol as usual created the necessary diversion. "What will you drink, Grace?" he said hastily. I nodded at the mint julep he was holding up, and turned to Colonel Primrose.

"I just met Elsie Carter in town," I said, firmly ignoring the instant flag of warning that he ran up behind his eyes. "I gather she's given you the low-down on the whole local situation."

He managed a smile, but it was not greatly amused. "I found her very helpful, Mrs. Latham," he said coolly.

"I'll bet you did," Jim Gould remarked. "Did you hear the one about Parran? He sent the bootlegger to the Cut for twenty years because he held a mortgage on the fellow's farm, and then he foreclosed on it."

"Or the one about Dr. Potter throwing a party at the club and putting something in the crab imperial to jog business up a bit?" George put in.

Colonel Primrose shook his head. "No," he said. "I didn't hear them."

He looked quietly at me for an instant, as if wondering for just a fraction of a moment about something.

"No," he repeated. "But I did hear the one about Miss Bishop and Sandra Gould meeting at the Goulds' gate Saturday night."

There was a tense sharp instant when everybody on that porch might have been in a state of suspended animation. Except Colonel Primrose. He was looking at Rosemary with calm deliberation, his eyes narrowed ever so slightly, catching the almost imperceptible pallor that hardened her lips a moment before it relaxed again.

"It seems rather a public place for a scene," he said. "In fact, I'm not sure I'd have believed her if I hadn't already found this there by the gate."

We sat there like eight graven images, watching him stretch a little so he could reach into his pocket and bring out his leather folder. Nobody moved while he opened it with maddening slowness and took out a piece of crumpled white tissue paper. He opened that. We stared at the two little blue velvet petals lying there on the tissue in his hand. He looked around from face to face, his eyes sparkling and terribly piercing.

"I lost the bunch of flowers," Rosemary said coolly. "At the clubhouse, I think."

159

Colonel Primrose shook his head. "That won't do, Miss Bishop. I found that too, you see. This is another piece of it."

I tried not to look at Alice Gould and I knew Colonel Primrose knew it.

"You see," he went on slowly, "there can't be any doubt that Sandra Gould had a primitive streak in her."

Rosemary flushed, her gray eyes almost black, her breath coming a little quicker in spite of herself. The flush receded from her forehead and throat and concentrated in two burning spots in her cheeks.

"Are you suggesting, Colonel Primrose," she said coolly, "that after she flew at me and ripped the flowers off my dress, *I* reverted to primitive type too?"

I looked at Jim Gould. He was shaking with anger, fists clenched, jaw clamped.

"You shut up, Rosemary," he said savagely. "Let me handle this."

Colonel Primrose looked mildly surprised.

"But I understood you weren't anywhere around, Gould," he said. "I understood you walked down to the lane from Mrs. Latham's front porch."

"Then forget it," Jim said curtly. "I met Miss Bishop at the gate just in time to keep my wife from making a bloody fool of herself."

"I see," Colonel Primrose said. He looked questioningly and deliberately from one to the other of them.

Nathan Kaufman jumped to his feet suddenly. "Now then, now then!" he said. "That'll be enough of this, Primrose!"

He brought the fist of his hand down on the table.

Jim took two steps across the porch. "Sit down!" he said. He planted his hand on Kaufman's chest and pushed him firmly into a low chair.

"Don't forget he's trying to save your neck, Gould," Paul Dikranov said quietly, under Nathan Kaufman's irate splutterings. He blew a nonchalant column of gray smoke through his full lips.

Jim looked down at the little lawyer for an instant, and turned to Dikranov. "Thanks!" he said. "When I need somebody to save my neck I'll call him in myself. And you'd better begin looking out for your own neck a little. And while I'm on your subject, you're not marrying Rosemary, do you get that?"

Rosemary got quickly to her feet. "Jim—stop it!"

160

"I told you to shut up. And I'm telling the whole bunch of you Rosemary's going to marry me—as soon as it's decent."

I looked anxiously at Colonel Primrose. He wasn't paying the slightest attention to Jim. He was watching somebody else, intently, his bright old eyes steady and unwavering. I couldn't make out just who it was. It was not Dikranov; he was standing easily against the white column of the porch, a smile in his eyes. As Jim spoke he bowed.

"I congratulate you, sir," he said suavely. "As a matter of fact, I'd thought of suggesting it myself."

I could not see George, but I heard his nervous laugh. Then Rodman Bishop got up abruptly. "Sit down, Jim," he said gruffly. "You're making it damned embarrassing for Rosemary."

"Quite the contrary, dad," Rosemary said quickly.

"That's because you're a shameless hussy," Rodman Bishop said. The tone of his voice showed how much he meant it. A quick grin lighted his savage old face for a moment and died. "Can't you young fools see this is just about all Colonel Primrose needs—"

There was a sudden sound from Lucy Lee. It was half sobbing.

"I wish Elsie Carter—"

Her mother leaned over towards her, but it was Colonel Primrose who interrupted actually and stopped her from going on.

"I'm very grateful to Mrs. Carter, really," he said calmly. "She gave me several extremely useful bits of gossip, Mrs. Thorp. Three that I'm especially grateful for. For instance: where was it that you said you were this morning, Mr. Barrol, between quarter to eleven and quarter past?"

George looked most startled. "I was—"

He remembered suddenly and blinked at Rodman Bishop.

"Oh," he said quickly. "I didn't get the time for a minute. I was down in the cellar bottling the blackberry wine."

I suppose if Rodman Bishop could have killed George just then without messing up the front porch, he'd gladly have done it.

Colonel Primrose shot a quick glance at Nathan Kaufman.

"And you, Dikranov—where were you?"

"At eleven o'clock also?"

"Yes."

"I was in my room, packing my things," Paul Dikranov said

161

imperturbably. "I have got urgent business in New York. I am sorry I cannot stay at this charming place longer. But business, you know . . ."

George tittered.

"Unfinished business," he said aside to Alice Gould, sitting by him on the swinging couch.

Rosemary and Jim looked at each other. Rosemary's eyes and his were a startling testimony of how shallow and insecure Sandra's hold had been.

Colonel Primrose frowned a little. Alice Gould went over to the porch rail and stood looking out. She knew better than anyone there, I suppose, the old adage about the slips between cup and lip. She stood there, fragile and elegant, her curly white hair shining in the sun, pleating and unpleating her handkerchief in her transparent trembling fingers. Lucy Lee was watching her. She was slumped down in a deep chintz-padded wicker chair, only her dark eyes alive. The rest of her was paralyzed with fear. I couldn't make Lucy Lee out then, and I couldn't later. You don't expect people like Lucy Lee to do odd things.

I've wondered since what would have happened if Nathan Kaufman had held his tongue the next moment. He got up—I imagine the third mint julep had something to do with it, though Colonel Primrose said he doubted it—and came out into the center of the little circle, rather as if he were mounting a rostrum. There was something a little forensic about everything he did.

"Colonel Primrose," he said sharply, "I see the way this investigation of yours is heading."

Which was very interesting, because, as I learned later, at that moment Colonel Primrose himself had only a glimmer of what way it was heading.

"I'm going to tell you now that the defense is suicide while of an unsound mind."

He shook his forefinger vigorously at the Colonel.

"You haven't got a leg to stand on, sir. I've seen Hawkins. His whole story has *collapsed*. He didn't hear anything except the radio that Sandra Gould was playing while the motor filled her lungs with carbon monoxide. Her family will tell you she never sat a moment of the day without the radio on. Mrs. Gould can tell you that she herself turned that radio off while she and Mrs. Latham were standing by the car. The station was dead but the instrument was still turned on."

I looked at Alice. She may have done it, of course. I certainly couldn't—and wouldn't—deny it.

"Because, you see, Colonel, Mrs. Gould had read that note Sandra Gould, her daughter-in-law, had left. She knew what was in her mind. And then, and above all, you've got that note itself—a note that's plain and specific, and that's genuine beyond all question. That handwriting's been identified by everybody here who had any knowledge of the subject whatsoever. You can't get around that note, Colonel. You can't even establish the fact of murder—let alone not having a shred of evidence against any specific person."

He paused for an instant, glaring a little heatedly across the floor.

Colonel Primrose shook his head suavely. "I beg your pardon! I beg your pardon!" he said politely. "I have a great deal of evidence. And that note—"

His eyes met mine for an instant, and he smiled a little sadly. My heart was icy.

"You attempt to deny its authenticity?" Mr. Kaufman barked triumphantly.

"No, no," said Colonel Primrose. "No, it's authentic. The only trouble with it, for present purposes, is that it was written —by Sandra Gould, of course—four and one-half years ago, when she came back from the hospital after her child was stillborn."

Jim Gould, completely and utterly speechless, stared across the porch at his mother. Alice swayed a little, and I could see her eyes close in pain. Her delicate unlined face was so old and ravaged that it looked as if she had pulled a mask suddenly down over it. Jim struggled to his feet. She opened her eyes and looked across at him.

"I know you'll never forgive me," she said slowly. "But it's true."

She looked painfully around at Colonel Primrose. "You found Ellen Stanley?"

He nodded.

"She was the only one who knew," she whispered.

She'd forgotten me, and I tried not to look as if I remembered the night she came out of that room and showed that note to me, and said, "I hope God will forgive me, Grace."

"I had the ink in the note tested," Colonel Primrose said, "and then I found her."

Jim was by his mother's side. She clung to him with one frail hand.

"I was angry with her. She kept going to pieces. I'd never let her see I knew she'd ruined my son's life, not until then, and then I told her things I shouldn't have, and left the room."

She brushed her lace handkerchief across her dry lips.

"I went to my room and got to thinking how unfair and cruel I'd been, when she was ill and nervous with no defense. So I went back to her room. She'd got up and gone to the bureau and had Jim's revolver in her hand. I took it away from her and talked to her a long time, and put her back to bed, and then Ellen Stanley came in, her nurse. She saw the letter before I did. I took it away with me, and I kept it . . . to remind me how near I'd been to murdering my son's wife. Because it would have been that."

She pressed her handkerchief to her lips and turned her head away.

Nobody had moved, not Lucy Lee nor Rodman Bishop—only Paul Dikranov was no longer there. I don't know when he'd gone.

Colonel Primrose leaned forward. Before he spoke the telephone inside rang loudly. It seemed strangely ominous, coming just then. It rang one long and three short.

"That's yours, Grace," George said.

I glanced at Colonel Primrose. He nodded.

"I'll answer it, then," I said.

"Right through to the left, in the library, Grace," Rosemary said.

I went into the hall, leaving them all behind me out there. The door to the Bishops' library was shut. I opened it and went into the big book-lined room and over to the desk. I sat down and pulled the telephone over to me. Outside I could hear them talking again. I took up the phone and said "Hello!"

"The Colonel ain' home, Sergeant, suh," I could hear Julius saying at my phone.

"This is Mrs. Latham, at the Bishops', Sergeant," I said. "Colonel Primrose is here. Would you like to speak to him?"

"Yes, ma'am," Sergeant Buck said stiffly.

"Hold on. I'll call him."

I had just started to take the receiver from my ear when I heard a sound that suddenly struck the blood cold in my veins. It was the familiar tiny sound of the murderer's clock. Tickety-tick, tickety-tock; tickety-tick, tickety-tock. I sat there for an instant frozen with dread. Then suddenly my heart gave a wild convulsive leap of joy. If I heard that terrible little sound now, with all the Goulds and all the Bishops out on the front porch not fifty feet from me, then it couldn't be one of them! All, of course, except Andy Thorp . . . and somehow I didn't care so much about Andy just then.

I opened my lips to call to Colonel Primrose, and stopped short, the words frozen in my throat. For I had taken the receiver away from my ear . . . and the sound of the murderer's clock still went steadily on. I looked about, half dazed, and there it was, on the desk, not two feet from my elbow. It ticked away, unmistakable, sinister, dreadful: tickety-tick, tickety-tock.

I sat there, trembling from my head to my feet.

Then I laid the receiver carefully down on the desk and picked up the clock as silently as I could. I put it in the bottom drawer of the desk under some papers, closed the drawer and took the key out.

I went back to the porch and told Colonel Primrose his sergeant was on the phone.

CHAPTER TWENTY-ONE

Lucy Lee watched Colonel Primrose until he had disappeared into the house. She stood up sharply as if the effort of waiting had been almost too much for her.

She came over to me and gripped my arm. "Who was it, Grace?" she demanded desperately.

My brain was still whirling and my veins icy cold at the discovery I'd made of that dreadful clock, ticking away there, monotonous and deadly, right on the Bishops' desk not a yard from me as I'd answered the phone. I controlled my voice as well as I could manage.

"Sergeant Buck, Lucy Lee."

She moistened her lips with a lightning flick of the tip of her tongue and pressed her cigarette out in the yellow bowl on the white table. We followed her to the screen door with disturbed eyes.

"I'm going home," she said abruptly.

The words sounded like a strip of hard cloth being ripped violently apart. She ran down the steps and across the lawn. Not until she'd stumbled and caught herself for the second time did we really understand, I think, that she was ready to crack up completely. Jim Gould must have caught up with her just inside my grounds, because he was off the porch and running past the two great magnolias before his mother had said good-by to Rosemary and Rodman Bishop and left, following them too.

We heard Colonel Primrose close the library door. Nathan Kaufman cleared his throat and said it was so hot in New York you could have fried an egg on the library steps at Forty-second Street the afternoon before, and Rodman Bishop said it was cooler down here than he remembered August usually was at April Harbor.

Colonel Primrose in the door glanced at the Goulds' empty chairs.

"They're probably worried about Andy," George said ingenuously, before Rodman Bishop could stop him.

166

A faintly amused light flickered in Colonel Primrose's eyes.

"They probably thought it was dinnertime," he said cheerfully. "Julius asked me to remind you, Mrs. Latham."

I gathered Sergeant Buck had said something fairly important that demanded Colonel Primrose's presence at once, for actually it was an hour before we ordinarily dined.

I got up promptly. We didn't go home, however. Halfway to the house he said, "Can you drive me to the village?"

"I take it the Sergeant has unearthed vital information?" I said. I was still horribly shaken by what I'd found in the Bishops' library.

He smiled.

"The last man that underestimated Sergeant Buck was electrocuted on June eighteenth at eight-four P.M., Mrs. Latham," he said placidly.

"Oh, dear!" I said. We got into the car. I put my foot on the gas. We went past the Bishops' place at fifty and crossed the bridge over April Harbor Narrows at considerably more.

"Where to?" I asked.

"Police station." Colonel Primrose smiled. "I presume from the way you drive you know where it is."

"We don't enforce laws at April Harbor," I said. Nevertheless, I stopped the car in front of the red brick building near the basement rear of the county courthouse, and pulled on the brake.

"Shall I wait?"

He looked around.

"This is too secluded a spot to leave anybody in who was murderously shot at less than twenty-four hours ago, Mrs. Latham," he said. "You come along."

We went into the bare damp room with its notices of wanted criminals and lost properties. There were spittoons on the dirty wood floor and a large white sign on the wall urging that they be used. To one side was the empty Magistrate's Court, in the rear a row of cells with two drunken negroes snoring loudly. The officer on duty took his feet off the littered table, straightened his screeching swivel chair, and said, "Howdy, Colonel; howdy, miss.

"The Sergeant said to tell you he'd gone up," he added. "There's steps at the end, or you can drive round."

"Where's Officer Flint?"

"He's up with the Sergeant, Colonel."

I followed them into the Magistrate's Court more bewildered than ever. The desk sergeant opened a door by the bench and

167

we went up two flights of stairs. Colonel Primrose must have been in better shape than he looked because I was the one out of breath when we came up to the evil-smelling corridor at the top.

The next to the last of the frosted-glass doorways had "A. L Shryock, County Coroner" printed on it. Colonel Primrose opened the door and we went in. Sergeant Buck was standing by the window, with him a raw-boned young man in a uniform that didn't fit or that he wasn't used to yet. The coroner's desk stood in a corner, behind it along the wall filing cabinets marked with the years and types of Mr. Shryock's professional activities: homicide, drowning, suicide, and so on. Mr. Shryock himself, I was glad to see, was not present.

Sergeant Buck introduced Officer Flint.

"All right, Flint," Colonel Primrose said briskly. "Let's hear it."

"I went on duty at midnight Saturday, Colonel. Around half past twelve I was at the White Lunch on account of a kid throwed a brick at his uncle and it landed in Teddy Pappas's window, square in the middle of a rhubarb pie. He beat it down the street an' I was chasin' him. I caught him an' brought him in, is why I was comin' round Church Circle an' happened to look over at Doc's place. An' all of a sudden I says 'Jeez!' "

Mr. Flint looked from one of us to the other.

"I couldn't figger it out. Certainly looked like Old Lady Potter, but what the hell, I says. So I came closer. I know her, all right, 'cause she sits in the window an' yells at the kids to keep off the grass. Then she's always callin' a cop to pull in a stray dog. 'Course, old Doc's a great guy."

Maggie Potter, I gathered, was not going to be mourned by the local constabulary.

"So there's no mistake about it?" Colonel Primrose said. "You're sure it was Mrs. Potter?"

"Oh, sure, Colonel. I know her. But I couldn't figger out what she was doin'. She came down the stairs, and first thing I know she's headin' off down the hill towards the dock. I got scared, Colonel—I thought she was goin' to kill herself, or somethin'. So I followed her."

"You'd got rid of the boy?"

"Yeah, I'd turned him in. Well, halfway down, about in front of Maxie's barbershop, the goin' wasn't so hot. I guess she was weak, not havin' walked so long. Then she got down to the phone booth outside Toplady's store an' went in. Stayed so

168

long I was beginning to get worried. It wasn't till quarter past one she came out. Then she went over to the dock."

Mr. Flint mopped his brow. Sergeant Buck was standing at somber attention in the corner. Colonel Primrose's black eyes were resting steadily on the red face of the perspiring young policeman, and I suppose I must have been staring at him like a zany.

"I figgered now's the time, but she didn't try to jump in, she just sat there. Course it was a swell night, after the storm, but Jeez, you don't just sit on the dock. Every once in a while she'd start back towards that phone booth and then she'd change her mind again an' go back. I figgered she was off her nut an' I'd call the Doc.

"So I sneaks over to the phone myself, but I couldn't raise him, an' Ella, she's the night operator, she says he's gone to Nag's Head an' he's been tryin' to raise his wife, an' why don't I go an' see if there's anythin' the matter with the old cat."

Mr. Flint grinned sheepishly.

"I says she ought to be ashamed of herself talkin' about a lady like that. I didn' tell her she was just out there settin' on the dock. I figgered there wasn't any call everybody in town knowin' it. Anyways, she looked like somebody with a heap of trouble on her mind, so I just stuck around. Wasn't anythin' else go do anyways. Well, sir, long about half past three she made it to the phone booth an' she stayed in there a long time. Then she headed home, pretty feeble, an' went in the house.

"I ducked back to the phone an' asked Ella who she was callin'. It was somebody at the Colony, Ella says, but she'd hung up again without talkin' to 'em. That makes Ella sore."

I didn't know then that Ella was Mr. Flint's sister. Not that it made any difference. The story sounded perfectly true, and he couldn't possibly have been mistaken in a woman whom everybody in town had known for years. I sat there, thinking as best I could in an almost complete mental fog, while Colonel Primrose was asking a few questions, making sure, as a sort of formality, I supposed, that Flint was sure.

For Flint's story was devastating. If Maggie Potter was sitting at the foot of Church Street from a quarter to one or thereabouts until half past three in the morning—plus the time it took her to get home—all directly under the eye of the night police, then she was not quarreling with Sandra outside the Goulds' garage. Neither was she being an eyewitness of a murder that had taken place at approximately one o'clock. Nor

169

could she have been on the spot at all, or even seen anyone who was.

I looked at Colonel Primrose dumbly. He was nodding his head and biting his lower lip with his upper teeth.

And when Sergeant Buck had escorted Officer Flint out, and come back in, he was still sitting there nodding silently, as if in some curious way he either saw some light in the Stygian gloom or saw none whatsoever—I couldn't tell which.

He looked over at me once. "She was confined to her house for a long time, wasn't she?"

"Seven years," I said. He nodded again and went on chewing his underlip.

Neither I nor the Sergeant spoke. We just watched him, Sergeant Buck with a sort of awed complacency. It was more than I felt. So far as I could see he was completely stymied. He had gone on the assumption that it was Maggie Potter that Hawkins and Andy had heard and seen respectively, and that her brutal, incredible murder in my own living room was the result of her having seen the killing of Sandra Gould and being seen by the murderer there outside the Goulds' garage. And now all that was most definitely out.

Colonel Primrose suddenly snapped out of his nodding meditation, looked absently at me for a moment and then, to my surprise, turned to the rows of cabinet files behind Mr. Shryock's desk. He looked at them for an instant, and turned back to me before I could ask what he expected to find there.

"I'll come back with Buck, Mrs. Latham," he said. "Don't wait dinner for us."

Sergeant Buck's dead pan lit up like an arc light. I was glad to be dismissed, for that reason if for no other.

I was having coffee on the front veranda when Colonel Primrose came back, alone. I found myself wishing Sergeant Buck were with him—there was no telling what new and distinctly ominous discoveries he was out making.

Colonel Primrose pulled up a chair and sat down. I poured him a cup of coffee.

"One lump or two?"

"Straight, please."

He took it from my hand and leaned back with it balanced precariously on his crossed knee. He looked tired. His mouth and chin had a grimness in repose that I hadn't noticed before. Neither of us spoke. I'd been thinking too seriously about the possible implications of Sergeant Buck's discovery to want to inquire into it until he indicated the direction it pointed. For just one thing, there *was* a woman at the garage Saturday night when Sandra Gould was murdered, and if it wasn't Maggie Potter, then it plainly must have been someone else—someone much closer to me than Maggie had ever been.

Colonel Primrose finished a second cup of coffee before he leaned forward and looked at me intently.

"Mrs. Latham—will you tell me one thing, honestly . . . with no hedging?" he asked.

"Probably not," I said.

"I know. This is quite serious for everybody.—Do you know who shot at you Sunday night?"

It was so plainly getting serious for everybody that in spite of my intentions I hardly hesitated.

"I don't like to say, for the simple reason that it just seems so ridiculous in the cold light of day," I began.

"It wouldn't have been so ridiculous if he hadn't missed you."

"I suppose it wouldn't. I thought it was Paul Dikranov. But I haven't any real way of knowing. I thought I smelled those Turkish cigarettes he smokes. It seemed to me I'd have to have more than that to go on. A reason for his doing it, for example."

"The reason's plain enough," he said shortly. "You presumably saw what went on Saturday night in the Goulds' garage."

"Furthermore," I said, "I smelled the cigarette smoke from the chairs on my lawn, and the empty case was way on the other side, by the hedge."

He looked intently at me, I thought a little startled.

"What do you mean?"

"The brass shell—didn't your men find it? It was there in the gap in the hedge when I went to the Goulds' and gone when you and I came back through, just before we found Maggie here."

Colonel Primrose stared at me, and drew a very deep breath. I imagine he was counting ten before he spoke, because when he did speak he was quite calm. In fact he managed a chuckle.

"I shall always remember you, Mrs. Latham," he said, "—apart from being a charming hostess—as the person who helped me the most, in this case.—Listen, Mrs. Latham. Doesn't the fact of that clock mean anything to you, under those circumstances?"

I swallowed the lump of sheer terror that rose in my throat.

"What do you mean?" I said.

"The clock, Mrs. Latham. The clock that you moved from the library desk at The Magnolias."

I stared at him, dumfounded.

"You mustn't think Buck and I are entirely devoid of senses," he said with a polite smile. "He heard it, of course, when he was talking to you, and he didn't hear it when he was talking to me. Well, there were only two possibilities; either someone was interested in your conversation and not in mine —which seemed rather pointless just at this time—or you'd done away with the clock. It was quite obvious where it had stood on the desk. Next time remember to scatter papers about, or you could dust the surface. Also don't forget to lock the drawer *above* the one you hide anything in."

He shook his head at me severely.

"You nearly did a terrible thing, Mrs. Latham. That clock is back in its place. I want it to stay there . . . and nothing is to be said about it. Do you understand that . . . and why?"

I nodded meekly. I expect I did have it coming to me.

"I don't seem to be able to make you see that we're dealing with a perfectly cold-blooded murderer," he went on, a little more kindly. "It's sheer fool's luck you aren't dead and in your grave this moment. I wish you'd try to see that. If it had become known that you'd moved the clock, and knew all that it . . ."

He shook his head.

"There's another thing. You understand now that the woman Sandra was heard quarreling with, just before she was killed, was not Mrs. Potter."

I nodded.

"And consequently that it was someone else."

"Then . . . why was Maggie killed?"

"Because she knew something that made her dangerous to a killer," he said shortly.

"But . . . I don't understand. If she wasn't here—?"

"It's curious," he said, rather oddly. "It still doesn't explain the attempt on your life.—Are you sure you didn't see Sandra Gould hit over the head?"

"I really didn't. I didn't go out of the house till after three o'clock."

"Did you let Jim Gould out—go out onto the porch with him?"

I shook my head. "No, he went too quickly, when he heard you coming. He didn't want to be caught in front of my fire in my husband's old dressing gown, I suppose."

172

Colonel Primrose thought that over a minute.

"It's got to be one of two things," he said. "Either you do know something, or somebody's made a mistake. The mistake could be either that you were the woman the murderer saw, Saturday night, and he thinks you saw him when you didn't, or that Sunday night you were mistaken for that woman."

He shook his head.

"I take it you really weren't there," he said slowly. "And with Mrs. Potter out . . . well, it leaves just one person. And when it gets out who she is, she may be in for trouble. Meaning that I've got to talk now to Lucy Lee."

I was silent a moment. "It was Lucy Lee who was there, quarreling with Sandra?"

He nodded.

"Andy knows it, probably—there's hardly any other reason for his hiding her slippers. Her mother knows it. I don't think anyone else does. I think I can depend on you for Lucy Lee's sake not to tell anyone—especially George, who'd be very likely to blurt it out before I'm ready."

"I won't mention it," I said.

He smiled.

"George's very special quality is inestimable, if it happens to be on your side. His mind is so concerned with present minutiae, and so concentrated on the main point, that he misses all the well-meant efforts to cloud the issue. This afternoon, for example."

He chuckled a little.

"I take it Lucy Lee's exit was violent and abrupt and the others followed in alarm. That in itself was about enough to give the Goulds away."

"What *do* you mean?" I asked.

"Let's see Lucy Lee and find out."

CHAPTER TWENTY-TWO

We went across the lawn and through the hedge. Lucy Lee was at her own cottage. She ran to the door when she heard us on the steps and stopped abruptly. "Oh!" she said. It had a curious deflated sound, as if someone had given her a sharp blow in the stomach. Nevertheless, she opened the screen door and said, "Come in!"

"Is your husband at home?" Colonel Primrose asked.

"I'm sorry. He's just stepped out. He'll be back any minute, unless he meets somebody and they have a drink. That might hold him up—"

She went bravely on. I suppose Colonel Primrose knew as well as I did that Lucy Lee had thought we were Andy and that he'd been gone a long time already.

"We'll wait, if you don't mind."

She gave him a stricken glance. "Not at all—won't you sit down? I can't imagine what's keeping Andy."

Her round lower jaw trembled a little. She caught her lip between her white even little teeth and batted her eyes to keep back the tears.

"I wonder if you know, Mrs. Thorp," Colonel Primrose said gently, "the reason your husband is acting the way he is?"

She stared at him desperately. "I don't know what you mean—"

"Perhaps I'd better explain. You see, it's the general opinion locally that your husband is acting like a first-class fool."

Lucy Lee flushed wretchedly.

"For instance: he's gone to the most extraordinary trouble to lie, and to conceal evidence, to protect an extremely ungrateful young woman who in my opinion needs nothing quite so much as a good sound spanking."

She stared at him with parted lips, breathlessly. Then she flushed violently.

"In the first place," Colonel Primrose went on deliberately, "she's allowed herself to get so involved in housekeeping that

174

she lets the lilies of the field completely absorb him. And now she's too much of a coward to come forward and tell the truth about Saturday night. You see—nobody has any doubt, my dear young lady, that it was you quarreling with Sandra Gould . . . or that your mother and your husband are both lying like troopers to protect you."

He leaned forward. Lucy Lee, flattened like some odd concave little figure in the corner of the sofa, stared at him, utterly fascinated.

"Well?" he said.

Lucy Lee nodded simply. "I hated her so," she said miserably.

"Was she dead when you went into the garage?" Colonel Primrose asked. His voice was still as kindly as at first.

Lucy Lee's dark eyes widened in horror.

"You did go in. There's grease on your slippers."

She stared frantically at him, and at me. "My slippers!"

Colonel Primrose nodded. "The ones your husband tried to clean, and buried when he found he couldn't."

I don't think that either he or I realized just what was happening behind her blank incredulous stare, or even that she was getting up until she was on her feet, halfway across the room, heading for her bedroom. She threw open the door and flew to the closet. I glanced at Colonel Primrose and followed her. She was throwing shoes, her own tiny ones and Andy's huge ones, out like a spaniel unearthing a rabbit.

Then suddenly she stopped and leaned against the doorframe, shaking with terror. "They're gone!" she whispered. "Where are they?"

"Mr. Parran has them," Colonel Primrose said quietly, from behind my back. "We also have the blue flowers. You know, Mrs. Thorp, I think if I were you I'd do something, just to keep Andy from barging into Parran's office and confessing to a crime he didn't commit just to save your skin—because I can tell you, if he did do that, he'd have a hard time laughing it off. For more reasons than one."

Lucy Lee pushed the mass of short chestnut curls back from her forehead and sat down limply on the edge of her bed, staring at us in a sort of dazed wretchedness.

I didn't say anything because I didn't know what to say. I couldn't say, "Tell him everything, all about it," because I didn't know what was in her mind. Since the Elsie Carter business I'd lost any notion that I was anything but the decoy Colo-

175

nel Primrose had called me—jokingly, as I'd fondly thought. Not so much a decoy, I thought now, as an entree into April Harbor's private lives.

She had already come to a decision by herself. "She was dead," she whispered.

"At what time?" Colonel Primrose said quickly.

She shook her head.

"I don't know. I'd waited so long for Andy, and he didn't come. She wasn't in either. I couldn't bear it. Jim didn't care, except for me. I tried to get him to go help me find them, but he wouldn't. So . . . I went alone."

She stopped, for so long that I thought she was in a sort of trance. I touched her hand, lying lifeless and cold on the tufted spread. She clung suddenly to my fingers.

"I took Jim's keys and went out Mother's back door. I was a little frightened. I'm a dreadful coward, but I had a flashlight. I looked around for something, some sort of a . . . weapon. I spotted Jim's big monkey wrench, lying in the grass. I picked it up and went on to the garage. I opened the side door . . . and I heard the engine."

Her face contorted with a spasm of pain.

"I thought it was Andy. I dashed around and opened the big doors and went in. Then I saw it was Sandra. I felt her pulse. I knew she was dead. And she had Rosemary's blue flowers clutched in her hand. I yanked them away and turned off the motor. Then I got to thinking—"

"Thinking what?" Colonel Primrose said quietly, because she'd stopped again and was staring straight ahead of her at the litter of shoes on the floor.

"Oh, everything. How easy it was, and where Andy was."

"What did you do?"

It was like talking to someone under a hypnotic spell.

"I closed the doors the way I'd found them and came out."

Lucy Lee twisted her fingers together in spasms of despair.

"I went up to Mother's and told her. We came back together. She wiped off the handle of the wrench—I'd left it on the running board—and put it on the floor. We switched on the motor again and closed up the garage and went back to the house. I thought she went to bed, but then she went back to find Grace."

Colonel Primrose looked at her silently for a moment, sitting there on the bed.

"And you thought Andy had killed her, of course?"

176

"Oh, I don't know. All I knew was she was dead . . . and I didn't care . . . I was glad!"

"Yes. And at twelve o'clock . . . when you'd waited for Andy, and he hadn't come, and you'd gone out to have a look for him?"

I must say he was much gentler with her than he had been with anybody else.

She stared at him for an instant as if he possessed some kind of second powers.

"I suppose they were only trying to be decent to me. I . . . I couldn't help it. I didn't mean to be so perfectly foul. I . . . I thought she'd gone, I didn't know she was coming back. I couldn't bear to hear her telling him how ghastly it must be to be married to me, and how wonderful he was, and Mother couldn't stop me. Oh, I didn't want her to get him away from me!"

She threw herself down on the pillow in a paroxysm of weeping.

"I didn't want her to! I love him! Oh, Andy, please come back!"

I looked at Colonel Primrose, virtually as shattered as Lucy Lee but for quite another reason. I was terribly sorry for her, but I couldn't help feeling still more upset at seeing her husband's and her mother's alibis knocked sky-winding at the drop of a hat.

"And Hawkins . . . ?"

She was quieter now as she raised her head and looked at him.

"Hawkins? He didn't come down. He just opened the window and said, 'Mis' Lucy, it ain' fitten for a lady to fight with a she-devil.' I guess he was right."

Colonel Primrose looked at me and shook his head.

We left shortly after that, only to run into young Andy, with a red leather overnight case in his hand, trudging down to the cottage from his grandmother's.

"Taking a trip, son?" Colonel Primrose inquired.

"I'm going to New York with Daddy if he hasn't gone yet," young Andy said sturdily, his blue eyes round and sober. He negotiated the steps on his fat short legs, tugging at the case.

"So he has gone," Colonel Primrose said. "I suppose it's what you'd expect. It's the trouble with young people now. They can't take it, I'm afraid."

I was a little annoyed. "I should think it would distress you

177

to recollect that it was your generation that produced these spineless jellyfish," I said. "Now look at young Andy. Why didn't you produce people like him?"

Colonel Primrose chuckled.

"He's what we were. The school-of-hard-knocks sort of thing."

"He'll coddle his children and complain about their being jellyfish," I said.

"Maybe. We've got to see Hawkins now. I should have known the truth wasn't in him. The way he practically accused Jim Gould of murder didn't prepare me for his lying to protect Lucy Lee."

Hawkins was in the Goulds' pantry wiping the dishes, his Bible propped up against the cookie jar on the shelf over the sink. He was mumbling the most unchristian sort of noises. He came out into the kitchen, head raised, more the shepherd of his flock than the Goulds' butler.

"Mis' Alice she lyin' down. The Lawd done struck 'em down!"

"Not Miss Alice!"

I was terribly startled for an instant.

"No, no! No, no! De 'Gyptians. Fayroh's daughter."

Which, I presumed, was Sandra. Though there was not much reason to think he was talking sense rather than his own brand of mumbo-jumbo.

"Hawkins," said Colonel Primrose. "I have been told it was Miss Lucy Lee you saw quarreling with young Mrs. Gould."

The old negro shook his head. "Ah don' recollect that, suh. Ah mus' have been asleep."

"You didn't see Miss Lucy Lee there, at about half past twelve?"

"No, suh. Ah didn' see nobody, Colonel."

"What about Mrs. Potter, Dr. Potter's wife? Have you seen her recently?"

"No, suh. Cain' say as Ah have."

"I mean this noon, Hawkins."

"Oh, Ah saw her this *noon*. Yas, suh. Ah saw her so plain this *noon* Ah just ain' worryin'."

"You didn't see her Saturday night."

Hawkins shook his old head. "Ah didn' even know she was out. It was mah impression she was a *confirmed* invalid."

We went on down the steps towards the garage.

"There's no use trying to get anything out of Hawkins he doesn't want to tell," I said.

178

"I suppose not," Colonel Primrose said absently. We went on down the brick walk.

"How do you suppose the monkey wrench got here?" he asked, stopping.

"Where?" I asked.

It was quite dark. I couldn't see any trace left by a monkey wrench that had lain there three days before.

"Lucy Lee said she picked it up lying on the ground on her way down. Buck found a reddish black spot on the grass just about here the next morning. Or hadn't I mentioned that?"

"No," I said. "But don't be disturbed—I'm sure it's only one of the things you haven't mentioned."

He grinned.

"Which, in view of your openhearted, generous assistance in such matters as the suicide note, the flowers and the clock, is certainly extremely low of me. Well, that's like life, Mrs. Latham."

"I suppose it is," I said.

"However, Buck did find a blood stain just along here in the grass Sunday morning."

I could see him cocking his head down and peering up at me in the dark.

"Would you take that to mean she was struck here, and dragged over to the garage, Mrs. Latham?"

I caught my breath. "I wouldn't take any part of it, Colonel Primrose. I just wouldn't know."

"It would mean she had to be carried or dragged a considerable distance."

He glanced over at the white corner of the garage. The light over the door was on, although none of the Goulds had had a car out. Hawkins, I knew, was still sleeping over it, which was odd, because normally he would have been most reluctant to sleep over violent death.

"Parran's case takes care of that better than mine," he added.

"Parran's case!"

"The State's Attorney. Didn't you know about him?"

I stared at him in amazement. "But I thought you—"

He shook his head.

"Parran's case is quite simple. Jim Gould came from your house, got as far as the back door there, heard a noise, picked up the wrench, which he says himself was there on the porch, went down to the gate, dragged his wife away from a blistering attack—actually physical, as the blue flowers show—on Rose-

179

mary Bishop, struck her over the head. He threw the wrench away, and he and Rosemary went off just leaving her there. Mrs. Gould and Lucy Lee found her when they were out, thought she was dead, and together, half dragging and half carrying her, got her to the garage and into Thorp's car and turned on the engine. That accounts for a good many things. The scratches on her legs. The fact that the wrench was removed from the back porch, the Goulds' continued misstatements. After all, theirs is really the only very powerful motive —from Mr. Parran's point of view."

"But . . . you don't think that, do you?"

He shook his head.

"No. That's why I said 'from Parran's point of view.' No, I take it Lucy Lee's story was quite true. I think they found her in the car. Or at any rate that Lucy Lee did. And I should say that if Mrs. Gould had known Sandra had been slugged with the wrench, she'd have been cool enough to wipe off the business end as well as the handle. And she'd have put it back neatly somewhere. No, I think that wrench points to incrimination, Mrs. Latham. Somebody did it exactly that way to point to somebody else. I haven't the slightest doubt the prints had been wiped off some time before Lucy Lee and her mother came along."

We had stopped in front of the garage. I could remember so dreadfully clearly tugging, Saturday night, at these double doors, trying to get them open so that Alice Gould and I could shut off the running engine. And with Alice, I thought now, knowing all the time what terrible thing awaited us inside, in Andy Thorp's car! And then, quite suddenly, something flashed into my mind that I had never thought of since that night.

"I know why somebody shot at me," I said.

He looked quickly over at me. "You've thought of something?"

"Yes. While I was standing there, after Alice had gone to get Jim, I heard something, or somebody, outside. I couldn't see anything, but couldn't that have been . . ."

"Probably."

Colonel Primrose nodded. "He could see you plainly, since you were just in the light there—"

"It was much brighter than that, I'd turned on the light in the garage."

"That's right. And he wasn't sure whether you could have

180

seen him—or she wasn't sure whether you could have seen her. Well, that's about it."

He stood looking up at Hawkins's window for a long time without a word. In fact he said nothing until we had got virtually to my porch.

"There's one more thing I think I can tell you," he said soberly. "Mrs. Carter saw Mr. Rodman Bishop going across the lawn from your house this morning, round eleven o'clock."

"That's probably what she meant when she said it was a public scandal the way he hangs around my house," I said.

He chuckled a little. "I don't know about that, Mrs. Latham —unless she's seen him there more than once. But it might be described as sort of a private scandal—just among ourselves— that the time she saw him this morning was the time in which he declared he was bottling his blackberry wine in his cellar."

"My dear Colonel," I said, "Elsie Carter could have seen him in North China when he was salmon fishing in Norway. You know she's—"

"I know," he said. "But it is rather odd that the blackberry wine was being bottled in the winter kitchen, isn't it?"

I didn't say anything for a minute. Things were piling up faster than I either liked or could keep track of.

"Sergeant Buck again, I suppose?"

"Precisely. The wine was moved to the cellar just before lunch."

It seemed so incredible to me that anyone could seriously suspect Rodman Bishop of murdering Maggie Potter. I said so.

"I know," he said. "It does sound ridiculous. But these are deep waters, Mrs. Latham. We're sounding far down."

"And anyway, aren't you connecting her murder with Sandra's any more?"

He looked a little surprised. "Oh, very definitely. They were most certainly killed by the same hand."

"But Rodman Bishop had no conceivable profit in killing Sandra—and could even Elsie Carter tell you a reason he had for killing poor Maggie Potter?"

He shook his head. "She couldn't, much to her regret, I think. Still, you underestimate Mrs. Carter."

"Rot," I said rudely.

"Yes, you do. I'm very much afraid if it hadn't been for her I shouldn't ever have got to the roots of this business."

"And have you?" I asked, sardonically and with a sort of amiable malice, just to hear him admit he hadn't.

181

"Yes, I rather think I have, Mrs. Latham."

I stopped short, my foot on the bottom step of my porch, utterly stupefied.

"You mean . . . you know who . . ."

He nodded.

"How simply ghastly!"

Colonel Primrose nodded again and smiled grimly.

"Ghastlier than you'd think, Mrs. Latham."

CHAPTER TWENTY-THREE

I can't remember spending any other period of my life that was as awful as the next few hours.

If he had only told me! But I'm not sure it would have helped. In fact, as I learned afterwards, he only told Sergeant Buck and Mr. Parran step by step. And of course if he *had* told me, I probably would have given it all away time after time.

It was nine o'clock when Colonel Primrose, complaining a little because he hadn't more time and hadn't more facilities for detection at his disposal, sent Sergeant Buck to the cottage to bring Lucy Lee. Buck found her, he said later, huddled with young Andy in a tear-stained heap fast asleep on the bed where we'd left her—and with the door wide open. Colonel Primrose's lips tightened a little at that. I gathered he hadn't been sure she was safe even then, which was why he'd sent Buck over instead of telephoning her. Why he waited to hear from the Sergeant I did not know, but he sat there until the telephone rang from the cottage. I didn't hear what he said, but after a few moments I heard him cranking my phone and asking the operator for the Goulds' house. Then he came back to the porch and waited until we saw a flashlight through the trees near the garage and heard Jim calling Hawkins to come down.

The phone rang again, and Colonel Primrose went in as if he'd been expecting it. After a bit I heard him wind the crank to signal, and ask for the Bishops' place. I heard him say, "Try again, operator, someone must be there." And I knew he'd been checking up on the clock.

He came back to the porch.

"I think we'll go inside, if you don't mind, Mrs. Latham," he said. "There are some faces I want to have a look at. Anyway, it might be a little dangerous to sit about in the dark."

I turned on the lights inside.

Then, while I was still getting in more chairs, people began turning up in a curious way, as if their coming was quite pointless and yet at the same time fraught with some dreadful

183

significance. Mr. Parran came with the coroner, Mr. Shryock. Sergeant Buck came with Lucy Lee, the Goulds came. Oddly enough, I thought, they had brought Hawkins with them. He looked—as he puts it—as if he knew what was going to happen so well he wasn't worrying. Which wasn't true of anyone else there. There's no doubt of it, Anglo-Saxons are worriers. Even the fish-gray eyes in Sergeant Buck's iron visage were troubled when they rested on Rosemary or Lucy Lee.

Lucy Lee was still pretty much of a mess, or perhaps she only looked it because Rosemary was so immaculately detached and casual and because Alice Gould was delicately and fragilely herself again. I didn't know then that the blue pinched look around her mouth came from anything more fundamentally wrong than worry over her two children. As Hawkins once remarked, "When you got children these days Ah tell you, Mis' Grace, you got sumpin'." I thought that was the trouble with Alice then.

Nathan Kaufman sat beside Rosemary, his jaw thrust out, his face flushed and mottled. It was pretty hot but not that hot. Rodman Bishop, still in his shrunk seersuckers, fuming a little, sat on the other side of Rosemary, and George Barrol fidgeted about until he grounded near the dining-room door by Alice Gould.

And then Colonel Primrose looked us all over, deliberately and quite as detached in his way as Rosemary was in hers.

"I'm taking unfair advantage of all of you," he said coolly, "for the simple reason that I want to teach you a lesson."

My eyes rested for a moment on Jim Gould, whose duty to his mother—and also the solid presences of Kaufman and Rodman Bishop, I imagine—kept him from being near Rosemary. He was gazing at her more like a devoted spaniel than a bitter and disillusioned young man who'd married a dance-hall girl destined to violent death.

Colonel Primrose went deliberately on, a bitter irony growing in his voice.

"The trouble with you people is that, desiring something, you can't imagine not going to the extreme of murder, even, to get it."

He looked at Jim.

"That's why it was so simple, apparently, for every person in this room—except one who had better knowledge—to believe that Jim Gould, an honest, honorable and even puritanical young man, could come back to his house after his wife and Rosemary Bishop had had an altercation, strike Sandra Gould

184

over the head and put her in the car in a closed garage with the engine running."

His level gaze fell on Rosemary.

"You didn't go out to meet Jim that Saturday night, of course, Miss Bishop. You went out to meet his wife, and you had a meeting with her—which we found out about with so much difficulty—in the course of which she, no doubt, demanded that you leave April Harbor at once, and you, no doubt, declined to do so till you had found out what Sandra Gould's connection with Mr. Dikranov had been. Possibly you'll tell us now how this meeting came about?"

"Just a minute," Jim Gould said quickly. He leaned forward, disregarding Rodman Bishop's scowl and shaking off Mr. Kaufman's restraining hand on his arm. "Where *is* Mr. Dikranov?"

"Mr. Dikranov is in New York. He had business."

"My brother-in-law had business in New York too."

"Mr. Gould," said Colonel Primrose, "you will have to take my word for it at the present that the situations were not the same.—And please do not interrupt me again."

He stared coldly at Jim for an instant and turned back to Rosemary. She was pale but perfectly self-possessed. It was her father and her lawyer who were disturbed.

"I don't mind telling you," she said, in her cool dusky voice. "Paul said you knew already, and there'd be no point in holding anything back."

I saw Rodman Bishop and Nathan Kaufman exchange uneasy glances.

"I came back from the dance with my father and Paul. It was hot and sultry and I went directly upstairs. I wanted a cigarette before I went to bed. There weren't any in the box, and I'd left my vanity and cigarette case in Paul's pocket, so I put on a dressing gown and went down to ask him for it. I heard Dad and Paul on the porch, having a nightcap. Their coats were hanging on the newel post. I put my hand in Paul's pocket to get my case, and I found the note."

"A note written, though neither addressed nor signed, by Sandra Gould," Colonel Primrose said curtly to all of us, "making an assignation in the Goulds' garage as soon as she got back. Yes, Miss Bishop—you read it."

"I read it," Rosemary said.

She shrugged her slim bare shoulders, brown against the pale blue of her cotton evening frock. It was a statement, not an excuse for her conduct.

"After what had been going on all evening I was pretty annoyed. I was hurt too, I suppose, because Paul had denied knowing her. I put the note back in his pocket, went upstairs, slipped my dress back on and went out. I don't know exactly what I thought I could do. I suppose I was spoiling for a fight with somebody . . . just to get everything off my chest."

A sudden smile danced in her gray eyes.

"Paul's coat was gone when I came back in at two. I supposed he'd gone to keep his rendezvous."

She smiled again, in amusement at herself. "I couldn't very well object, because I'd been keeping one with Jim. But we weren't near the garage, Colonel Primrose. We went to a place we used to go to, on the beach, after he'd sent Sandra away. We had a sort of 'Last Ride Together' notion, I suppose."

She paused, and said simply: "We didn't kill Sandra. It would have killed everything for us, either alone or together, if we had. I did say I wished he'd drowned her when he had the chance, and he said I didn't, really, because . . . well, things don't work out when they're got—that way. And of course I didn't wish it, really."

Colonel Primrose smiled faintly. He turned to Rodman Bishop.

"And you, Mr. Bishop?" he said pleasantly. "Where were you when all this was going on?"

"I was in bed asleep," Rodman Bishop said aggressively, beetling his shaggy brows.

"You didn't hear Dikranov go out?"

"I didn't."

"Did you, Mr. Barrol?"

George looked uncomfortable.

"Well, as a matter of fact, you see I don't often drink anything after dinner, and what they gave me at the club, and the excitement and the heat and all that sort of knocked me out. So I wasn't myself exactly."

"Darling, you were boiled," Rosemary said amiably. "I accused you of it then and you said you were cold sober."

"That's not so, Rosemary. I was sleepy, and my stomach was a little upset."

"Is that why Paul had to carry you upstairs and put you to bed?"

Everyone smiled, even Sergeant Buck. George blinked.

"I was sober enough to hear Paul go out," he said stoutly. "At least I supposed it was Paul, if Uncle Rod was in bed. You clump, Rosemary, but not that heavily."

186

I thought Rodman Bishop would quietly explode. Instead his face, at first purple with fury as George was talking, turned suddenly gray when Colonel Primrose turned back to him.

"You bottled the wine in the winter kitchen, Mr. Bishop," he said. "Not in the cellar. And not at eleven o'clock. You were seen at that time in Mrs. Latham's garden—not long after Mrs. Potter had come here."

"Just a minute," Nathan Kaufman said sharply. His red bulbous nose jutted out towards Colonel Primrose. "My client has nothing to say at this time, Colonel."

"Ah," Colonel Primrose said politely. "We have at last discovered who your client is?"

He looked placidly at Rodman Bishop, whose tough old face was again inflamed with rage. He shook his head.

"It doesn't make much difference where you bottled the wine, Mr. Bishop," he said. "I don't think the mere fact that like all Americans you mistrust foreigners—especially suave ones—and that your daughter was headed for unhappiness would be enough to make you kill the woman who had prevented her happiness. No, there's something deeper, and quite different, at the bottom of all this."

He looked slowly around the circle of motionless faces there in my living room.

"There has been one outstanding problem in this case from the beginning," he said. "There are always two main problems in every case. Who had the motive to kill? Who had the opportunity? In this case the answer to the second question was almost absurdly simple."

He hesitated for a moment, still looking slowly from face to face.

"The answer to the question of opportunity was . . . everybody. Jim Gould, Mrs. Gould, Mrs. Thorp, Andy Thorp; Miss Rosemary Bishop, Mr. Bishop, Mr. Dikranov; Dr. Potter, Mr. Barrol here; Mrs. Latham, even Mrs. Potter whose dead body was found in this room Monday morning.

"There was one other person," he continued, "who also had the opportunity . . . and who, oddly enough, nobody has even thought of."

I think no one in the room moved, even to look at anyone else.

"Now, when opportunity leads you nowhere, the question of motive in any case becomes very important. In this present case it has been paramount from the beginning. The point has always been, What was the motive from which Mrs. Sandra

187

Gould was murdered? And here again we have an odd situation. For while there are not so many people who could have a motive to commit that act, there are nevertheless far too many. Allow me to point them out to you.

"Mr. Jim Gould. The motive is obvious. He wanted to free himself from a wife who refused him any legal release.

"Miss Bishop. To free the man she obviously is still in love with.

"Mrs. Alice Gould. Again obvious. To free her son.

"Mr. Bishop. Obvious too. To enable his daughter to marry the man she is in love with.

"Mrs. Lucy Lee Thorp. Equally obvious. To free herself from a rival or supposed rival.

"Mr. Dikranov. To free himself of an incumbrance.

"So far these motives have—all of them—one thing in common," he went on quietly. "They are all calculating. Some of them are selfish, some unselfish. They would all lead, in a greater or less degree, to a planned act of murder. There is another possible murderer of Mrs. Sandra Gould, who could have had both the motive and the opportunity—Andy Thorp. That motive would be blind passion, jealous fury . . . and it would be the only uncalculating motive of the whole lot."

Colonel Primrose stopped, smiling a little.

"I've tried to find a motive for Mr. Barrol," he said.

George gulped, horrified. *"Me?"* he gasped. "Oh, my goodness!"

"We can't presume he was in love with Sandra, when he'd not met her until noon that day. If he had, for some odd reason, suddenly felt impelled to kill her, you'd imagine he would have managed to do it out there in the water, when all he had to do was hold her head under for a while."

I couldn't, try as I would, visualize (as Sergeant Buck says) George being consumed by a grand passion. Neither could George, I'm afraid.

"So the problem was always clear," Colonel Primrose went on. "There was no point in worrying about *a* motive. The problem has always been to find *the* motive. The *one* motive that led directly to Sandra Gould's murder—just as there was one plain motive that led to Mrs. Potter's."

"What was that?" Nathan Kaufman said brusquely.

"Fear. Fear of what she'd come to tell. Panic too. And there was another point about Mrs. Potter's murder, easy to answer in her case, which must be answered about Sandra's too. Why was she killed at that particular time? Why not a month before, or a year before, or two weeks later? Mrs. Potter was killed because she had to be stopped at once from communicating with me. Why was Sandra killed when she was?

"Now, we all realize that Miss Rosemary's return is the obvious answer. It's the single new thing that happened that could, for instance, bring things to a head. Such things, for example, as the desperate unhappiness in 'Jim Gould's soul, in her own certainly, probably in her father's and in Mrs. Gould's."

The room was perfectly silent. I could hear the grandfather clock on the landing going, "Tick, tock, tick, tock," heavily and evenly. Suddenly it brought into my mind that other clock with its tickety-tick, tickety-tock; tickety-tick, tickety-tock. I tried, desperately, to keep it out of my consciousness.

"A second fusing point was Sandra Gould's meeting with Mr. Dikranov, the business of the boat was still a third—for Andy Thorp and Lucy Lee Thorp. However, there is another kind of timeliness that crimes can have—they can be psychologically timely, the culmination of a long train of emotional factors. They can be acts performed as a result of the sudden collapse of a person's endurance of—for instance—continued resentment, or even continued envy or exasperation. No particular sudden act is needed to set such passions in action. They pile up . . . and someday the dam bursts.

"It's here," he went on slowly, "that you run into the borderline of passion and ignorance and prejudice that breaks out into hysteria. I told you that one person who had the opportunity to murder Sandra Gould was one that none of us had thought of. That person also had a motive of the sort I'm describing. It's strange we didn't think of him . . . because from the beginning he has purposely lied to us, misleading us from the very start.

"When we arrived at the garage, Saturday night, someone was already there, and had been there for some time. When we came here after Mrs. Potter was killed, that person had been here. That he was in both places occurred to nobody, it was taken entirely for granted. And this person is the only one, of all the persons in this room, who steadily and openly denounced Sandra Gould, and kept on doing it, steadily and openly, after her death as well as before. He has tried by lying to give Jim Gould and the other Goulds—as well as himself—unbreakable alibis, by lying about the time of the murder and the woman whom he heard quarreling with Sandra in the garage."

189

Colonel Primrose turned suddenly to the corner of the room, his voice swelling in the utter silence.

"He is a worshiper of a God, and his God is a God of vengeance, whose hand strikes down the evildoer!"

As Colonel Primrose spoke a strange and blood-chilling thing happened. Old Hawkins rose to his feet, his white kinky head trembling, eyes shining through his gold-rimmed spectacles, lips moving fervently, hands clasped on his breast; and when Colonel Primrose stopped he said, "Amen, Lawd, amen!"

And as Sergeant Buck put one hand on his arm his old voice rolled out again, strong and sonorous: "An' de city of Babylon was crumbled to dust! Amen, Lawd, amen!"

Mr. Parran followed them out, in a silence such as I trust I shall never hear again.

Then Alice Gould got up. "Not *Hawkins?*" she cried softly. "How did you *know?*"

"By many things, Mrs. Gould," Colonel Primrose said somberly. "Including information left by the hand of the dead. I have just learned that Mrs. Potter spent that last morning in writing, before she came out here to her death. I haven't seen what she wrote yet—it's at her house. I'll get it in the morning. I have no doubt it is her account, as an eyewitness, of the information she possessed that led up to her death."

He shrugged his shoulders wearily.

"Well," he said, "I must apologize—"

And just then I couldn't stand any longer not being able to understand one particular thing.

"But, Colonel Primrose," I cried, "the—"

The words faltered on my lips as I spoke them. I hadn't realized what a strain this must have been on him. He raised one hand sharply to his heart, stared at me in speechless pain for an instant, stumbled forward, knocking a large vase of gladiolus winding and crashing to the floor, and then fell back in his chair in a dead faint.

I think I was by his side first. "Call Dr. Potter, Jim!" I cried. "Where's Sergeant Buck?"

Sergeant Buck, I've known since then, has genie blood in him. You don't have to rub a lamp or touch a ring; you simply touch the Colonel and there he is.

He had Colonel Primrose lying on the floor, collar undone, in an instant.

"You'd best leave him be, miss—excuse me, ma'am," he said

stiffly. "I can't visualize a woman taking care of the Colonel. So if you'd just as leave scram, ma'am."

I scrammed, out onto the porch. When the others had gone and I came back, Sergeant Buck had moved him. He had also cleaned up the broken litter of one of my great-grandmother's vases.

CHAPTER TWENTY-FOUR

I picked up the evening paper, still unopened where Julius had left it with the afternoon mail, and sat down to read it, not knowing anything else to do. My brain was still whirling. It all seemed so shapeless, someway. I couldn't understand anything, and I tried to clear it all out of my mind and not think about it.

I was terribly distressed, naturally, about Colonel Primrose, and I had some vague notion of seeing Dr. Potter when he came in to find out if there was anything I could do for him— in spite of Sergeant Buck. The night was incredibly still. I heard a car start somewhere, and another came along the road. It didn't occur to me that Dr. Potter could have got out so quickly, not until I heard someone on my back stairs and a car started in my own back drive.

The Sergeant, I thought, had probably guessed I was waiting to waylay Dr. Potter and had smuggled him in through the back. I sat there a few moments more, and went upstairs. The hall was quiet . . . too quiet, I realized with a sudden sinking feeling in the pit of my stomach. I hurried along it and tapped on Colonel Primrose's door. There was no answer. I opened it; the room was empty.

It seems strange to me now that I should have been so upset about it, but of course I was frightfully upset already, about everything. If Colonel Primrose had to be ill, there was no doubt that the hospital was the best place for him, but their not even telling me was dreadfully annoying. Even a hotelkeeper would be notified, I thought. It was more than exasperating, it was simply maddening. The man could be dying for all I cared, but the idea of his wretched sergeant sneaking him out was a little too much. And, after all, he was my guest.

I went back to my room, got out my car keys and went downstairs. My car was in the drive. I got in and switched on the motor, and ten minutes later I stopped in front of the tiny memorial hospital next to the courthouse.

The nurse at the desk, her face a sea-sick green from the

shade over the switchboard, shook her head. "No patient for Dr. Potter this evening. Perhaps he took him to his house."

If I had had any sense at all I would have gone home then, immediately. But there isn't anything more determined, or senseless, than an officious woman. I'd often said just that about Elsie Carter, and now not even Elsie herself could have strode more officiously across the narrowest street and marched into Dr. Potter's house, bent on being of assistance where none was wanted.

I was inside the hall before I realized that the house was as still as death, and moreover that I hadn't seen either Colonel Primrose's car or Dr. Potter's in the street. I took a step forward in the dimly lighted hall, and then stopped dead in my tracks as a sudden panicky intuition struck me completely aghast.

It was all perfectly obvious. The whole business of Hawkins, impossible from the beginning, as I'd so clearly recognized at least in my subconscious mind, was a blind, Colonel Primrose's sudden illness when I was about to mention the clock was a farce. They had called Dr. Potter out to confront him with his guilt and trap him into confessing it. And I understood now why Colonel Primrose had been so interested in Elsie Carter— Elsie with her conviction that the poor man had been slowly killing his wife for years.

Then it was Sandra that was killed in fear, because she'd found it out, and Maggie was killed later, even though she knew it was coming and was struggling to Colonel Primrose to save herself.

I leaned against the stair rail. The picture of that woman sitting down there at the foot of Church Street, in the dark, trying to make up her mind to tell somebody, afraid to be in the house . . . It made me sick to think of it.

The idea of going home was worse still. I had to sit down and think it over. I went over to the room to my right, Maggie's sitting room. There was no light there. I had just had the unpleasant thought that Maggie's ghost must certainly haunt this room where for seven years she'd spent all her waking hours—and in what terror I could only guess. I stepped inside, and then suddenly, without the faintest warning, a light went sharply on.

I was staring, blinded for an instant and utterly aghast, into the horrified face of Colonel Primrose.

I dimly saw Sergeant Buck towering behind him, but all I

had eyes for was the Colonel and the expression on his face. Emotions passed over it so transparently and so kaleidoscopically that I could have laughed if I had not been terrified out of my wits. There was amazement and shock on it, horror and incredulity.

I saw his lips move almost mechanically as he stared at me.

"*Grace Latham!*" he said. "*What—*"

The telephone on the desk rang noisily.

Then I saw Mr. Parran, in the shadows behind Sergeant Buck, and staring at me like all the rest of them, in dumfounded consternation.

He moved towards the telephone. Colonel Primrose's hand raised quickly. "No!" he said. He turned to me, his black eyes boring into mine.

"What are you doing here, Mrs. Latham?" he asked. His voice was tense and hard.

I opened my mouth to answer him, but for a moment I couldn't speak. "I . . . I came to see what was the matter with you," I said then. "I've just been to the hospital—"

The telephone rang again.

Colonel Primrose's face cleared. He motioned to Sergeant Buck who turned off the glaring light in the sitting room. The bell rang again and again, incessantly.

"Get over here, Mrs. Latham," he said. I could see him dimly in the faint light from the hall. "Behind the sofa. Get down . . . down on the floor. Stay there, and for God's sake keep quiet. Get back, Parran.—I thought he'd phone to make sure."

I got back behind the little Victorian sofa in the corner. There was a quiet movement of feet, then silence and darkness in the room again. My throat was so parched with terror that it ached painfully, my heart was pounding violently.

How long we waited there I don't know. It couldn't have been long—no longer than it took for anyone to get from the telephone booth at the foot of Church Street to the Potters' house at the top. It seemed ages to me, cramped there behind the high-backed horsehair sofa in the musty airless room where Maggie Potter had spent her days. And then, sounding through the silent house with a queer dreadful sinisterness, came another ring. It was not the telephone, it was the bell at the front door. Then there was another silence, agelong; and then the sound of a window, somewhere near by, opening gently. And a foot somewhere touching the bare floor.

I don't know whether I could hear someone coming stealthily but swiftly nearer and nearer, or whether it was terror lending sounds to my imagination. But suddenly I knew there was someone in the room, moving across it, nearer and nearer, even before I could actually hear. I tried to hold my breath, to keep my heart from beating so dreadfully that it seemed to fill the house. Then a sharp little splatter of sound as someone struck a match, and I could hear the noise of drawers being pulled, hastily, frantically, out of a desk. Then the sharp rustle of papers. Another match struck, the papers rustled again . . . and then I could hear a breath sharply drawn and a choked snarl that was half a cry of dread and horror.

Suddenly the glaring light went on and there was a rush of feet. I crawled up, crouching, leaning against the wall behind me, and looked over the high back of the sofa. Across from me, on the other side of the room, stood Paul Dikranov, as suave and unmoved as ever. He was not looking at me. His eyes were fastened on the figure at Maggie Potter's desk.

I grasped desperately at the back of the sofa and stared, shivering with fright and quite unbelieving, at the man crouching at bay there, glaring at us in a fury of terror, one hand holding a revolver pointed directly at Colonel Primrose in the doorway, the other desperately clutching a crumpled mass of papers.

For an instant no one spoke. Then Colonel Primrose moved slowly in from the doorway, and Sergeant Buck's great form loomed to my left.

The man at his desk shrank back, his face white and dreadful with fear. His quivering lips opened. "It's a trap!" he screamed.

Colonel Primrose took another step towards him.

"It's a trap, Mr. Barrol," he said. "And you're in it. You might as well give up, Mr. Barrol. I knew you'd come, because you're a coward—you were afraid of her, afraid of what she'd written and left behind her, even after you'd murdered her to keep her still."

The revolver in George Barrol's hand shook. He stared, horribly. Colonel Primrose took another step into the room.

"That's why you killed Sandra Gould too. You were a coward—and when you thought you were going to be drowned out there Saturday night, you confessed to her, you told her what you'd done seven years ago, the thing that's been on your soul ever since . . . because you couldn't face death with it burning there."

Sergeant Buck moved silently forward a step.

195

"Because it's all down in the coroner's report, Barrol. You did it the same way—the blow on the head, the clothes soaked with whisky, the empty bottle by his side . . . that's the way you made it appear that Chapin Bishop had been drowned, two months before he inherited your aunt's money that you shared instead . . . just the same way you killed Sandra Gould. That's why you've stuck to the Bishops, you were afraid they might find out. And you killed Maggie Potter because you thought, when you knew she was trying to get me on the telephone and when you saw her coming in to Mrs. Latham's, that she'd seen you kill Sandra Gould—but you never knew till this moment, Mr. Barrol, that Maggie Potter had seen you, that night seven years ago, strike Chapin Bishop over the head and put him face down in the pool and pour the whisky on his clothes . . . You are a murderer threefold, Mr. Barrol, and you are a coward. Put down that gun!"

Then Colonel Primrose and Sergeant Buck and Paul Dikranov moved slowly forward, towards that dreadful cornered figure by the desk. But George Barrol, staring for an instant horribly from one to another of them, screamed again, an inarticulate scream of terror, and raised the revolver to his head. Through the smoke and the heavy smell of cordite I saw him lurch forward on to the rug.

I remember just two things before I fainted . . . Colonel Primrose bending down and taking the mangled papers out of that clutching hand, and Mr. Parran coming slowly in from somewhere outside, wiping his forehead with a soiled handkerchief and saying, "Well, I'll be a son of a gun."

CHAPTER TWENTY-FIVE

When I came to I was lying on the Victorian sofa and Sergeant Buck was bending over me, as dead-panned as ever, if one can be that and at the same time a granite monument of disgust. "Never saw one yet you couldn't count on to pull something like this," he was saying.

I could dimly hear Colonel Primrose: "He was an old friend, Buck," and the Sergeant again: "I can't visualize a berry like that havin' friends."

I opened my eyes again.

"You shouldn't ought to have come, ma'am," Sergeant Buck said, not unkindly.

"You're telling *me,*" I said. I tried to sit up. "Believe me, I'm really sorry."

Colonel Primrose gave me a worried glance.

"Are you all right, Mrs. Latham?"

"I'm all right."

I leaned back on the sofa and took all my courage in hand to look round the room. Paul Dikranov and Parran had gone, and I could guess what they were doing, for there was nothing else in the room—only Colonel Primrose, Sergeant Buck and I.

The crumpled papers that Colonel Primrose had taken out of George's hand were lying on the low table in front of me. I could see the spidery uneven scrawl in the green ink on pink note paper that Maggie always used.

"Maggie really wrote that?" I whispered. "It really says that about George?"

Colonel Primrose looked steadily at me. The smell of cordite was still heavy in the close little room though somebody had opened a window.

"The answer is yes and no," he said. "It really says that. Mrs. Potter didn't write it. She didn't write anything, so far as I know. I'm an engineer, Mrs. Latham, and I used to be a very good draftsman."

"You . . . you wrote them yourself?"

He nodded.

"But—how did you know?"

He looked down at me with genuine concern on his face.

"You're sure you're all right?—Why, I guessed it, in part. Aided in doing so by a good deal of information and misinformation from your friends. You see, there wasn't any other way to do it. I *knew* Barrol was the killer; I was perfectly certain about it. But you can't *prove* a man was knocked unconscious and left face down, apparently drunk, in shallow water seven years ago. That's where Maggie Potter came in. When things began pointing definitely to Barrol—as they did from the very beginning, if people hadn't just assumed it couldn't possibly be him—it was plain there was something in the past to demand such conduct on his part. I reconstructed. You saw how it worked out."

I shuddered. "But I *don't* see—"

"Think back, Mrs. Latham. Barrol didn't want to come here, he only came back when Rosemary forced it. He came before the rest, no doubt to have a look around and see if anything had turned up. There was no other point in it—they had a caretaker on the place. He's incredibly careful of his person and his health, yet it turns up, as Rosemary told me, that he's always refused to have a simple appendectomy for fear he'll talk while he's under the anesthetic.

"So much about George generally. Now the particulars. When Sandra took him out and nearly drowned him, his first reaction on the dock was fear and a wild hope that she hadn't been rescued. His story that she'd been hit on the head by the jib came after the bruise on her head had been discovered. It was a pure invention. His yarn about holding her up was also an afterthought, and ridiculous on the face of it. Jim Gould, swimming out there, of course found her in perfect shape and holding George up. And Sandra was completely changed from the moment she got back to the clubhouse. At dinner she'd phoned Dikranov, I suppose imploring him to take Rosemary away. They were both angry. Before the boat episode she was sullen, sultry and . . . vicious, I'd say. Now, after she got in from the bay, she went to the powder room—singing happily, laughing to herself, gloating about something—and wrote a note.

"That note, of course, was on the whole the most vital point of the whole business. It was a giveaway of the very deadest kind, so to speak, and I was terribly afraid you would see it was, when we were there in the powder room. The point isn't just that there *was* a note—it's the matter of when and where and to whom it was written. Why was it done? There was no conceivable point in her writing it to Dikranov . . . but George Barrol was with Andy Thorp, and she couldn't ask him to meet her secretly with Andy right there."

"But . . . the note *was* to Dikranov, of course?"

He shook his head.

"I never for an instant thought it was for Dikranov. It was in his pocket, but it was obvious that it was intended either for one of the Bishops or for George."

"But why—"

"My dear Mrs. Latham, those people are both Georgian. When she talked to Dikranov over the telephone, as Jim Gould told us, she spoke in their own language. She wouldn't conceivably have written a secret note to Dikranov in English. Furthermore, there was hardly any point in writing to him at all. She could easily have spoken to him. No, that note was written to George Barrol, and he most foolishly put it in Dikranov's pocket . . . thinking that he wouldn't put his linen dinner jacket on again till the next night."

"What a foul trick!" I said.

"Ah, yes. The old gnat-straining business, Mrs. Latham. Murder you didn't object to, but a social treachery like that . . ."

He shook his head.

"If Barrol had had the coolheadedness to destroy that note . . . But that's the point about the hysterical criminal. Well, when Dikranov remembered Rosemary's cigarette case and found the note that Saturday night, he was on his guard. Without knowing anything about all this, he suspected, naturally, that somebody was trying to implicate him in something, and he was worried, both for his own sake and for Rosemary's. Hence his prowling about at night. He didn't suspect George, because that Saturday night, when he'd got back from being seen by you in your garden, he found George quite drunk and asleep by Bishop's desk."

I tried desperately to think.

"But Sandra, and the wrench, and Mrs. Potter?"

Colonel Primrose chuckled.

"It's a long story, Mrs. Latham. I suspect that when Andy Thorp sees fit to show up he'll remember—things being as they are now—that Sandra picked the wrench up herself, off the back porch, when she went down to meet George at the garage. George, after using it, left it in the grass near the Goulds' back door for Jim to explain as best he could.

"Then Mrs. Potter. She was the human crux of the whole thing, in a way. You see, I found out easily enough where those mysterious silent calls came from, and it was just as easy for George to do it. The first one of them came just two hours after the murder—before George was found at the desk. He wasn't at the garage, by the way, when you were there. You heard something else—or imagined you did. Have you figured out yet why he shot at you?"

Colonel Primrose chuckled again. "It's not flattering."

I shook my head. I had no remote idea.

"Why, he mistook you for me, Mrs. Latham. We were both wearing white. It was quite dark. He fired, panic-stricken, at a white blur walking up towards the house. It was easy enough to be smoking one of Dikranov's cigarettes."

"Well," I said philosophically, "it's occurred to me before that I really ought to diet."

"Don't," he said. "You don't need it . . . and I'm too old to worry about *my* figure. Well, Barrol was really a coward, nervous, panicky, frightened constantly—as well he might be. That's why he spied on Potter leaving after his interview with me, that's why he spotted Maggie Potter coming to your place. And when he saw her, the hysterical idea he'd formed that she might have seen him kill Sandra—why else should a bedridden woman actually struggle out there, after being too frightened to talk over the telephone?—sprang instantly into his mind. And he acted instantly on it. He had to, from his point of view."

I nodded. "He saw her from the winter kitchen, of course."

"My dear Mrs. Latham, so far as I know he was never in the winter kitchen in his life. Rodman Bishop, to save himself from having to admit that he'd seen his daughter leaving his house, definitely upset, and presumably *after* Mrs. Potter had been killed, just plain lied about where he was. He was outside in your garden. So, in giving himself an out, he struck on the idea of bottling the wine . . . and in quite accidentally picking a witness he gave George Barrol an alibi too. He knew George wouldn't dare not support him. And not supporting him was the last thing in the world George would want to do. It was providential for him.

"However, the minute that clock turned out to be in the Bishops' house—and I couldn't myself find out where it was without running the risk of giving the whole show away —it was perfectly evident that it pointed to one of the four people there. And with everything else pointing to George already . . ."

Colonel Primrose shrugged.

"I framed my little trap. I'd worked out the business of Sandra. You may remember my pointing out early in the evening that there must always be a reason for a crime taking place *at a specific time*. Well, there was a supremely good reason of that sort here. George Barrol, drowning out there in the bay, in that storm, utterly terrified, paralyzed with fear, confessed his murder of Chapin Bishop to Sandra . . . and he *had* to close her mouth at the earliest possible moment. It all worked out."

He shook his head a little, regretfully.

"I made one mistake," he said.

"Dear me," I said. "Sergeant Buck told me—"

"Oh, it wasn't serious. In fact it was just as good as not being one. And it was very ironical. I thought George killed Mrs. Potter because she knew about Chapin—but it was because he thought she knew about Sandra. He had no idea, really, that she knew about his first murder seven years ago. I didn't realize that until I heard that sheer gasp of horror he gave when he read Mrs. Potter's memoirs."

He touched the little mass of papers.

"And how do you know she did, really?" I asked.

Colonel Primrose smiled.

"Deduction, Mrs. Latham, greatly aided by your friend Elsie Carter. I told you you'd underestimated her. She was convinced that Chapin Bishop had been murdered. Not by George, of course. By Dr. Potter."

"By Adam Potter?" I gasped.

"According to Mrs. Carter, Maggie Potter, seven years ago, was carrying on—in one degree or another, it doesn't matter— with Chapin Bishop, who was considerably younger than she was. She'd gone to meet him clandestinely at the inlet, Potter had followed and killed him. Since then Mrs. Potter lived in a borderline state of compounded hysteria and a sense of guilt and what not."

He shook his head soberly.

"The dreadful trouble about people like Elsie Carter is that they're often half right. *And she was*—you saw what happened when George was suddenly confronted with her story."

"With *your* story," I said.

"With my *correct* story. There's no doubt that's exactly what was the matter with Maggie Potter. She wasn't sick, as Potter told us himself. If she had been, she couldn't have got out here. And she couldn't tell anybody about it—not because her husband had done it and had her terrified, as Elsie Carter thought —but because she *was* doing a clandestine act that she didn't dare admit. Until, of course, the murder of Sandra with its precisely similar details, as I found in the coroner's report and as Mrs. Potter read in the papers. That was too much, and she tried hysterically to get in touch with me.

"Well, I wasn't interested in Potter as Chapin Bishop's murderer. It was simple enough to see that a person who I already thought had killed Sandra profited enormously by Chapin's death. I take it a quarter of a million was enormous, even before nineteen-twenty-nine. And that was our friend George. The rest of it followed as the night the day. It wasn't too sharp and exact—it took some reconstruction. But it was good enough. It was all true."

We were silent a moment there in the little room.

"And *poor* Hawkins!" I said.

Colonel Primrose chuckled quite callously.

"My dear Mrs. Latham, that was the supreme moment of his life. He probably actually thought, at that moment, that he'd really done it. I had to do it that way, you see. There was no evidence against Barrol that a shrewd fellow like Nathan Kaufman couldn't have torn to bits in front of a jury. I had to make George think the case was closed—he was in no danger at all, *except from one thing, which he could forestall.* But that danger was terrific. I don't know whether you've realized how very subtle my statement of the case against Hawkins was. As I stated the criminal's motive, it was a precise statement of George's, in the abstract and leaving out the details framed around Hawkins—the motive no one suspected and so on. Hence the infallibility of the trap baited with Maggie Potter's papers. George couldn't help but see that he was just on the very verge of detection, that it was a pure miracle I'd picked on Hawkins. He wouldn't dare not take the risk of getting those papers. He simply had to get them. The least little shred of evidence and he was done for.

"Well, you nearly ruined everything by starting to ask me about the clock, which would have given it all away. I imagine you were just about to remind me also that of course Mrs. Potter really wasn't an eyewitness. Fortunately I have a very bad heart. The shock was too much for me."

"You nearly scared the wits out of me," I said.

"That was the idea. I'd thought of doing something of the kind anyway. It served the very useful purposes of letting George know Potter would be out of his house and I confined to yours. But imagine my *real* shock, Mrs. Latham, when you turned up here! We thought for a moment you'd come after the papers yourself."

I stared at the pleasant gray-haired rotund little man placidly lighting a cigar.

"Then you . . . you *expected* him to kill himself!"

"That was certainly my hope, Mrs. Latham," he said cheerfully. "After all, he was a gentleman. And, by the way, I'll be glad to get you another vase."

"That was my great-grandmother's!" I said weakly.

"I'll give you one of my *great*-great-grandmother's."

I left my car in the kitchen drive and went into the house. There was a curious empty feeling inside me, and the house seemed strangely silent and forlorn, like a stage after the last curtain has fallen and gone up again on a deserted theater. I picked up a little piece of glass that had landed under the pleated edge of the chintz slip cover in the living room and put it in an ash tray. Then I sat down and closed my eyes, utterly and unbelievably weary.

I opened them again when I heard someone coming in the porch door. It was Jim.

He dropped into a chair and sat there, staring down between his knees at the rug, as completely dejected a figure as I've ever seen.

"Well," I said, "it's all pretty foul."

He nodded.

"When did he come back?" he asked.

"George?"

"Dikranov."

"Oh. He never went. He was helping Colonel Primrose to keep an eye on George. I take it Mr. Dikranov's something pretty swell in his country."

"Thanks," Jim said.

I sat up . . . with an effort.

"Jim, what's the matter?"

He laughed, bitterly. "Nothing. I guess I'm just all wet. And nineteen kinds of a jackass. Anybody not a conceited swine could have seen she'd got way out past me."

I felt even worse than I'd felt during that dreadful scene in Maggie Potter's sitting room.

203

I couldn't think of a single thing to say. I said, "Do you want a drink?"

"No."

He got up, stood there for a moment and went wretchedly to the door and on out.

I don't know how long I stood miserably there, watching the dark spot in the night where I'd lost sight of him. One thing was good, I thought. There wasn't a Palais de Danse about, where he could go and get potted and marry another Sandra. Not that night anyway.

Then the kitchen door slammed, and I heard somebody calling me, and the hall door flew open, and then the front door, and Rosemary burst through it.

"Grace!" she said. "Where's Jim?"

"Oh," I said, "I'd leave him alone, darling. He's feeling rotten enough."

All the fire and life went out of her suddenly. She sat down on the porch chair.

"Then he really did love her, didn't he?"

I think I glared at her.

"My God," I said, "somebody's raving mad around here, and it can't be me. Are you going to marry Paul?"

"Oh, no!" she gasped. "That's all out! It has been for days!"

"Then go and find your Jim before he casts himself into the sea!"

I pushed her down the porch steps. A flying wisp of blue was the last I saw of Rosemary that night. Alice Gould, coming up the flagged walk, watched her go too, and smiled.

"Journeys end in lovers' meetings," she said.

We stood for a moment looking out into the night where Rosemary had gone.

"Andy's home," Alice said. "So is Lucy Lee. I feel rather lonely, just now. I think I'll go over and see Rodman. He was fond of George."

I went back into the house and through to the kitchen.

Colonel Primrose was just coming in, his sergeant behind him. I had just started to say anything—I don't know what—when Sergeant Buck cleared his throat.

"Could I speak to you, alone, ma'am?" he asked stiffly.

"Surely," I said.

Colonel Primrose looked puzzled, hesitated a moment, and went on into the living room. Sergeant Buck's hard lined lantern-jawed face turned slowly to a dull brick-red.

"I just wanted to say, ma'am," he began doggedly, "that the Colonel seems to think pretty well of you."

I was more than a little surprised, for certainly I'd had no idea of it. Sergeant Buck cleared his throat again.

"I wanted to say that . . . if the Colonel should ask you to marry him, ma'am, I'd regard it as a personal favor if you'd say nothing doing."

I suppose I must have looked still more surprised, for he swallowed hard and turned still redder.

"The Colonel's had a hard life—no offense intended, ma'am —and you see, we ain't marryin' men."

There was a loud bang on the pantry door, and Colonel Primrose then pushed it open.

"Buck," he demanded, "what the devil are you up to?"

He looked at us with a suspicious frown.

"Not anything, sir," Sergeant Buck said promptly.

"He's just warning me about the primrose path," I said. "Who'd like a drink?"